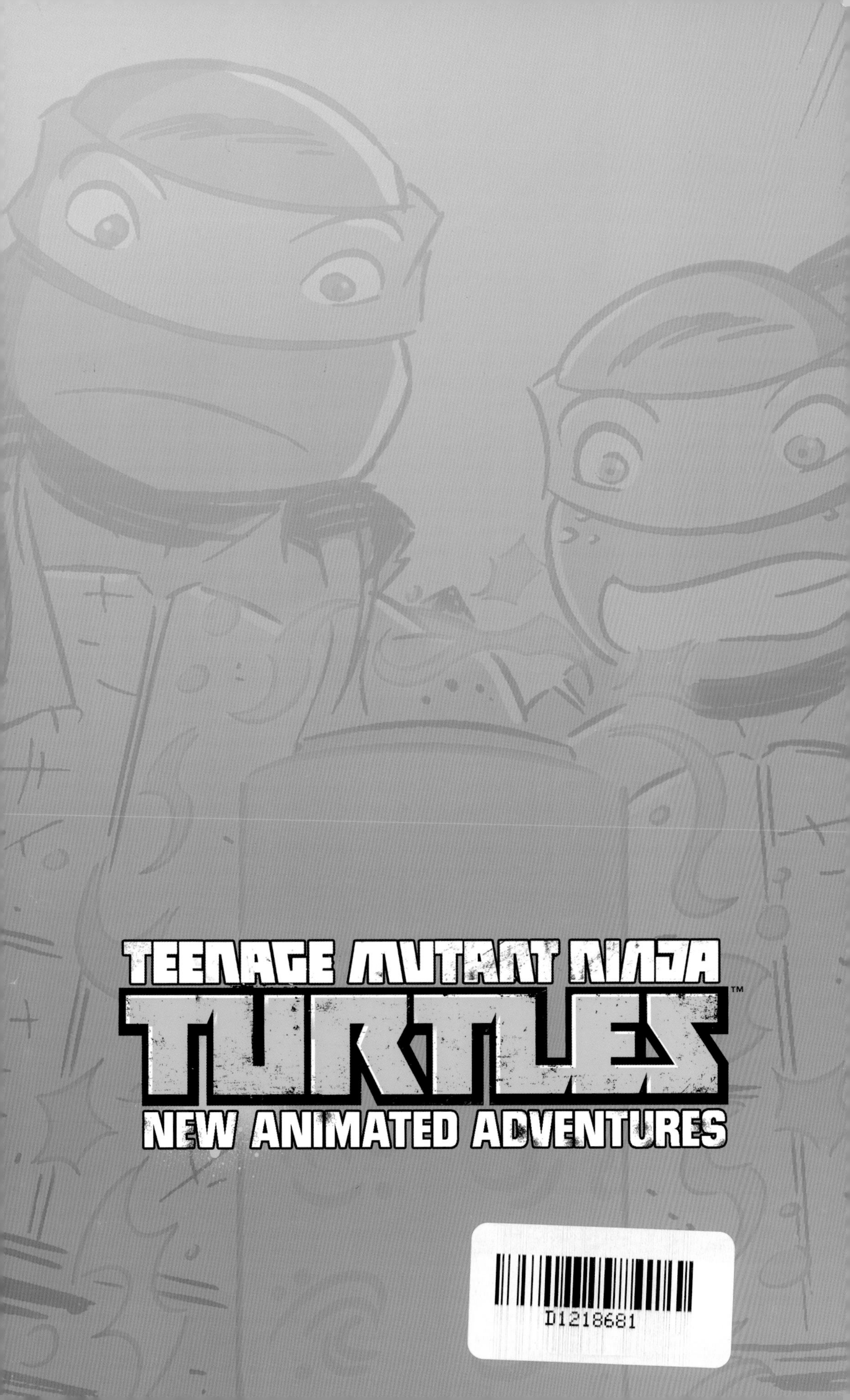
TEENAGE MUTANT NINJA
TURTLES™
NEW ANIMATED ADVENTURES

WRITTEN BY **KENNY BYERLY** (CHAPTERS 1 & 4),
CULLEN BUNN (CHAPTER 2),
AND **BRIAN SMITH** (CHAPTER 3)

ART BY **ADAM ARCHER** (CHAPTER 1),
DARIO BRIZUELA (CHAPTERS 2 & 4),
AND **CHAD THOMAS** (CHAPTER 3)

COLORS BY **HEATHER BRECKEL**
LETTERS BY **SHAWN LEE**
SERIES EDITS BY **BOBBY CURNOW**

COVER BY **FELIPE SMITH**

COLLECTION EDITS BY **JUSTIN EISINGER**
AND **ALONZO SIMON**

COLLECTION DESIGN BY **SHAWN LEE**

Special thanks to Joan Hilty, Linda Lee, and Kat van Dam for their invaluable assistance.

ISBN: 978-1-61377-962-0

17 16 15 14   2 3 4 5

www.IDWPUBLISHING.com
IDW founded by Ted Adams, Alex Garner, Kris Oprisko, and Robbie Robbins

Ted Adams, CEO & Publisher
Greg Goldstein, President & COO
Robbie Robbins, EVP/Sr. Graphic Artist
Chris Ryall, Chief Creative Officer/Editor-in-Chief
Matthew Ruzicka, CPA, Chief Financial Officer
Alan Payne, VP of Sales
Dirk Wood, VP of Marketing
Lorelei Bunjes, VP of Digital Services
Jeff Webber, VP of Digital Publishing & Business Development

Facebook: facebook.com/idwpublishing
Twitter: @idwpublishing
YouTube: youtube.com/idwpublishing
Instagram: instagram.com/idwpublishing
deviantART: idwpublishing.deviantart.com
Pinterest: pinterest.com/idwpublishing/idw-staff-faves

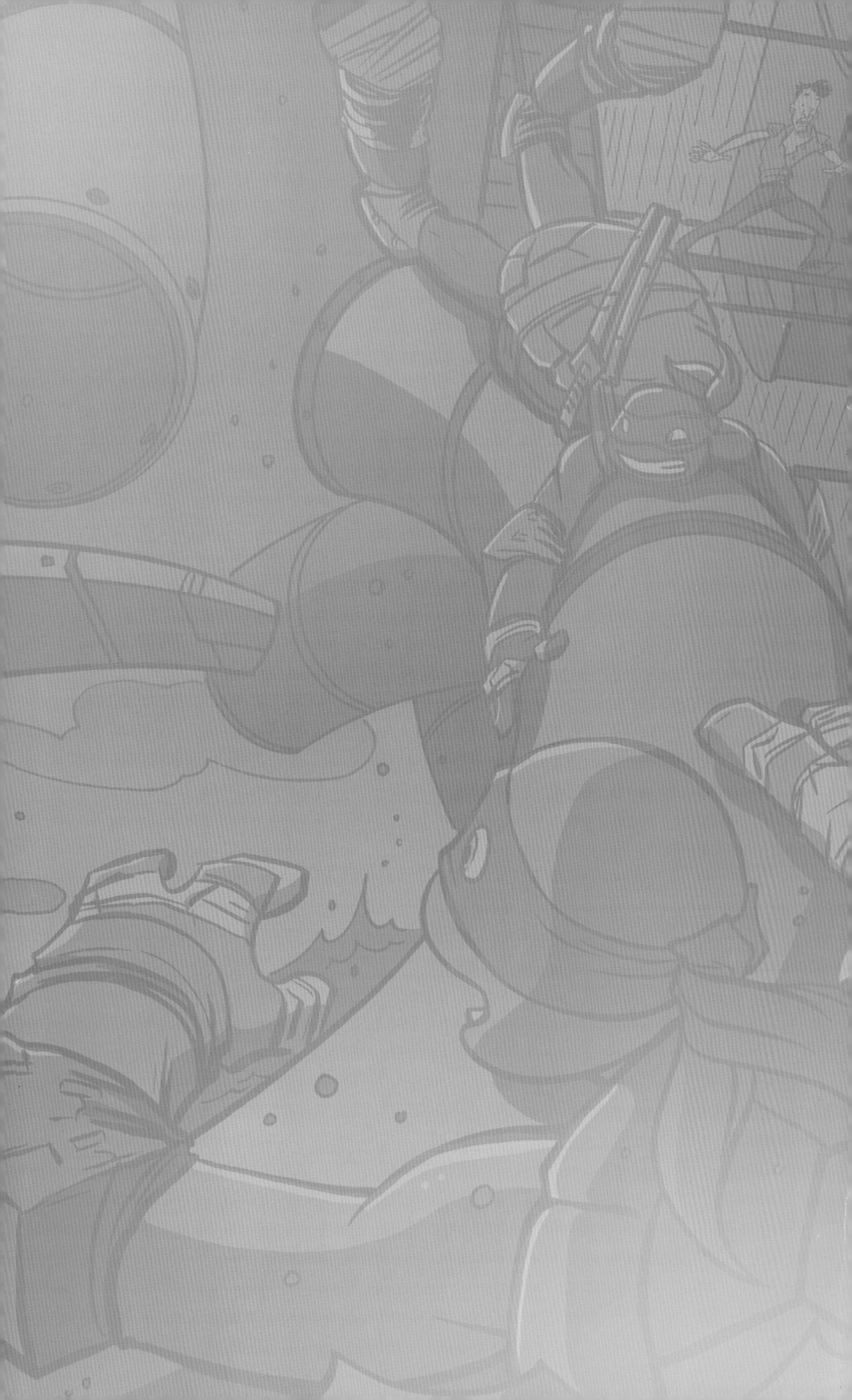

ART BY DARIO BRIZUELA

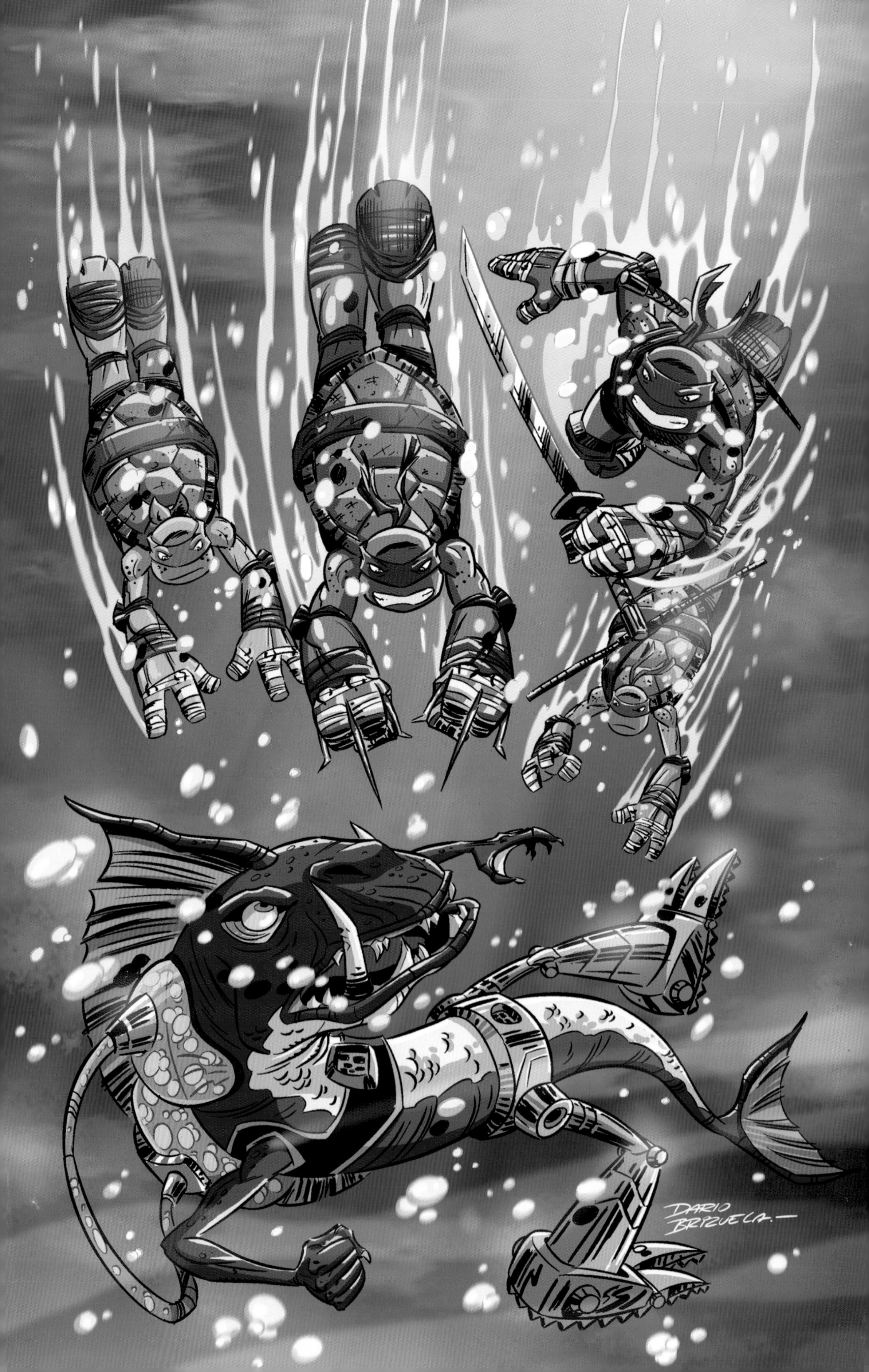
DARIO BRIZUELA

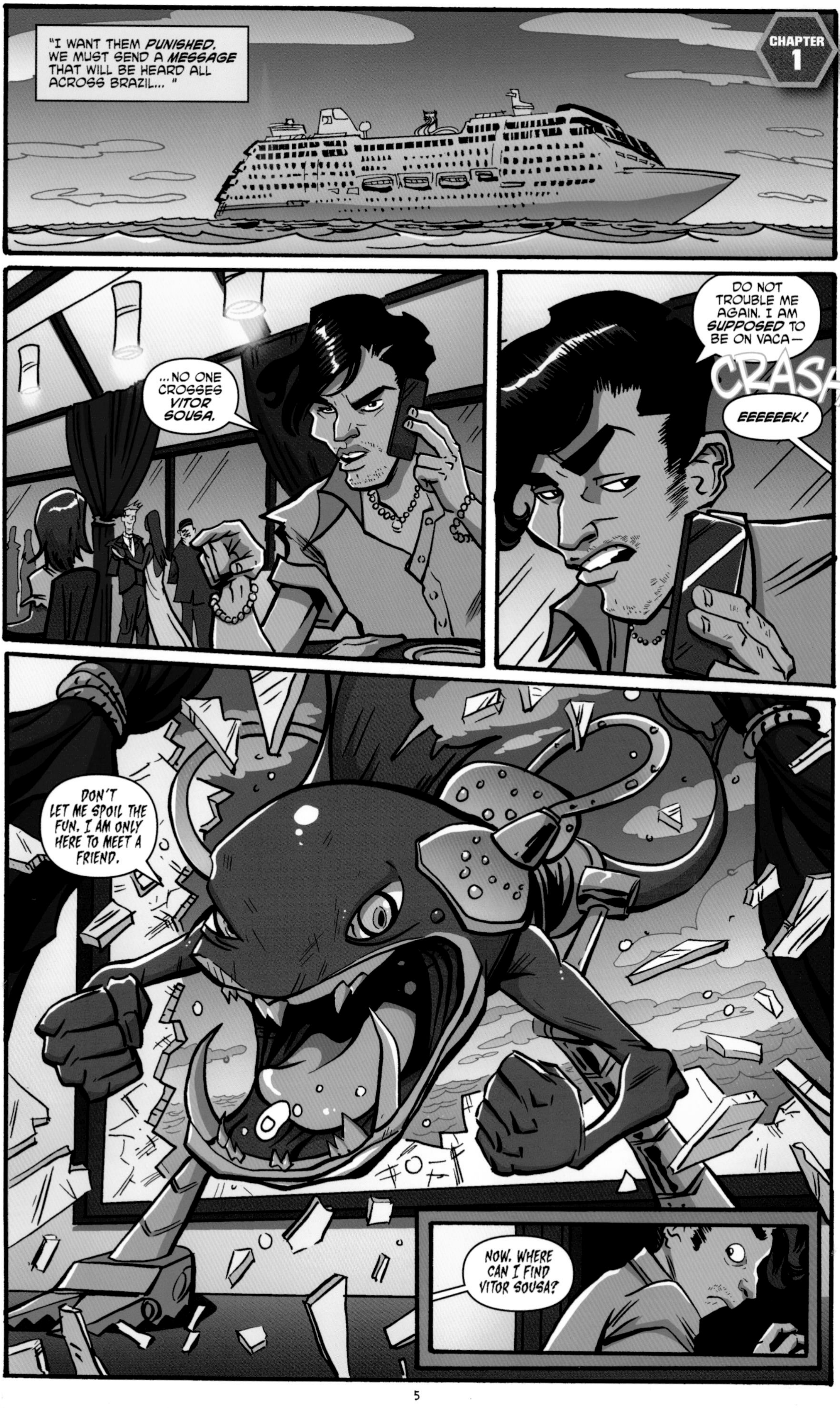
CHAPTER 1
"I WANT THEM PUNISHED. WE MUST SEND A MESSAGE THAT WILL BE HEARD ALL ACROSS BRAZIL... "
...NO ONE CROSSES VITOR SOUSA.
DO NOT TROUBLE ME AGAIN. I AM SUPPOSED TO BE ON VACA—
CRASH
EEEEEEK!
DON'T LET ME SPOIL THE FUN. I AM ONLY HERE TO MEET A FRIEND.
NOW. WHERE CAN I FIND VITOR SOUSA?

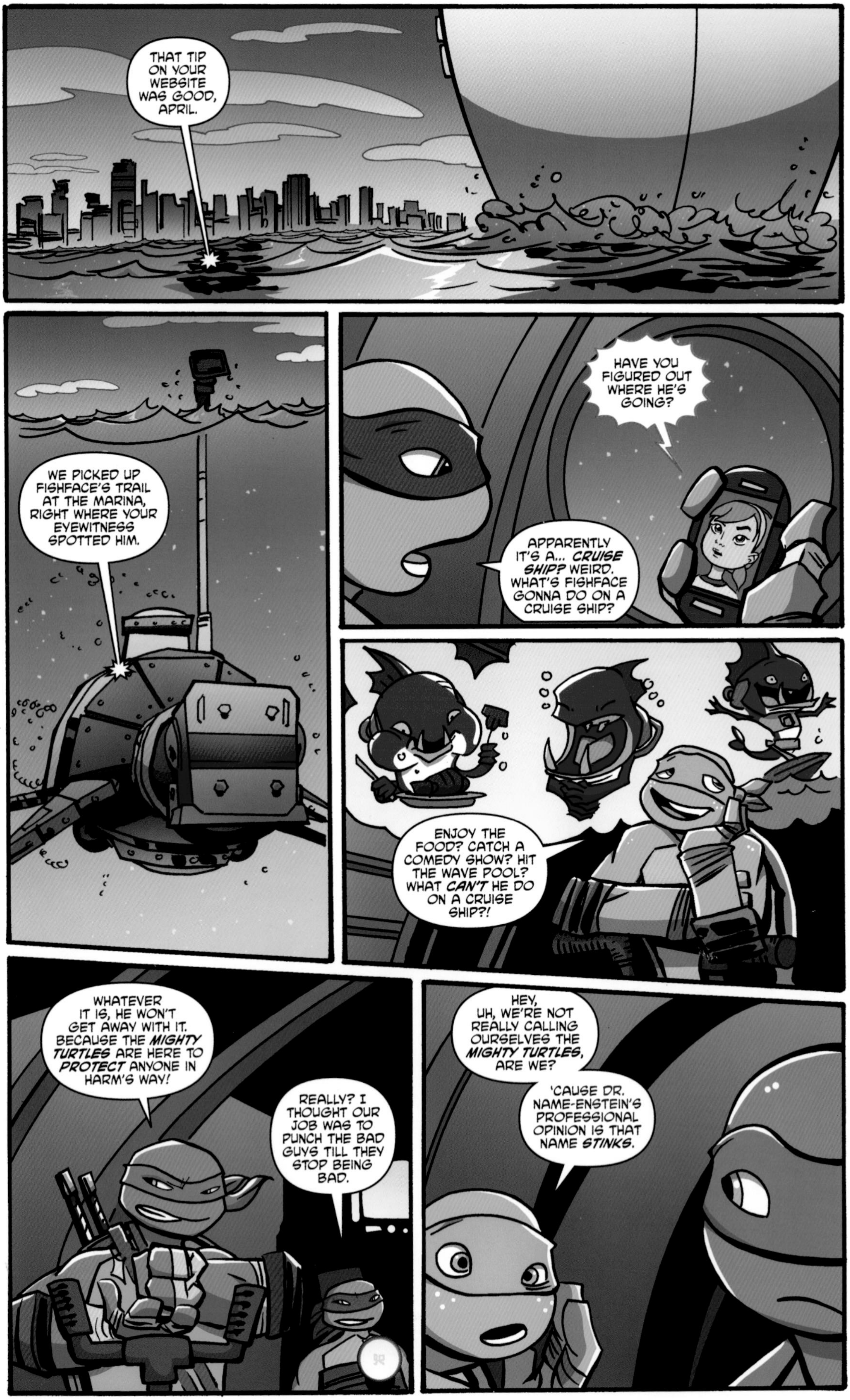
THAT TIP ON YOUR WEBSITE WAS GOOD, APRIL.
WE PICKED UP FISHFACE'S TRAIL AT THE MARINA, RIGHT WHERE YOUR EYEWITNESS SPOTTED HIM.
HAVE YOU FIGURED OUT WHERE HE'S GOING?
APPARENTLY IT'S A... *CRUISE SHIP?* WEIRD. WHAT'S FISHFACE GONNA DO ON A CRUISE SHIP?
ENJOY THE FOOD? CATCH A COMEDY SHOW? HIT THE WAVE POOL? WHAT *CAN'T* HE DO ON A CRUISE SHIP?!
WHATEVER IT IS, HE WON'T GET AWAY WITH IT. BECAUSE THE *MIGHTY TURTLES* ARE HERE TO *PROTECT* ANYONE IN HARM'S WAY!
REALLY? I THOUGHT OUR JOB WAS TO PUNCH THE BAD GUYS TILL THEY STOP BEING BAD.
HEY, UH, WE'RE NOT REALLY CALLING OURSELVES THE *MIGHTY TURTLES*, ARE WE?
'CAUSE DR. NAME-ENSTEIN'S PROFESSIONAL OPINION IS THAT NAME *STINKS*.

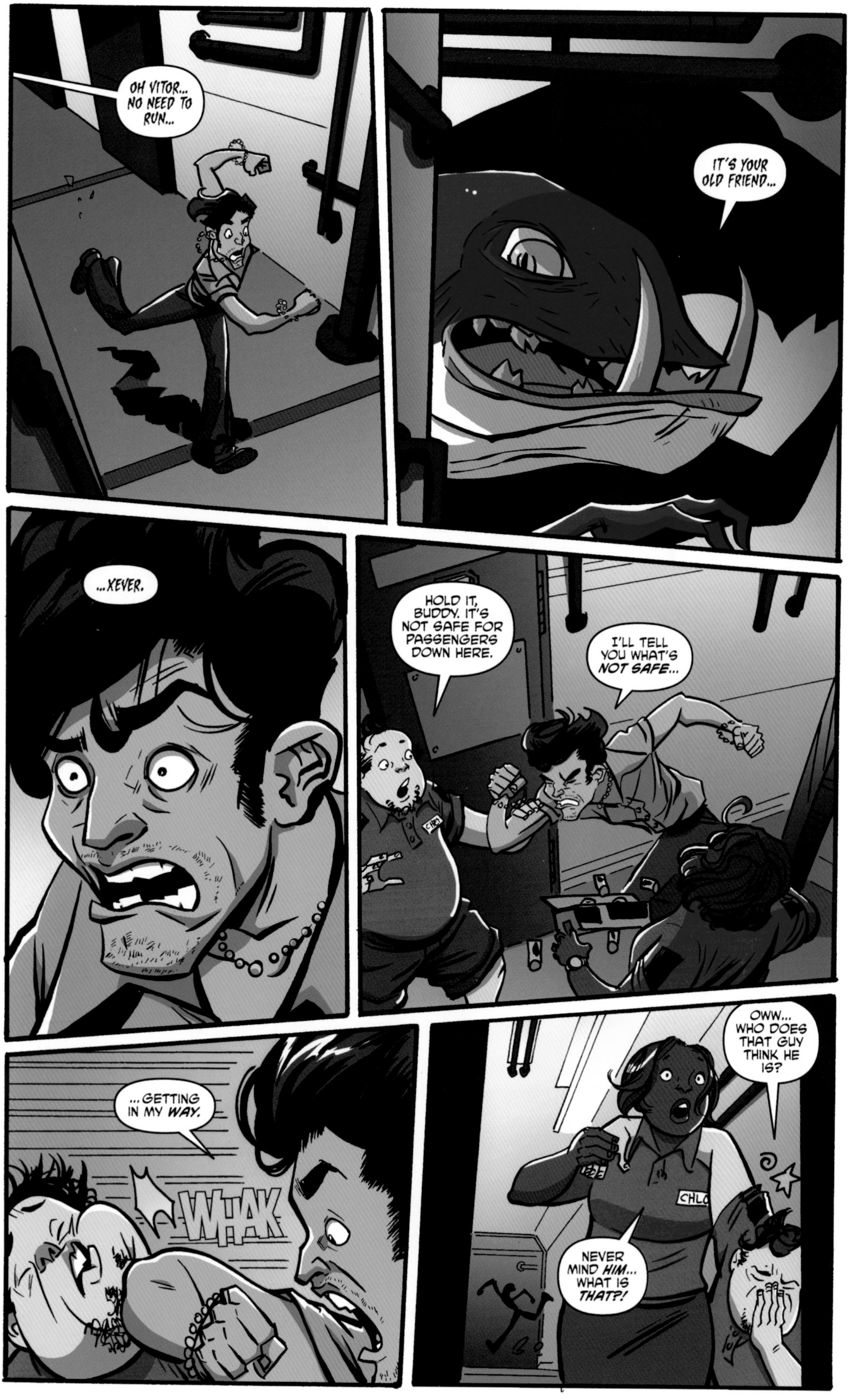
OH VITOR... NO NEED TO RUN...
IT'S YOUR OLD FRIEND...
...XEVER.
HOLD IT, BUDDY. IT'S NOT SAFE FOR PASSENGERS DOWN HERE.
I'LL TELL YOU WHAT'S NOT SAFE...
...GETTING IN MY WAY.
WHAK
OWW... WHO DOES THAT GUY THINK HE IS?
NEVER MIND HIM... WHAT IS THAT?!

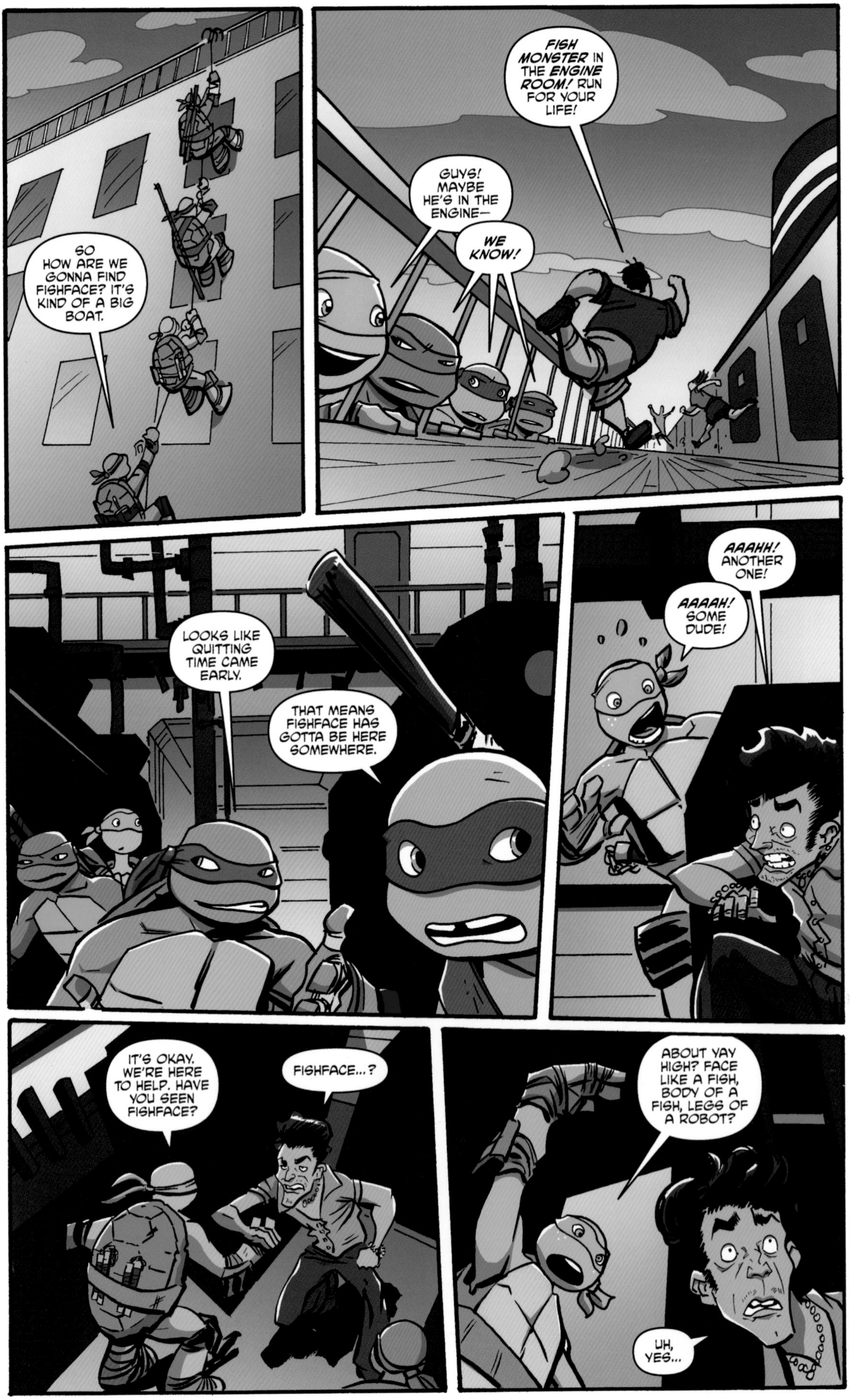
SO HOW ARE WE GONNA FIND FISHFACE? IT'S KIND OF A BIG BOAT.
FISH MONSTER IN THE ENGINE ROOM! RUN FOR YOUR LIFE!
GUYS! MAYBE HE'S IN THE ENGINE—
WE KNOW!
LOOKS LIKE QUITTING TIME CAME EARLY.
THAT MEANS FISHFACE HAS GOTTA BE HERE SOMEWHERE.
AAAHH! ANOTHER ONE!
AAAAH! SOME DUDE!
IT'S OKAY. WE'RE HERE TO HELP. HAVE YOU SEEN FISHFACE?
FISHFACE...?
ABOUT YAY HIGH? FACE LIKE A FISH, BODY OF A FISH, LEGS OF A ROBOT?
UH, YES...

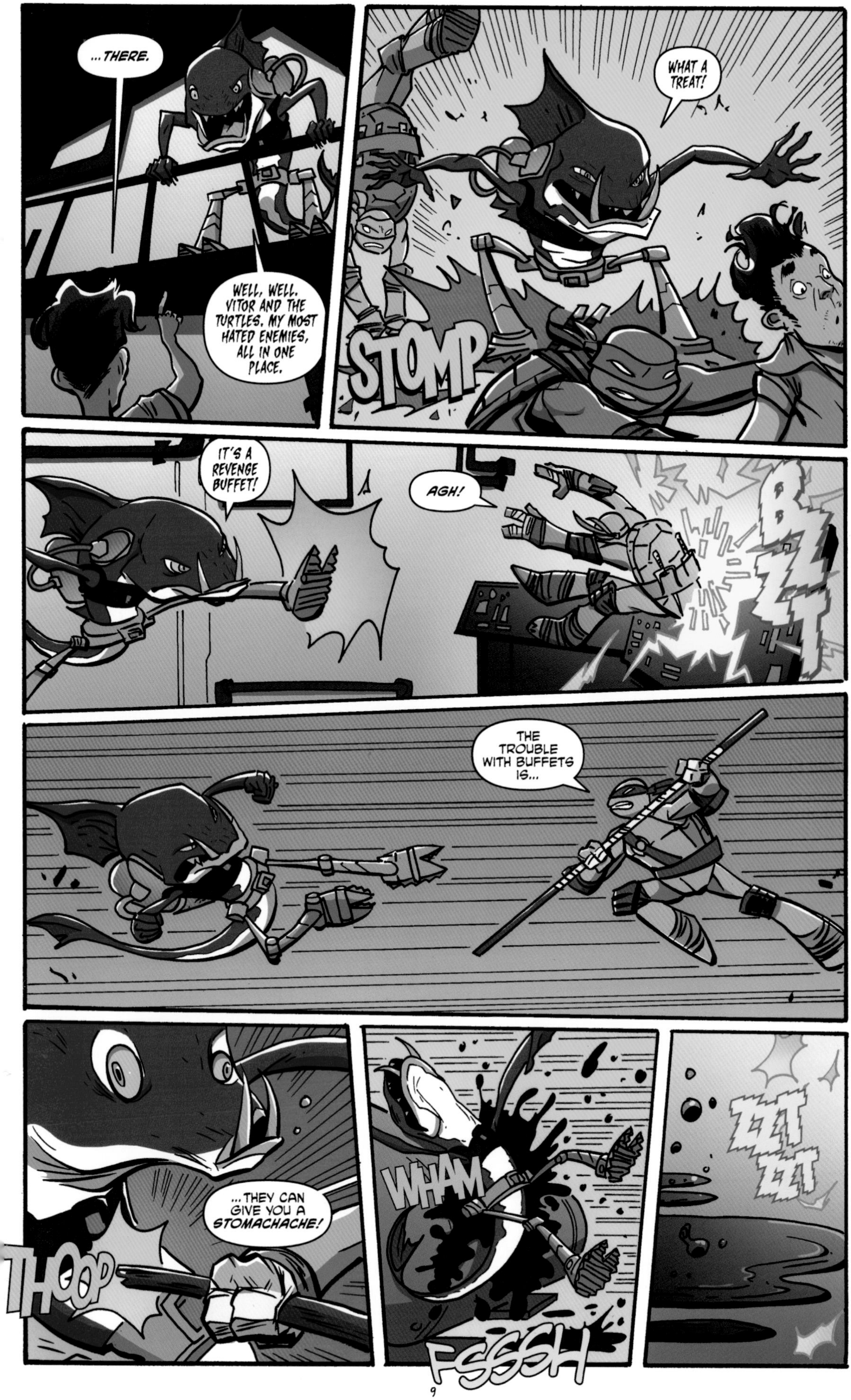
...THERE.
WELL, WELL. VITOR AND THE TURTLES. MY MOST HATED ENEMIES, ALL IN ONE PLACE.
WHAT A TREAT!
STOMP
IT'S A REVENGE BUFFET!
AGH!
BZZT
THE TROUBLE WITH BUFFETS IS...
...THEY CAN GIVE YOU A STOMACHACHE!
THOOP
WHAM
FSSSH
ZZT ZZT

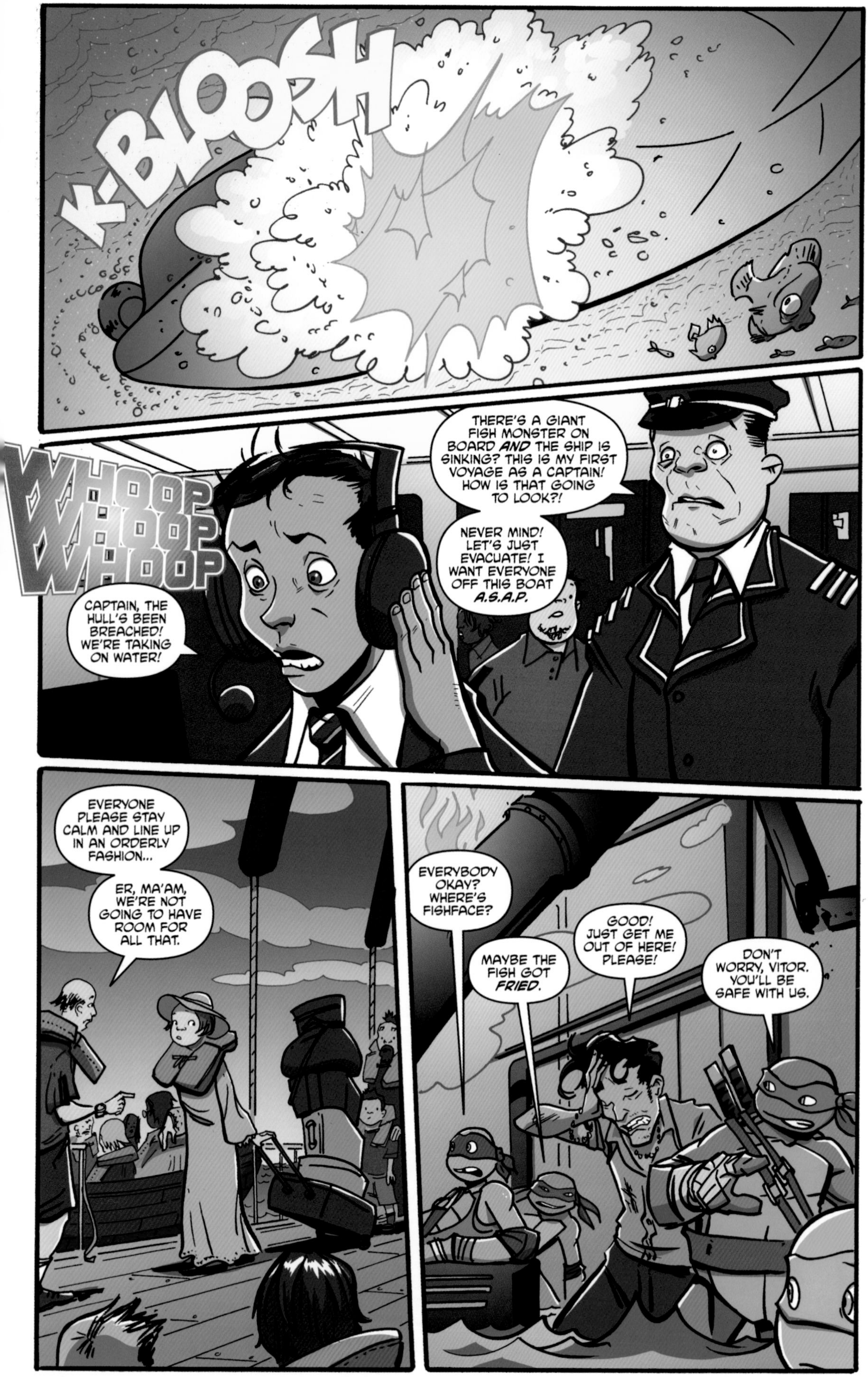
K-BLOOSH
WHOOP WHOOP WHOOP
CAPTAIN, THE HULL'S BEEN BREACHED! WE'RE TAKING ON WATER!
THERE'S A GIANT FISH MONSTER ON BOARD AND THE SHIP IS SINKING? THIS IS MY FIRST VOYAGE AS A CAPTAIN! HOW IS THAT GOING TO LOOK?!
NEVER MIND! LET'S JUST EVACUATE! I WANT EVERYONE OFF THIS BOAT A.S.A.P.
EVERYONE PLEASE STAY CALM AND LINE UP IN AN ORDERLY FASHION...
ER, MA'AM, WE'RE NOT GOING TO HAVE ROOM FOR ALL THAT.
EVERYBODY OKAY? WHERE'S FISHFACE?
MAYBE THE FISH GOT FRIED.
GOOD! JUST GET ME OUT OF HERE! PLEASE!
DON'T WORRY, VITOR. YOU'LL BE SAFE WITH US.

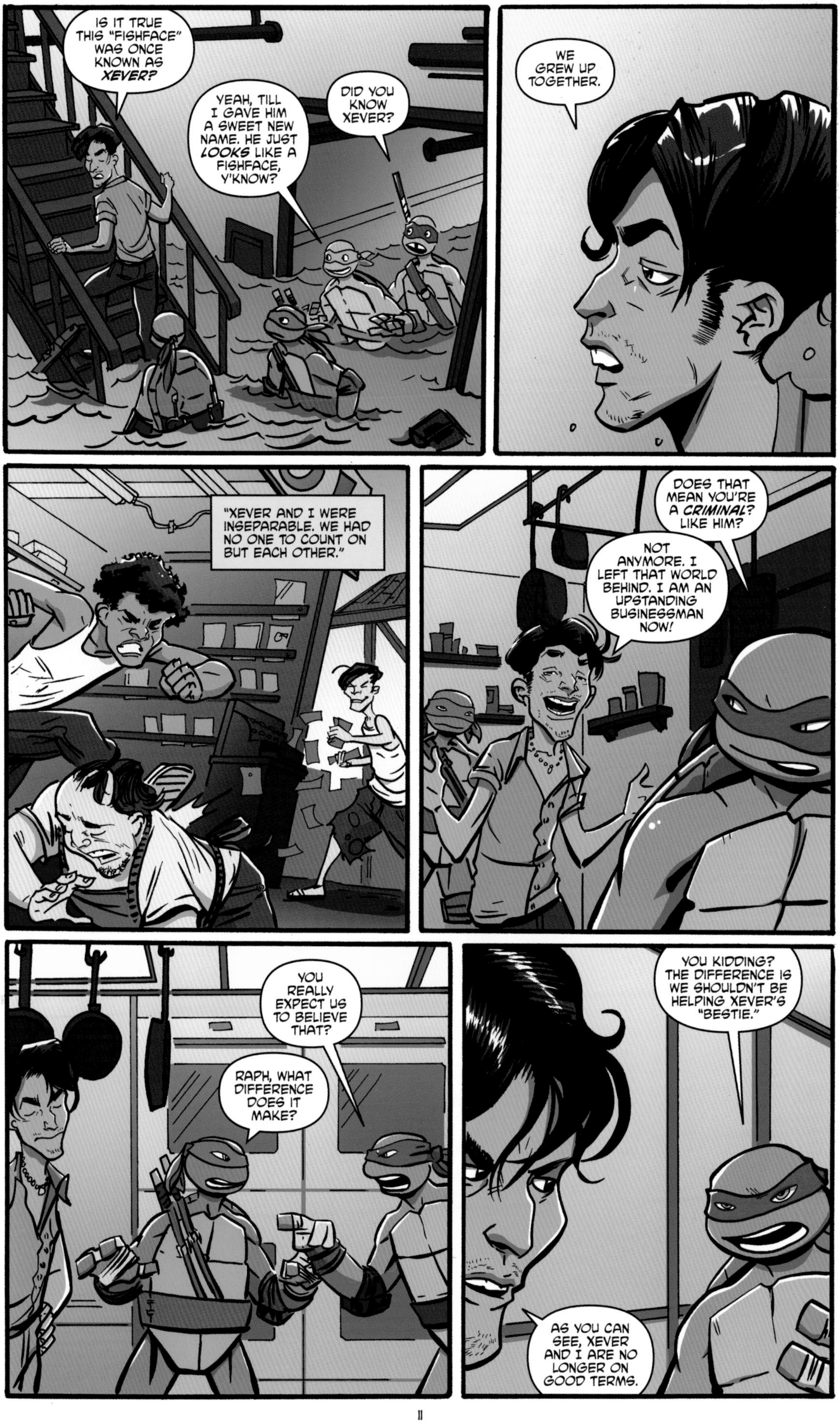

IS IT TRUE THIS "FISHFACE" WAS ONCE KNOWN AS XEVER?
YEAH, TILL I GAVE HIM A SWEET NEW NAME. HE JUST LOOKS LIKE A FISHFACE, Y'KNOW?
DID YOU KNOW XEVER?
WE GREW UP TOGETHER.
"XEVER AND I WERE INSEPARABLE. WE HAD NO ONE TO COUNT ON BUT EACH OTHER."
DOES THAT MEAN YOU'RE A CRIMINAL? LIKE HIM?
NOT ANYMORE. I LEFT THAT WORLD BEHIND. I AM AN UPSTANDING BUSINESSMAN NOW!
YOU REALLY EXPECT US TO BELIEVE THAT?
RAPH, WHAT DIFFERENCE DOES IT MAKE?
YOU KIDDING? THE DIFFERENCE IS WE SHOULDN'T BE HELPING XEVER'S "BESTIE."
AS YOU CAN SEE, XEVER AND I ARE NO LONGER ON GOOD TERMS.

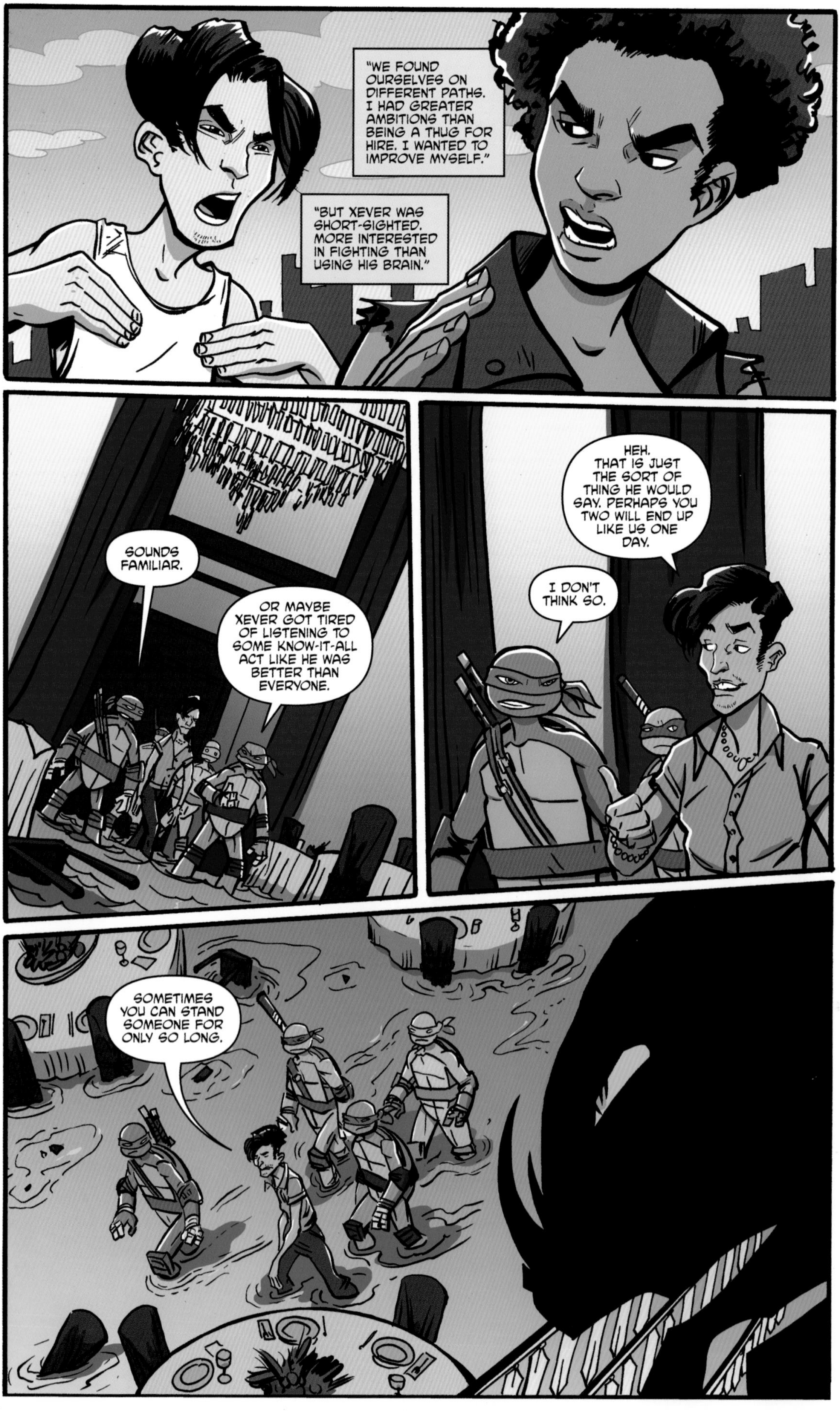
"WE FOUND OURSELVES ON DIFFERENT PATHS. I HAD GREATER AMBITIONS THAN BEING A THUG FOR HIRE. I WANTED TO IMPROVE MYSELF."
"BUT XEVER WAS SHORT-SIGHTED. MORE INTERESTED IN FIGHTING THAN USING HIS BRAIN."
SOUNDS FAMILIAR.
OR MAYBE XEVER GOT TIRED OF LISTENING TO SOME KNOW-IT-ALL ACT LIKE HE WAS BETTER THAN EVERYONE.
HEH. THAT IS JUST THE SORT OF THING HE WOULD SAY. PERHAPS YOU TWO WILL END UP LIKE US ONE DAY.
I DON'T THINK SO.
SOMETIMES YOU CAN STAND SOMEONE FOR ONLY SO LONG.

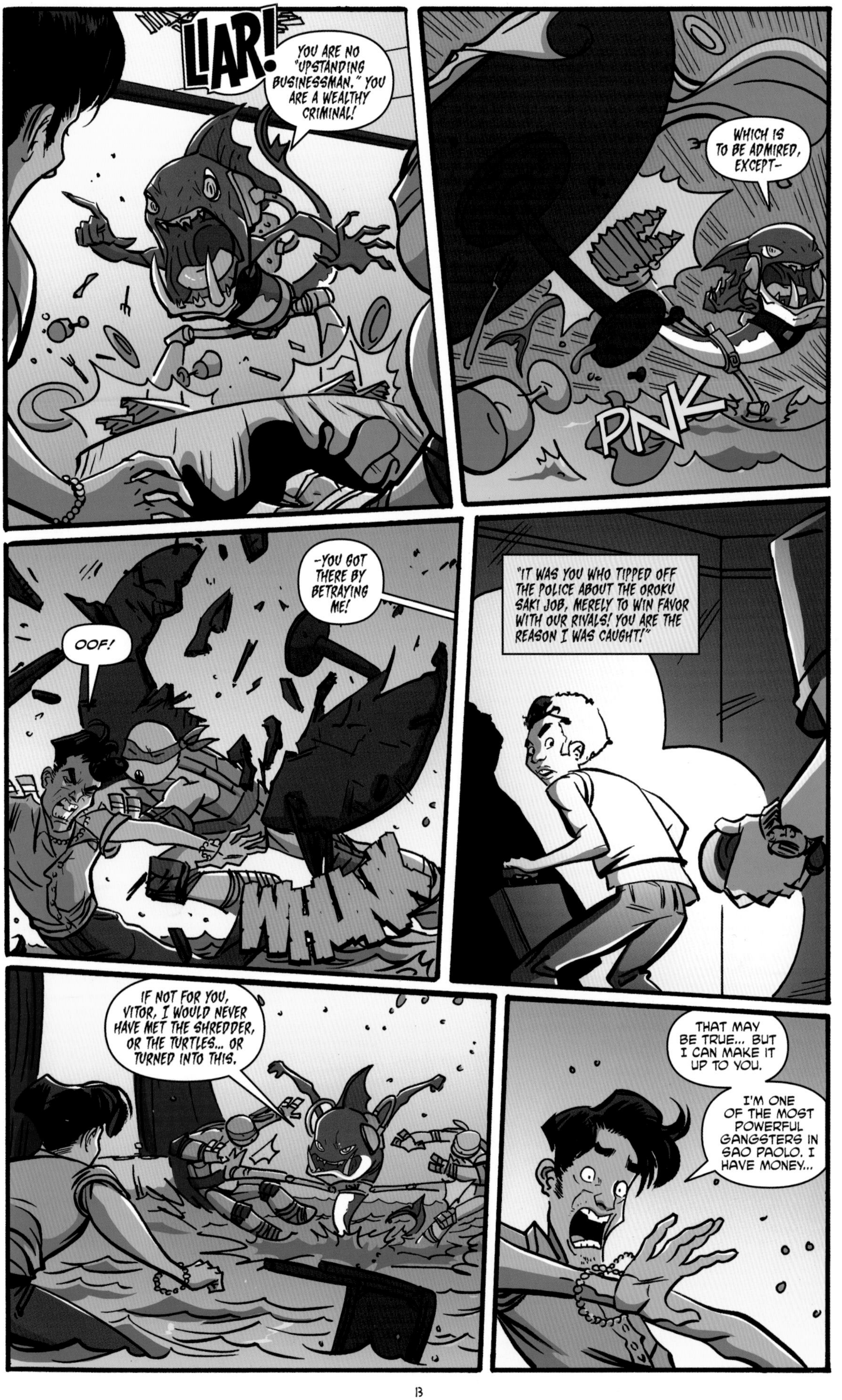
LIAR!
YOU ARE NO "UPSTANDING BUSINESSMAN." YOU ARE A WEALTHY CRIMINAL!
WHICH IS TO BE ADMIRED, EXCEPT-
PNK
-YOU GOT THERE BY BETRAYING ME!
OOF!
WHUN
"IT WAS YOU WHO TIPPED OFF THE POLICE ABOUT THE OROKU SAKI JOB, MERELY TO WIN FAVOR WITH OUR RIVALS! YOU ARE THE REASON I WAS CAUGHT!"
IF NOT FOR YOU, VITOR, I WOULD NEVER HAVE MET THE SHREDDER, OR THE TURTLES... OR TURNED INTO THIS.
THAT MAY BE TRUE... BUT I CAN MAKE IT UP TO YOU.
I'M ONE OF THE MOST POWERFUL GANGSTERS IN SAO PAOLO. I HAVE MONEY...

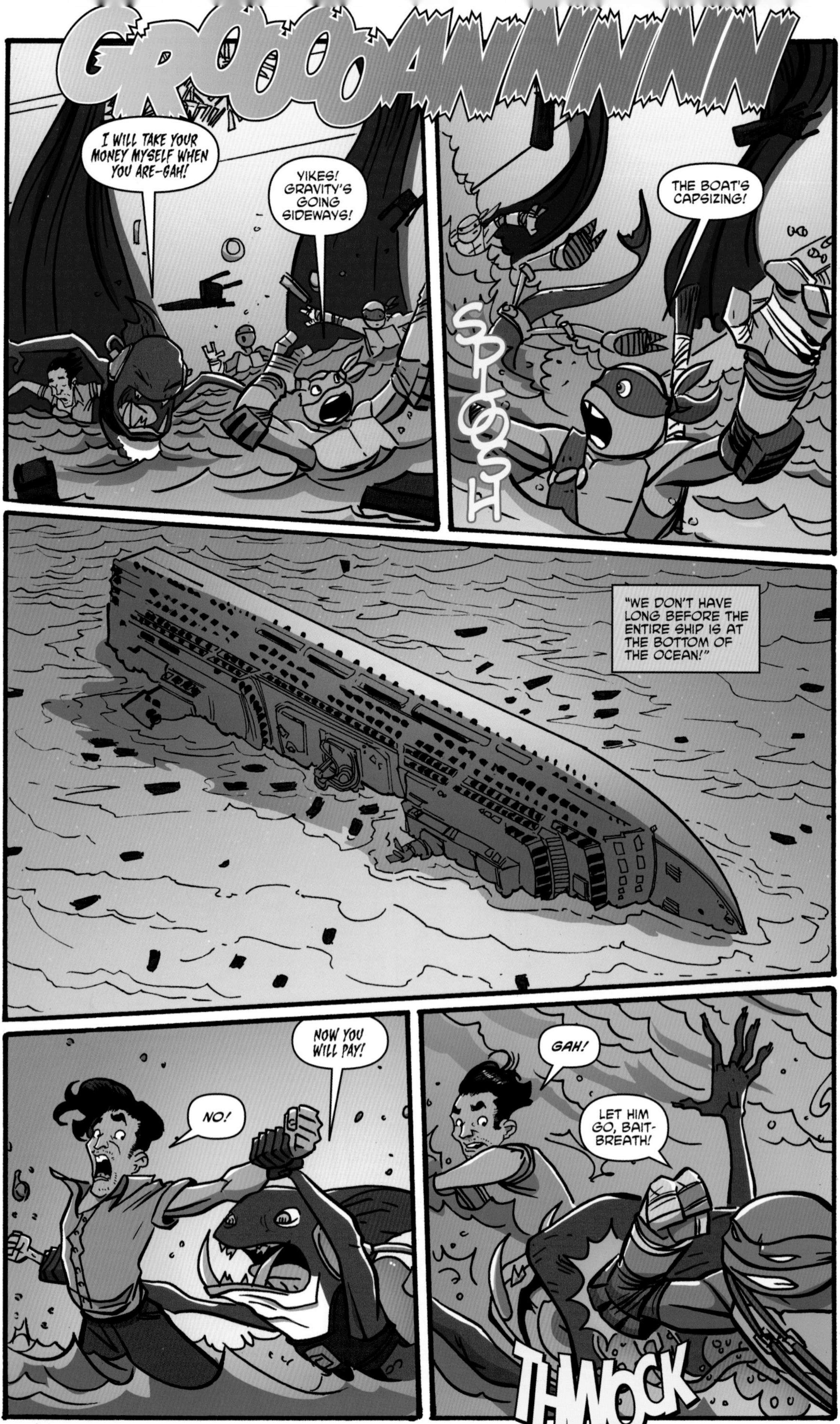
GROOOOANNNNNN
I WILL TAKE YOUR MONEY MYSELF WHEN YOU ARE–GAH!
YIKES! GRAVITY'S GOING SIDEWAYS!
THE BOAT'S CAPSIZING!
SPLOOSH
"WE DON'T HAVE LONG BEFORE THE ENTIRE SHIP IS AT THE BOTTOM OF THE OCEAN!"
NOW YOU WILL PAY!
NO!
GAH!
LET HIM GO, BAIT-BREATH!
THWOCK

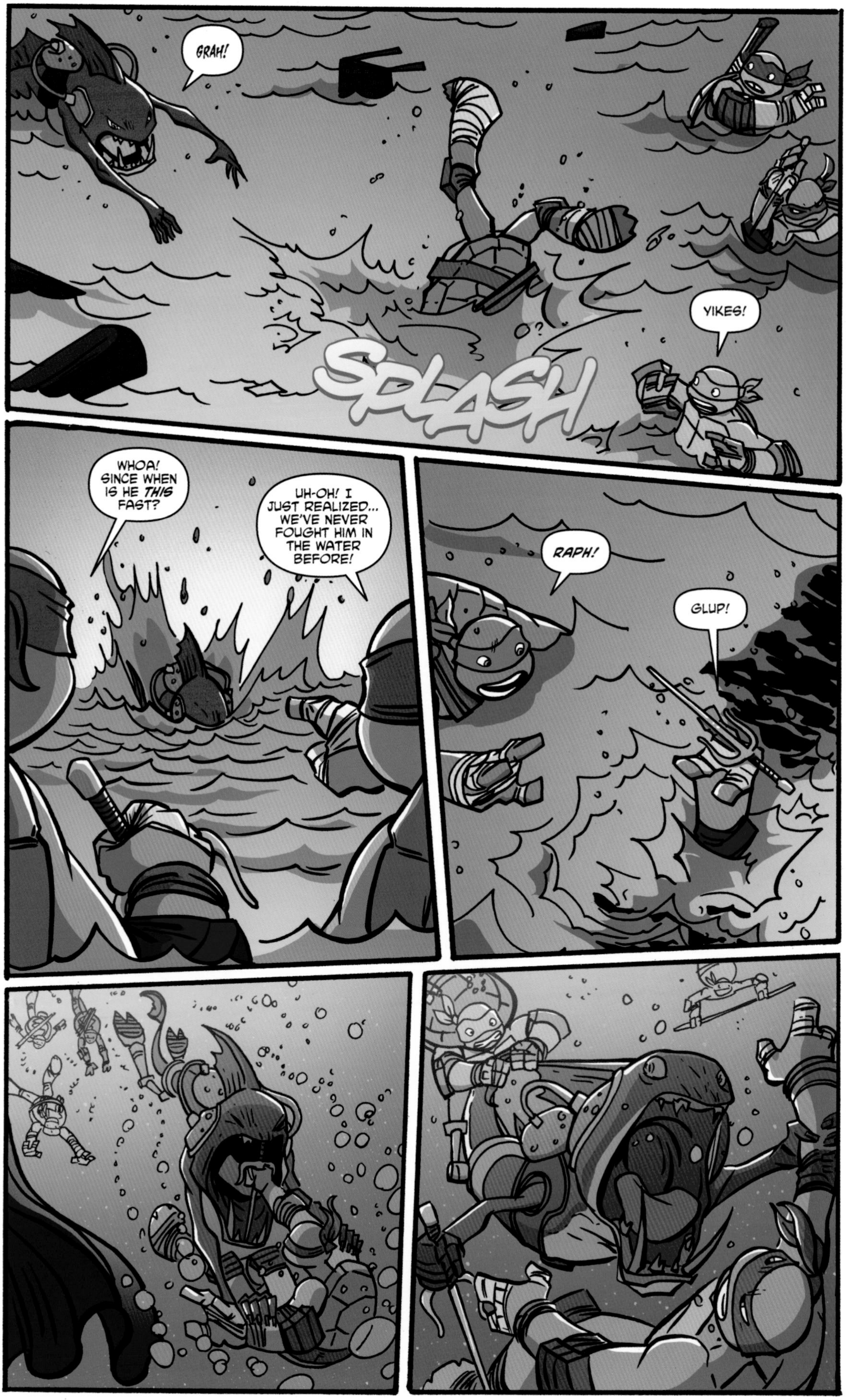
GRAH!
YIKES!
SPLASH
WHOA! SINCE WHEN IS HE *THIS* FAST?
UH-OH! I JUST REALIZED... WE'VE NEVER FOUGHT HIM IN THE WATER BEFORE!
RAPH!
GLUP!

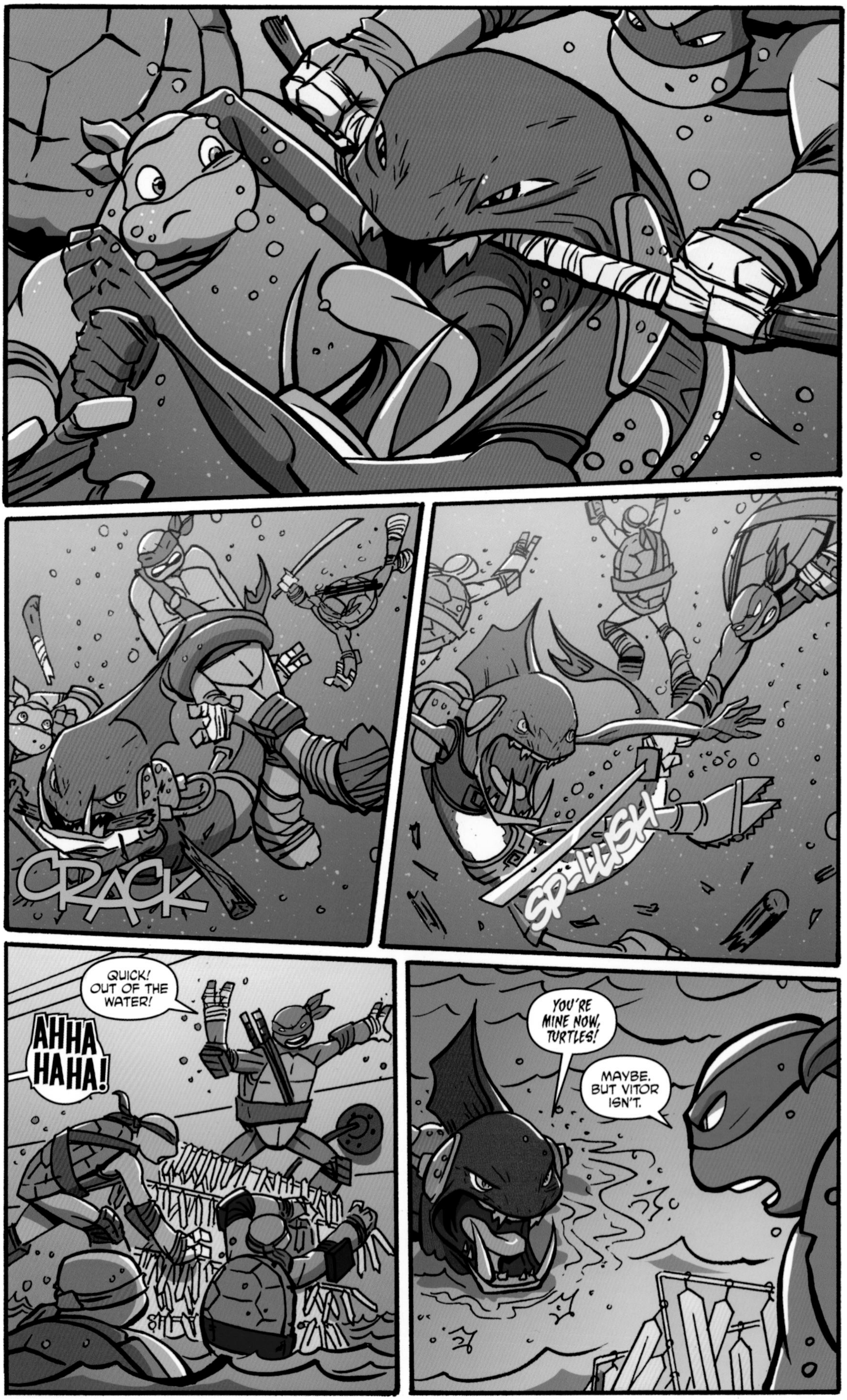
CRACK
SP-LUSH
QUICK! OUT OF THE WATER!
AHHA HAHA!
YOU'RE MINE NOW, TURTLES!
MAYBE. BUT VITOR ISN'T.

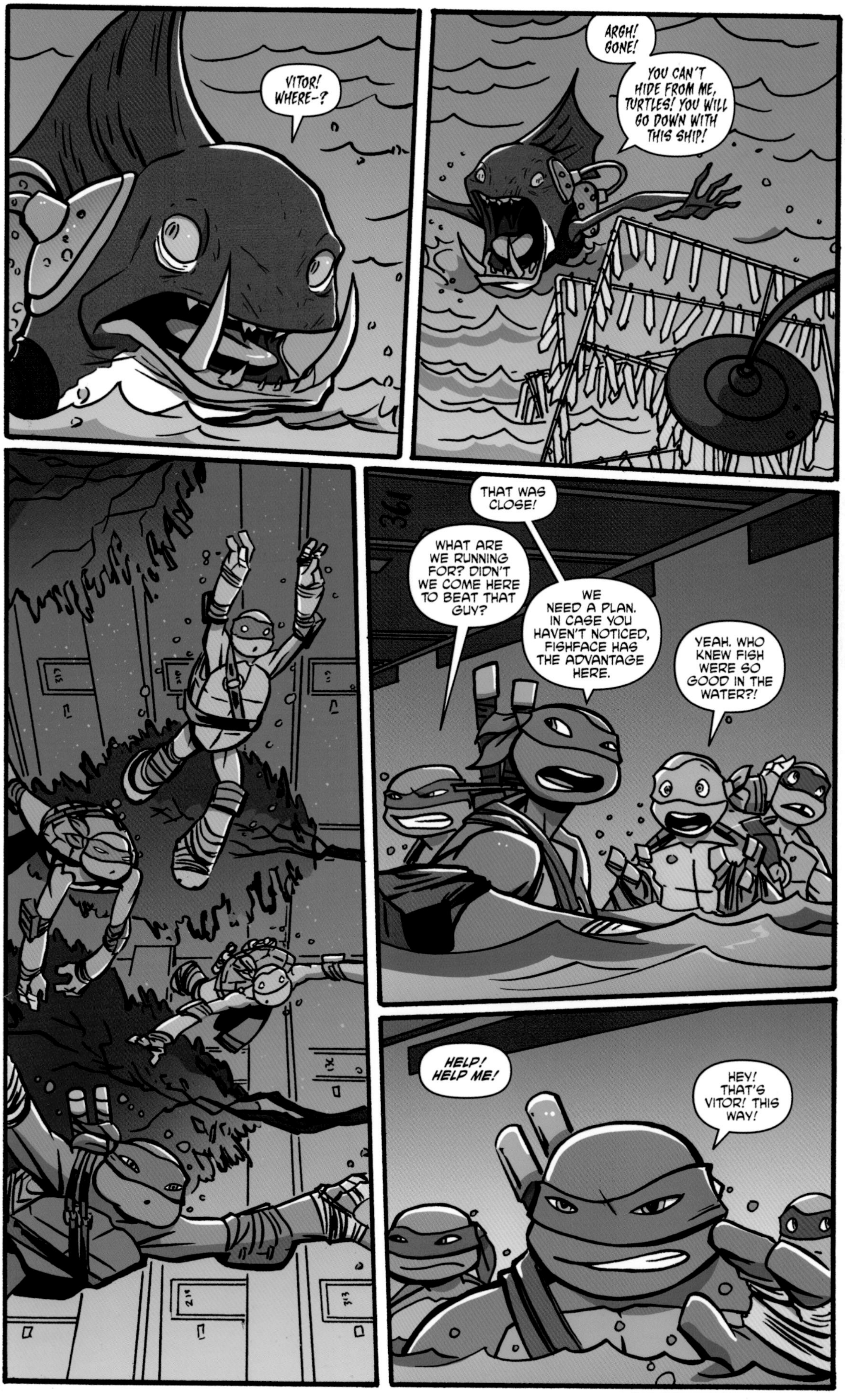
VITOR! WHERE-?
ARGH! GONE!
YOU CAN'T HIDE FROM ME, TURTLES! YOU WILL GO DOWN WITH THIS SHIP!
THAT WAS CLOSE!
WHAT ARE WE RUNNING FOR? DIDN'T WE COME HERE TO BEAT THAT GUY?
WE NEED A PLAN. IN CASE YOU HAVEN'T NOTICED, FISHFACE HAS THE ADVANTAGE HERE.
YEAH. WHO KNEW FISH WERE SO GOOD IN THE WATER?!
HELP! HELP ME!
HEY! THAT'S VITOR! THIS WAY!

WHY WOULD WE HELP HIM? HE LIED TO US. WE CAN'T TRUST THAT GUY ANY MORE THAN FISHFACE!

WE CAN'T JUST LEAVE HIM. HE COULD DROWN ON THIS SHIP!

HELP!

HE'S A *BAD GUY*, LEO. WHO KNOWS HOW MANY PEOPLE HE'S HURT? "SAO PAOLO'S TOP GANGSTER" CAN TAKE CARE OF HIMSELF.

WE *DON'T* IGNORE PEOPLE IN DANGER.

GIMME A BREAK! YOU JUST WANT TO BE ALL NOBLE AND PERFECT LIKE SOME COMIC BOOK HERO!

SENSEI TAUGHT US THE MISSION COMES FIRST. WE'RE *NINJA* TURTLES, NOT "HERO TURTLES."

WELL, MAYBE WE *SHOULD* BE HERO TURTLES!

I DUNNO, DUDE. DOESN'T HAVE MUCH OF A *RING* TO IT.

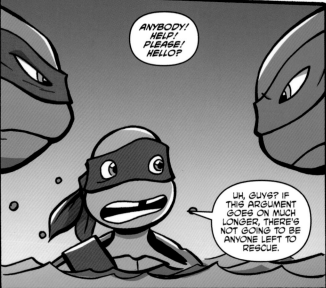

ANYBODY! HELP! PLEASE! HELLO?

UH, GUYS? IF THIS ARGUMENT GOES ON MUCH LONGER, THERE'S NOT GOING TO BE ANYONE LEFT TO RESCUE.

OKAY, RAPH. YOU DON'T WANT TO HELP VITOR? WE'LL DO IT WITHOUT YOU...

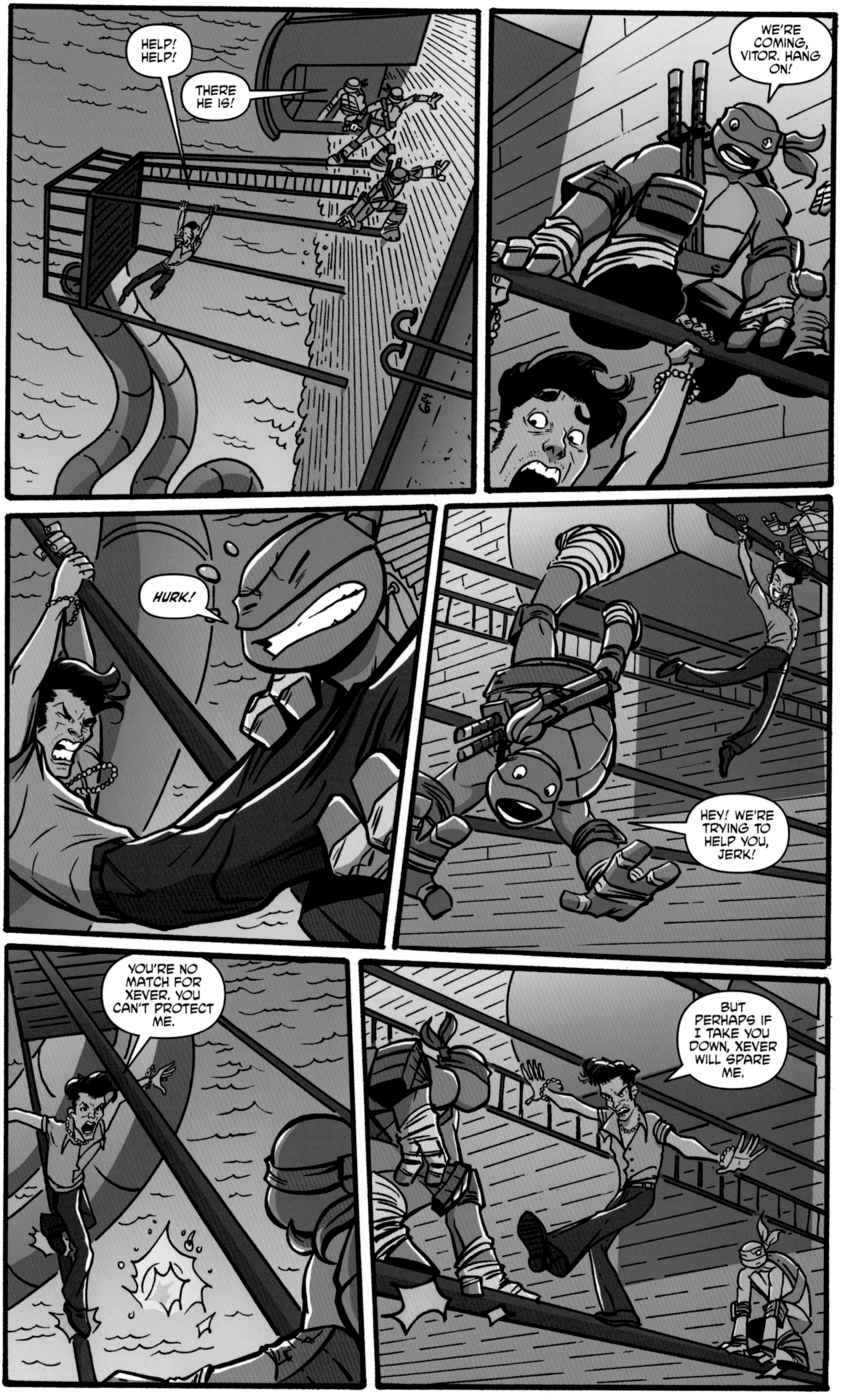
HELP! HELP!
THERE HE IS!
WE'RE COMING, VITOR. HANG ON!
HURK!
HEY! WE'RE TRYING TO HELP YOU, JERK!
YOU'RE NO MATCH FOR XEVER. YOU CAN'T PROTECT ME.
BUT PERHAPS IF I TAKE YOU DOWN, XEVER WILL SPARE ME.

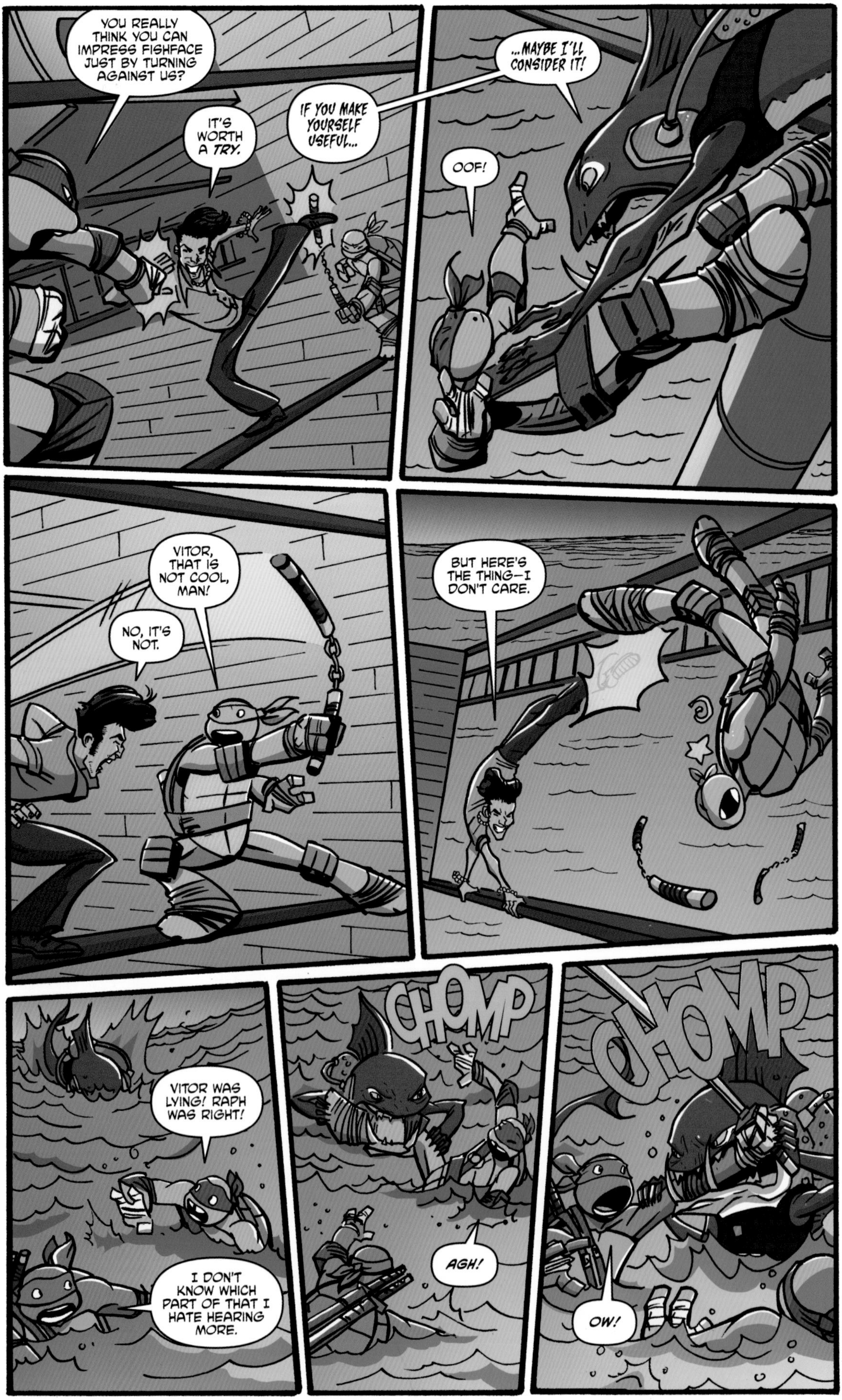
YOU REALLY THINK YOU CAN IMPRESS FISHFACE JUST BY TURNING AGAINST US?
IT'S WORTH A TRY.
IF YOU MAKE YOURSELF USEFUL...
...MAYBE I'LL CONSIDER IT!
OOF!
VITOR, THAT IS NOT COOL, MAN!
NO, IT'S NOT.
BUT HERE'S THE THING—I DON'T CARE.
VITOR WAS LYING! RAPH WAS RIGHT!
I DON'T KNOW WHICH PART OF THAT I HATE HEARING MORE.
CHOMP
AGH!
CHOMP
OW!

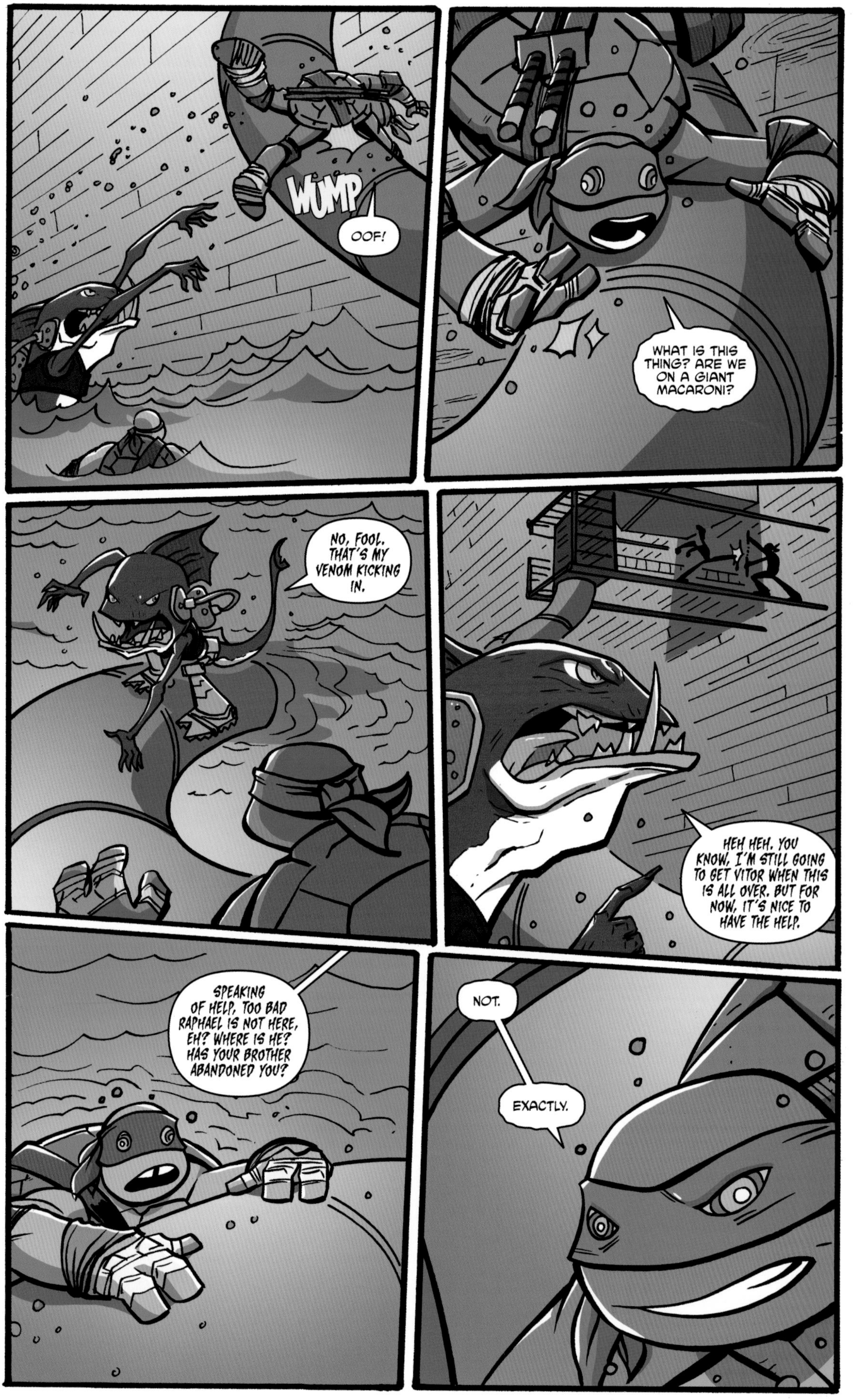
WUMP
OOF!
WHAT IS THIS THING? ARE WE ON A GIANT MACARONI?
NO, FOOL. THAT'S MY VENOM KICKING IN.
HEH HEH. YOU KNOW, I'M STILL GOING TO GET VITOR WHEN THIS IS ALL OVER. BUT FOR NOW, IT'S NICE TO HAVE THE HELP.
SPEAKING OF HELP, TOO BAD RAPHAEL IS NOT HERE, EH? WHERE IS HE? HAS YOUR BROTHER ABANDONED YOU?
NOT.
EXACTLY.

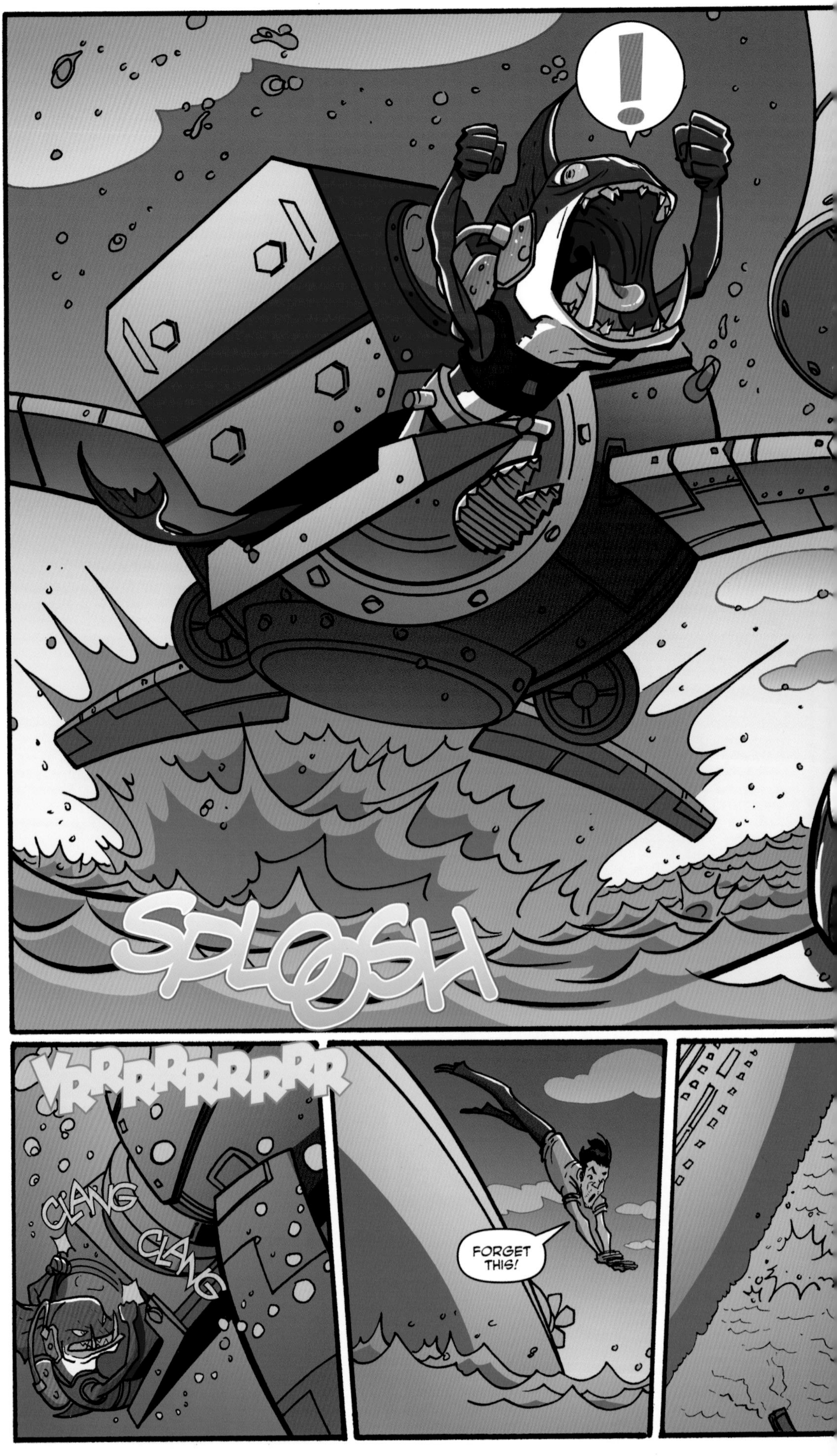
!
SPLOOSH
VRRRRRRRRRR
CLANG
CLANG
FORGET THIS!

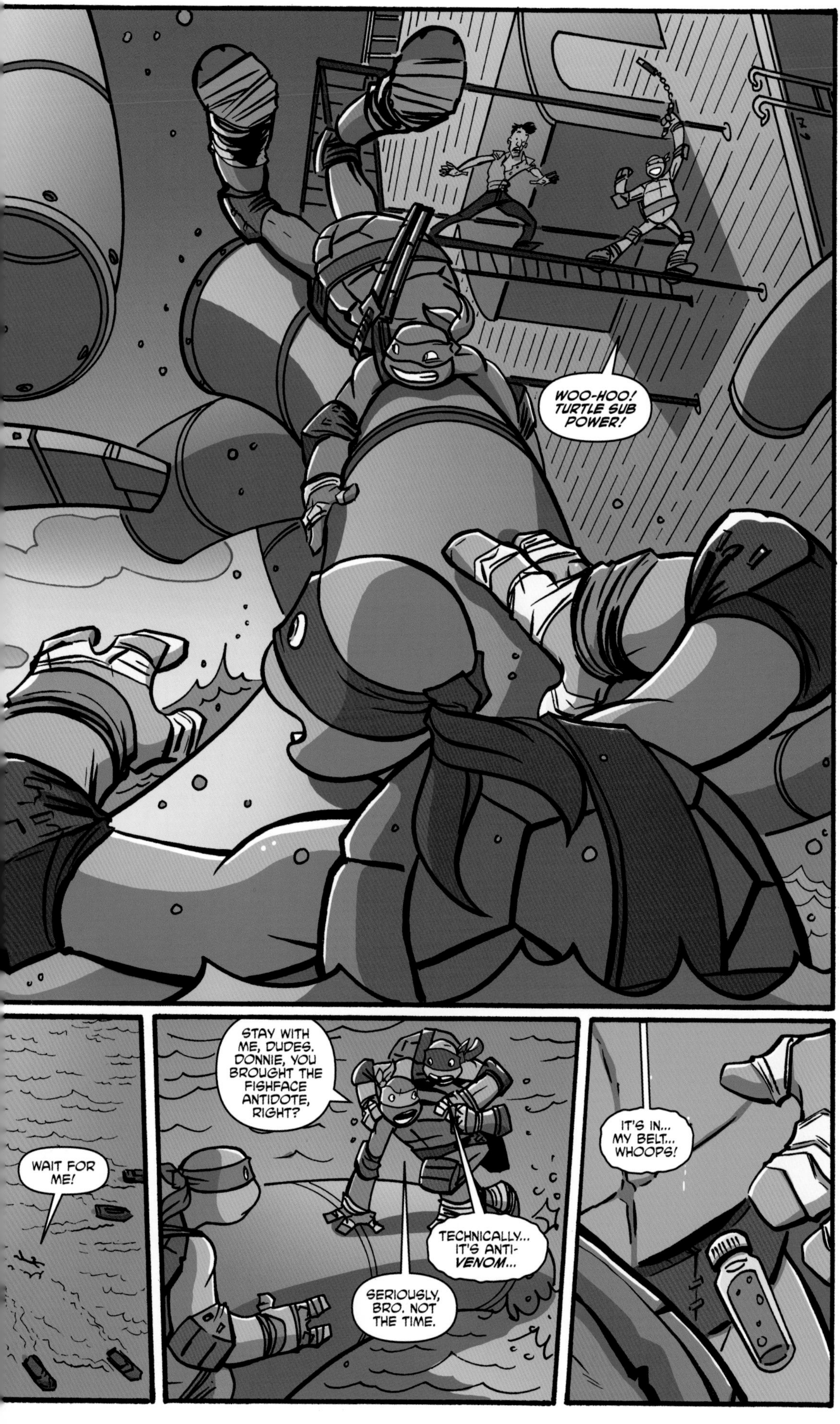
WOO-HOO! TURTLE SUB POWER!
WAIT FOR ME!
STAY WITH ME, DUDES. DONNIE, YOU BROUGHT THE FISHFACE ANTIDOTE, RIGHT?
TECHNICALLY... IT'S ANTI-VENOM...
SERIOUSLY, BRO. NOT THE TIME.
IT'S IN... MY BELT... WHOOPS!

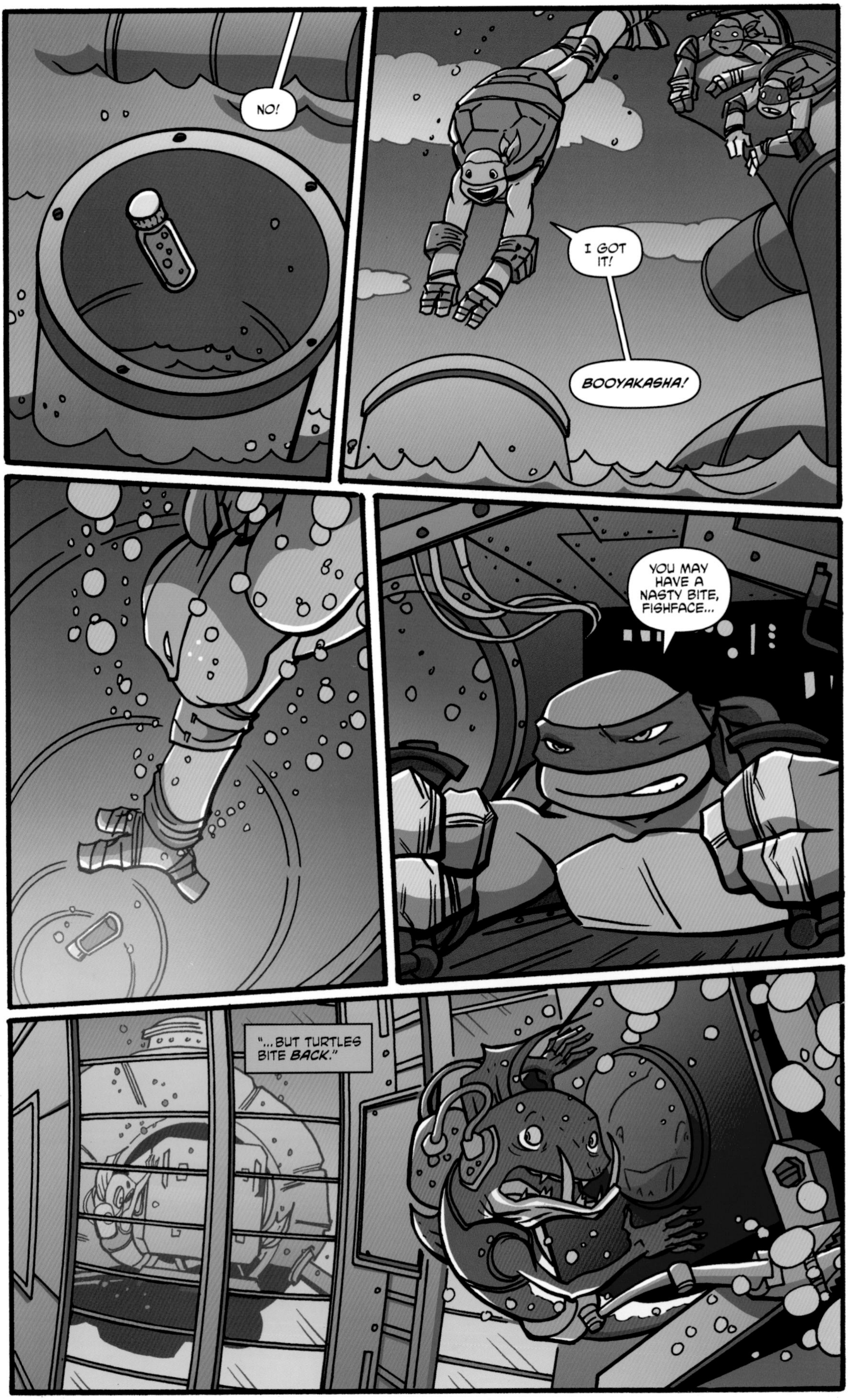
NO!
I GOT IT!
BOOYAKASHA!
YOU MAY HAVE A NASTY BITE, FISHFACE...
"...BUT TURTLES BITE BACK."

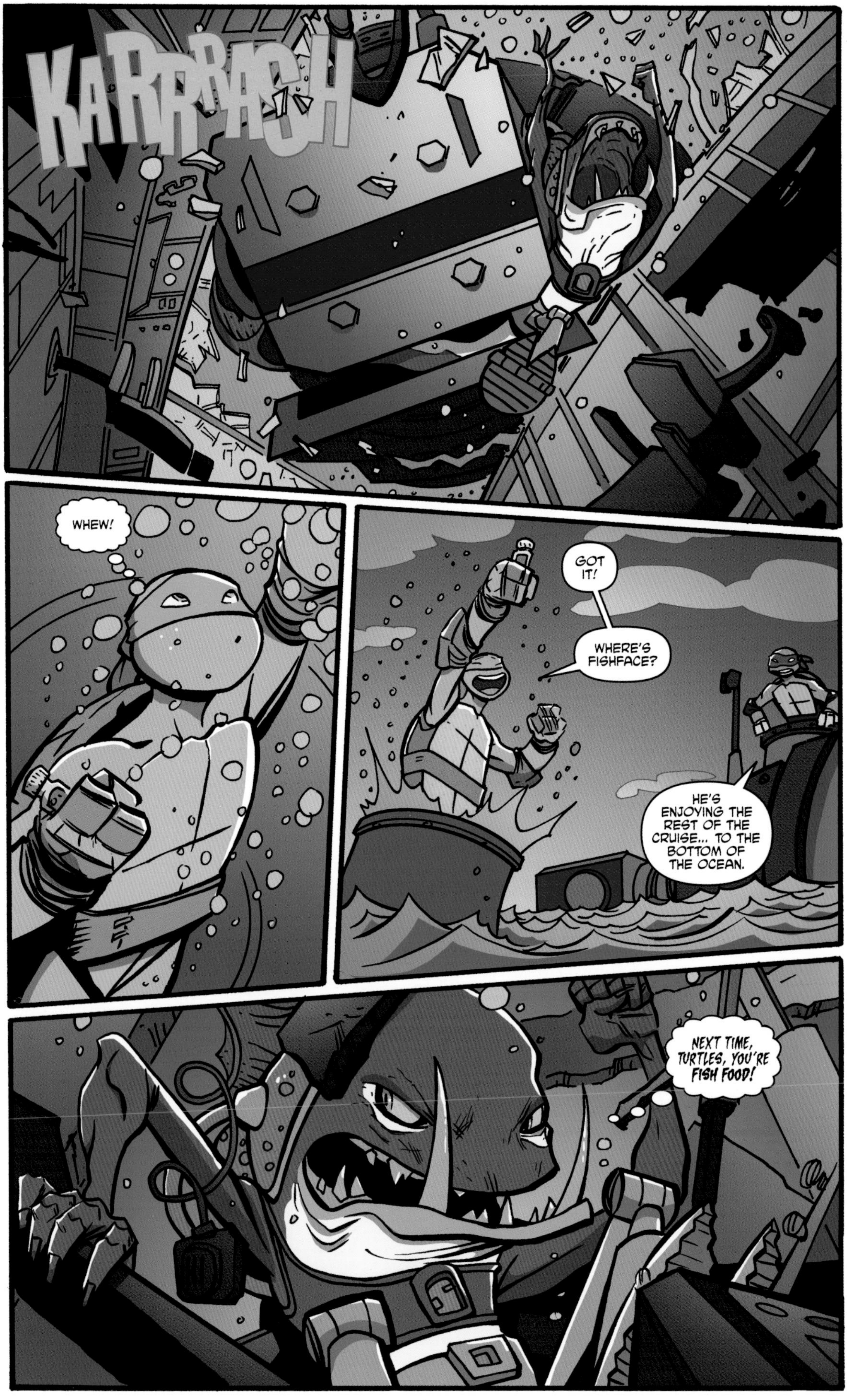
KARRRASH
WHEW!
GOT IT!
WHERE'S FISHFACE?
HE'S ENJOYING THE REST OF THE CRUISE... TO THE BOTTOM OF THE OCEAN.
NEXT TIME, TURTLES, YOU'RE FISH FOOD!

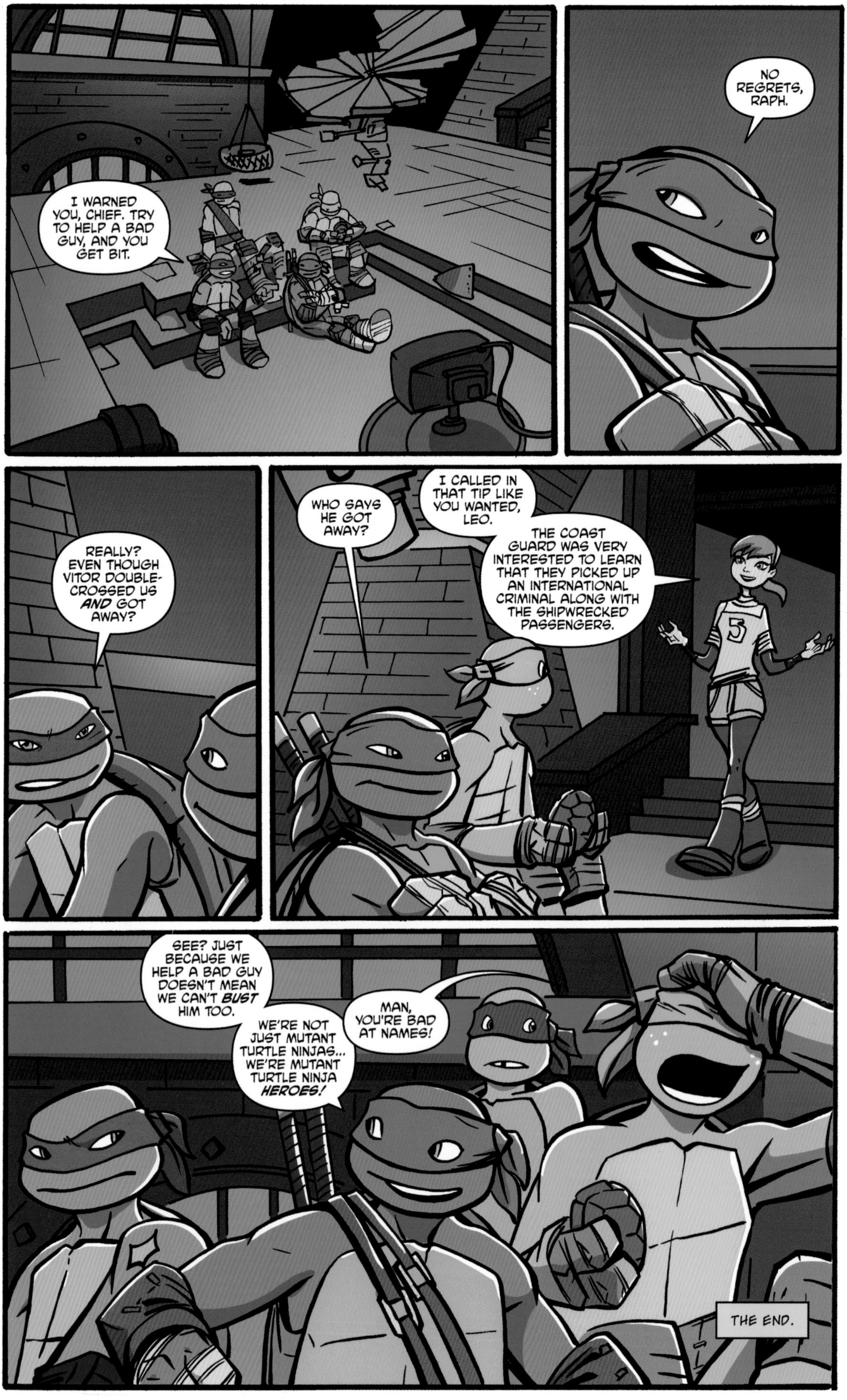
I WARNED YOU, CHIEF. TRY TO HELP A BAD GUY, AND YOU GET BIT.
NO REGRETS, RAPH.
REALLY? EVEN THOUGH VITOR DOUBLE-CROSSED US *AND* GOT AWAY?
WHO SAYS HE GOT AWAY?
I CALLED IN THAT TIP LIKE YOU WANTED, LEO.
THE COAST GUARD WAS VERY INTERESTED TO LEARN THAT THEY PICKED UP AN INTERNATIONAL CRIMINAL ALONG WITH THE SHIPWRECKED PASSENGERS.
SEE? JUST BECAUSE WE HELP A BAD GUY DOESN'T MEAN WE CAN'T *BUST* HIM TOO.
WE'RE NOT JUST MUTANT TURTLE NINJAS... WE'RE MUTANT TURTLE NINJA *HEROES!*
MAN, YOU'RE BAD AT NAMES!
THE END.

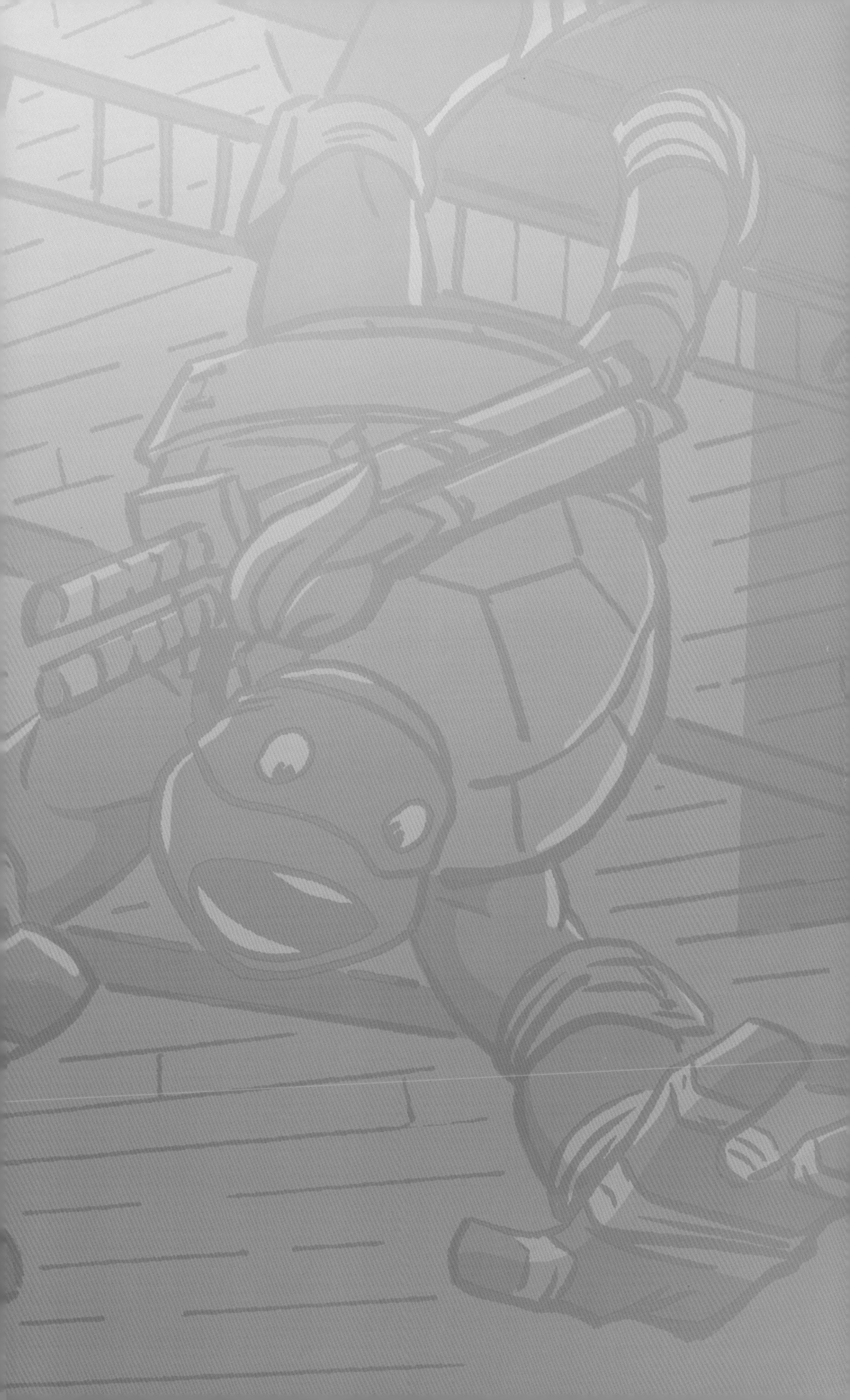

ART BY **DARIO BRIZUELA**

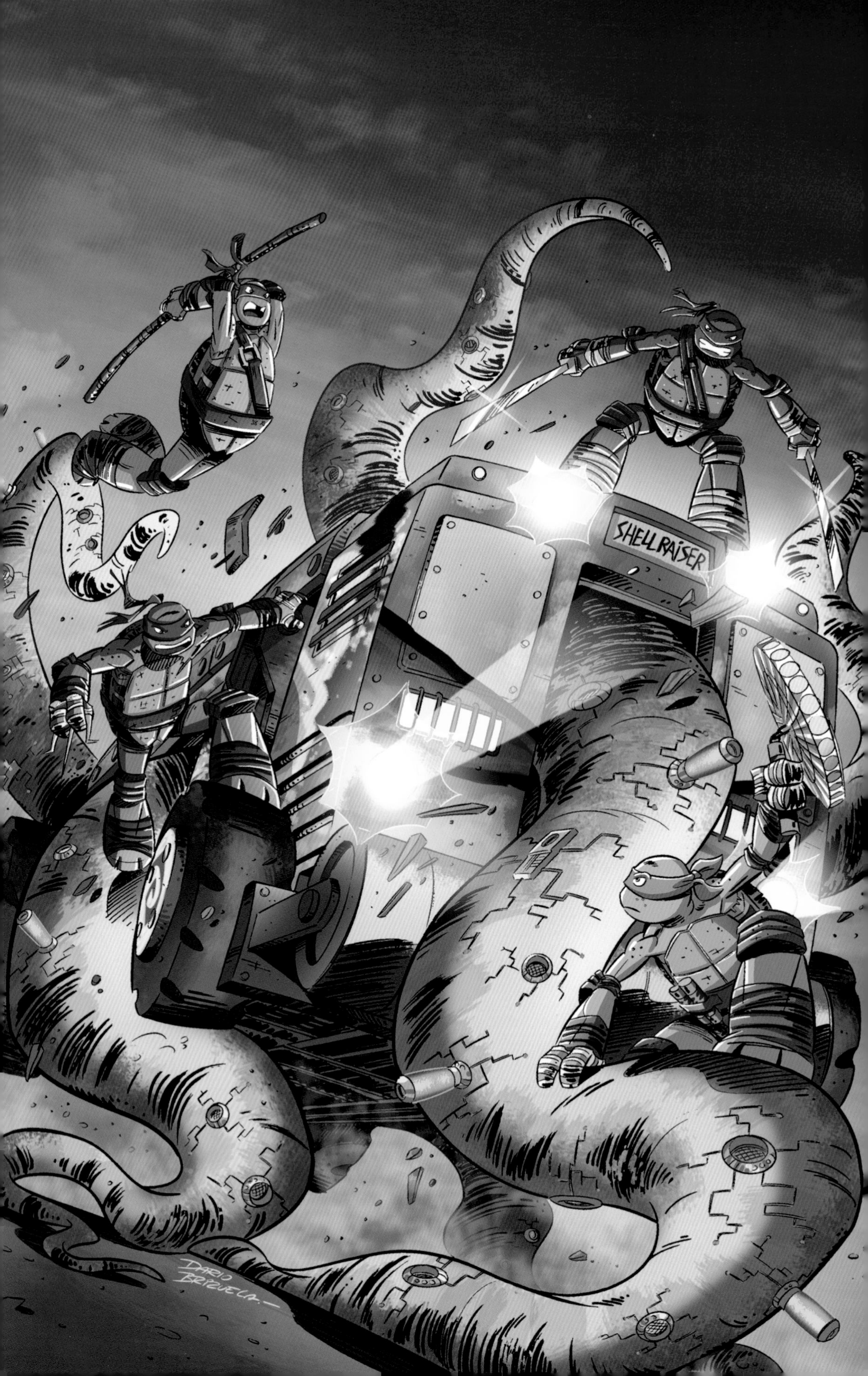
SHELLRAISER
DARIO BRIZUELA

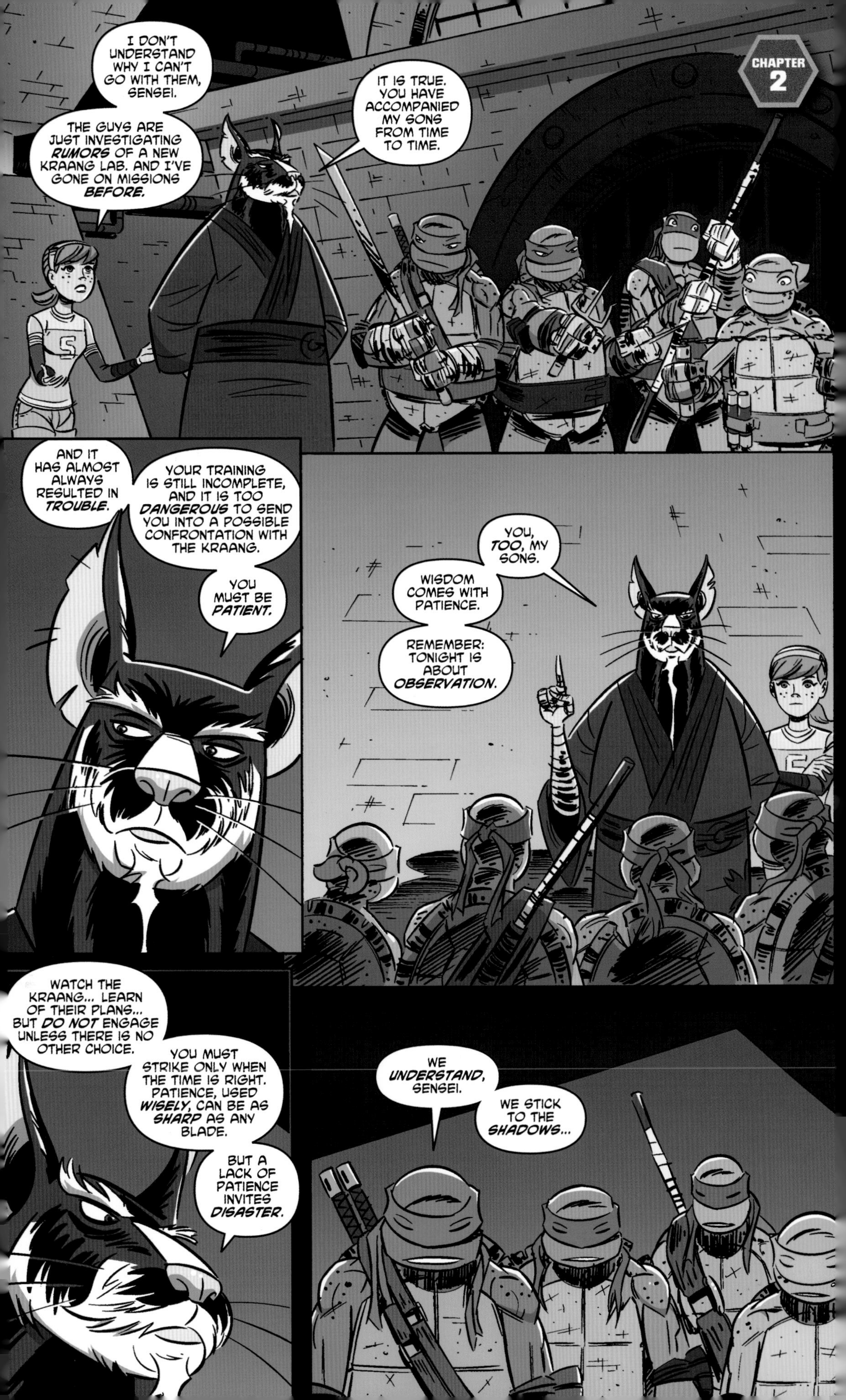
CHAPTER 2
I DON'T UNDERSTAND WHY I CAN'T GO WITH THEM, SENSEI.
THE GUYS ARE JUST INVESTIGATING RUMORS OF A NEW KRAANG LAB. AND I'VE GONE ON MISSIONS BEFORE.
IT IS TRUE. YOU HAVE ACCOMPANIED MY SONS FROM TIME TO TIME.
AND IT HAS ALMOST ALWAYS RESULTED IN TROUBLE.
YOUR TRAINING IS STILL INCOMPLETE, AND IT IS TOO DANGEROUS TO SEND YOU INTO A POSSIBLE CONFRONTATION WITH THE KRAANG.
YOU MUST BE PATIENT.
YOU, TOO, MY SONS.
WISDOM COMES WITH PATIENCE.
REMEMBER: TONIGHT IS ABOUT OBSERVATION.
WATCH THE KRAANG... LEARN OF THEIR PLANS... BUT DO NOT ENGAGE UNLESS THERE IS NO OTHER CHOICE.
YOU MUST STRIKE ONLY WHEN THE TIME IS RIGHT. PATIENCE, USED WISELY, CAN BE AS SHARP AS ANY BLADE.
BUT A LACK OF PATIENCE INVITES DISASTER.
WE UNDERSTAND, SENSEI.
WE STICK TO THE SHADOWS...

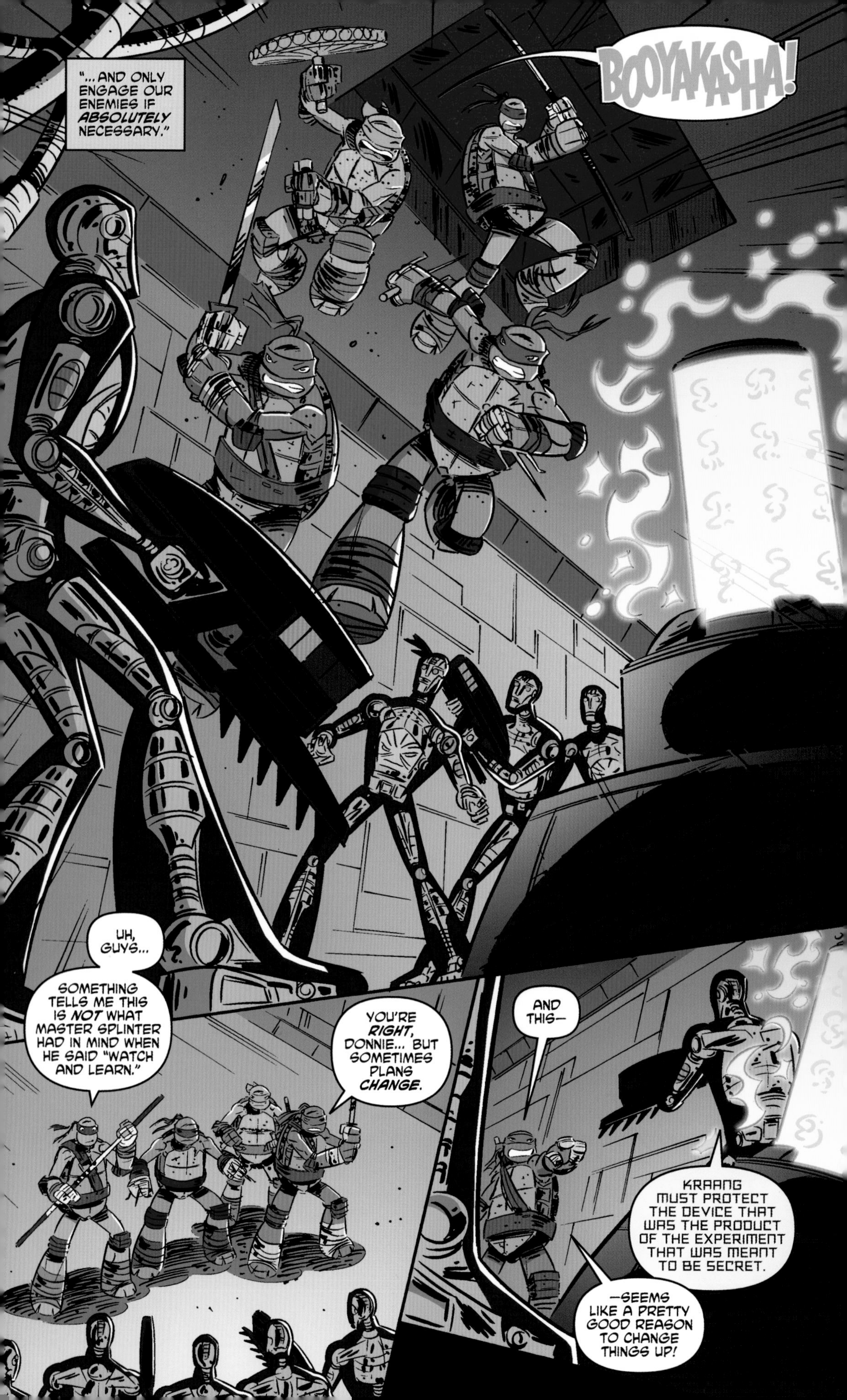
"...AND ONLY ENGAGE OUR ENEMIES IF *ABSOLUTELY* NECESSARY."
BOOYAKASHA!
UH, GUYS...
SOMETHING TELLS ME THIS IS *NOT* WHAT MASTER SPLINTER HAD IN MIND WHEN HE SAID "WATCH AND LEARN."
YOU'RE *RIGHT*, DONNIE... BUT SOMETIMES PLANS *CHANGE*.
AND THIS—
KRAANG MUST PROTECT THE DEVICE THAT WAS THE PRODUCT OF THE EXPERIMENT THAT WAS MEANT TO BE SECRET.
—SEEMS LIKE A PRETTY GOOD REASON TO CHANGE THINGS UP!

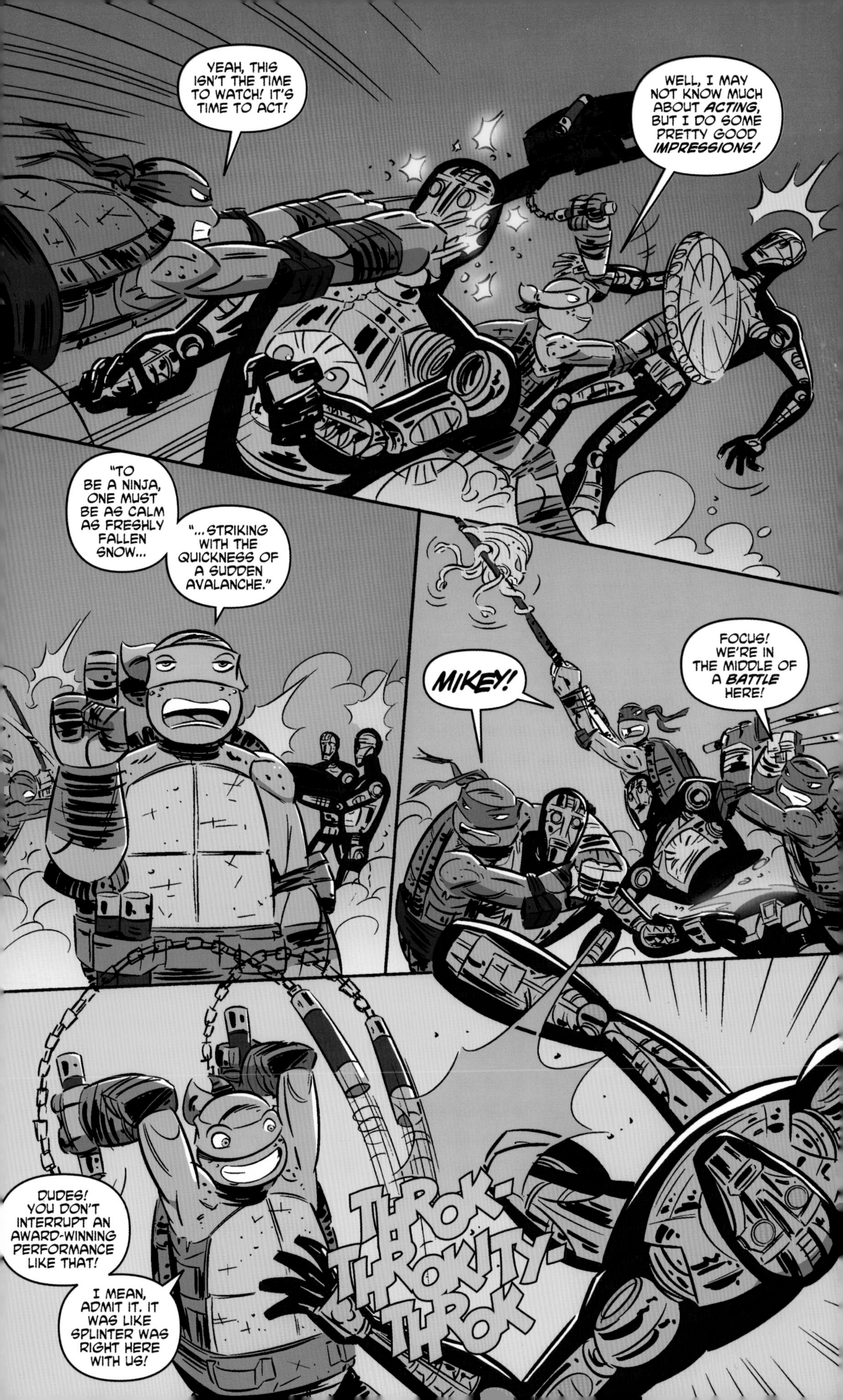
YEAH, THIS ISN'T THE TIME TO WATCH! IT'S TIME TO ACT!
WELL, I MAY NOT KNOW MUCH ABOUT *ACTING*, BUT I DO SOME PRETTY GOOD *IMPRESSIONS!*
"TO BE A NINJA, ONE MUST BE AS CALM AS FRESHLY FALLEN SNOW...
"...STRIKING WITH THE QUICKNESS OF A SUDDEN AVALANCHE."
MIKEY!
FOCUS! WE'RE IN THE MIDDLE OF A *BATTLE* HERE!
DUDES! YOU DON'T INTERRUPT AN AWARD-WINNING PERFORMANCE LIKE THAT!
I MEAN, ADMIT IT. IT WAS LIKE SPLINTER WAS RIGHT HERE WITH US!
THROK-THROKITY-THROK

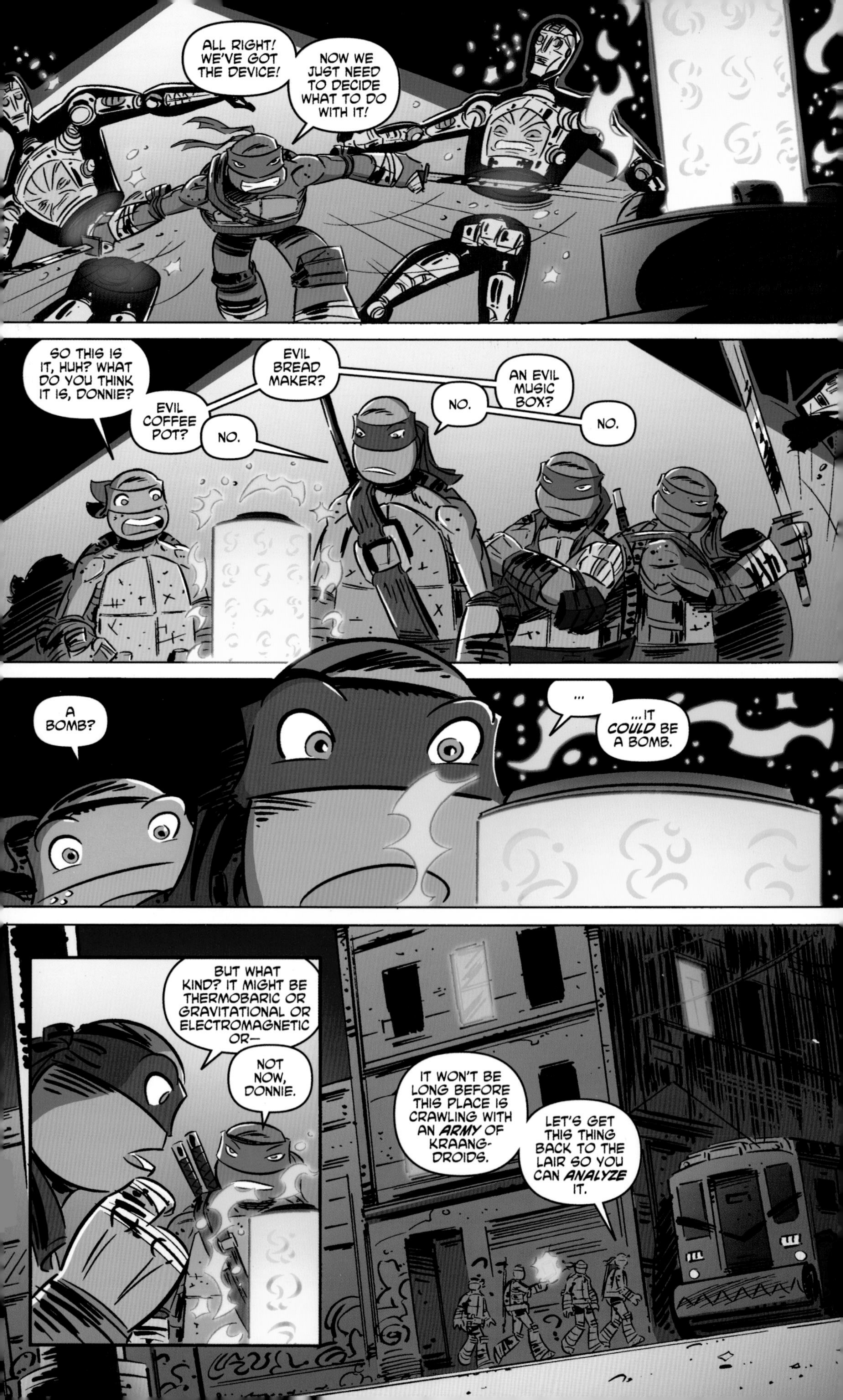
ALL RIGHT! WE'VE GOT THE DEVICE!
NOW WE JUST NEED TO DECIDE WHAT TO DO WITH IT!
SO THIS IS IT, HUH? WHAT DO YOU THINK IT IS, DONNIE?
EVIL COFFEE POT?
NO.
EVIL BREAD MAKER?
NO.
AN EVIL MUSIC BOX?
NO.
A BOMB?
...
...IT COULD BE A BOMB.
BUT WHAT KIND? IT MIGHT BE THERMOBARIC OR GRAVITATIONAL OR ELECTROMAGNETIC OR—
NOT NOW, DONNIE.
IT WON'T BE LONG BEFORE THIS PLACE IS CRAWLING WITH AN ARMY OF KRAANG-DROIDS.
LET'S GET THIS THING BACK TO THE LAIR SO YOU CAN ANALYZE IT.

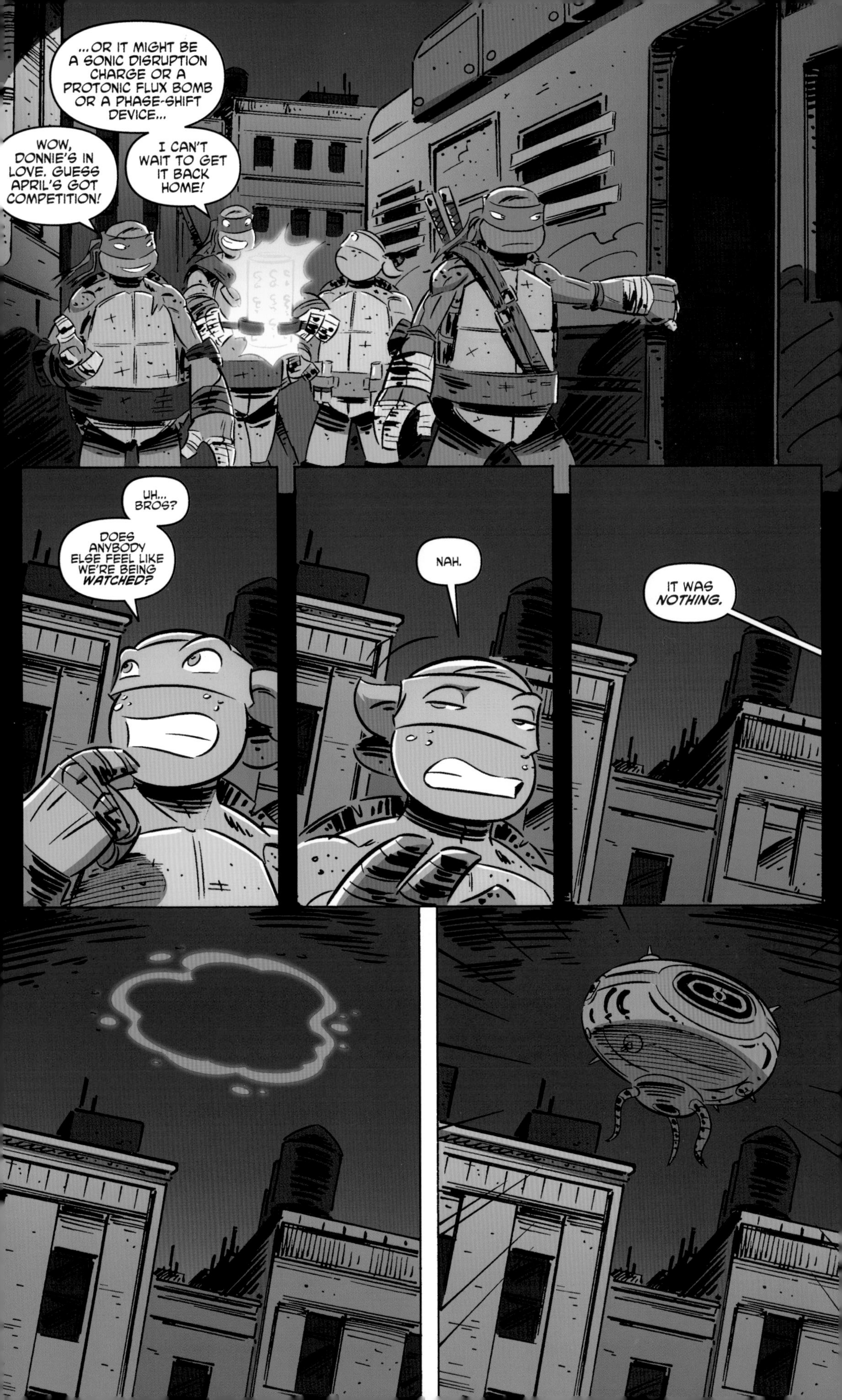

...OR IT MIGHT BE A SONIC DISRUPTION CHARGE OR A PROTONIC FLUX BOMB OR A PHASE-SHIFT DEVICE...
WOW, DONNIE'S IN LOVE. GUESS APRIL'S GOT COMPETITION!
I CAN'T WAIT TO GET IT BACK HOME!
UH... BROS?
DOES ANYBODY ELSE FEEL LIKE WE'RE BEING WATCHED?
NAH.
IT WAS NOTHING.

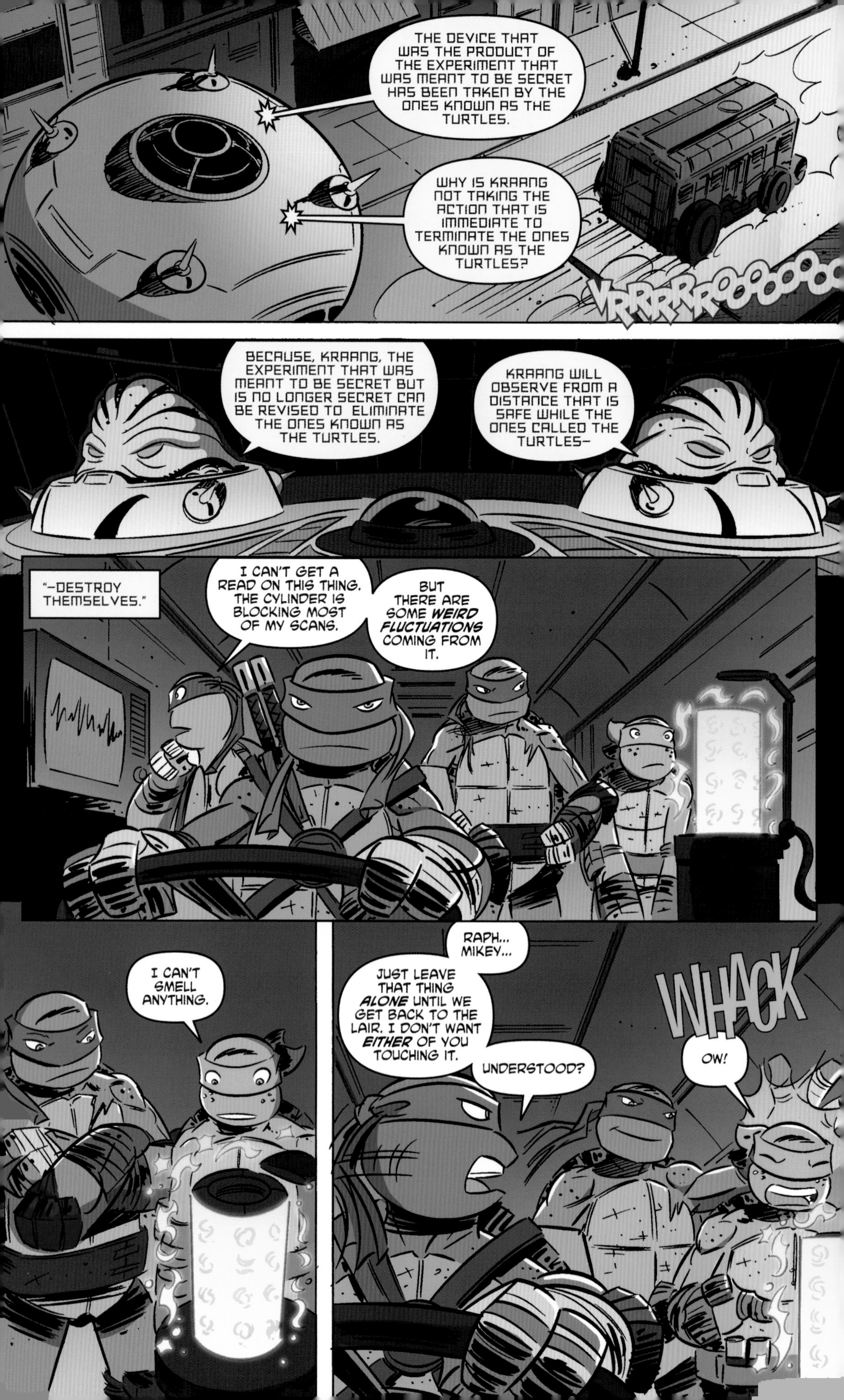
THE DEVICE THAT WAS THE PRODUCT OF THE EXPERIMENT THAT WAS MEANT TO BE SECRET HAS BEEN TAKEN BY THE ONES KNOWN AS THE TURTLES.
WHY IS KRAANG NOT TAKING THE ACTION THAT IS IMMEDIATE TO TERMINATE THE ONES KNOWN AS THE TURTLES?
VRRRRROOOOOOO
BECAUSE, KRAANG, THE EXPERIMENT THAT WAS MEANT TO BE SECRET BUT IS NO LONGER SECRET CAN BE REVISED TO ELIMINATE THE ONES KNOWN AS THE TURTLES.
KRAANG WILL OBSERVE FROM A DISTANCE THAT IS SAFE WHILE THE ONES CALLED THE TURTLES–
"–DESTROY THEMSELVES."
I CAN'T GET A READ ON THIS THING. THE CYLINDER IS BLOCKING MOST OF MY SCANS.
BUT THERE ARE SOME WEIRD FLUCTUATIONS COMING FROM IT.
I CAN'T SMELL ANYTHING.
RAPH... MIKEY...
JUST LEAVE THAT THING ALONE UNTIL WE GET BACK TO THE LAIR. I DON'T WANT EITHER OF YOU TOUCHING IT.
UNDERSTOOD?
WHACK
OW!

GASP!

RAPH DID IT! HE TOUCHED IT!

POKE

THAT'S RIGHT. AND NOTHING—

EE-BE
EE-BE
EE-BE
EE-BE

UGH! I SEE WHAT YOU MEAN ABOUT THOSE *FLUCTUATIONS!*

HSSSSSSSSSSSSSSSSSS

WHEW! SMELLS LIKE MIKEY'S FEET!

DEFINITELY *NOT* A BOMB.

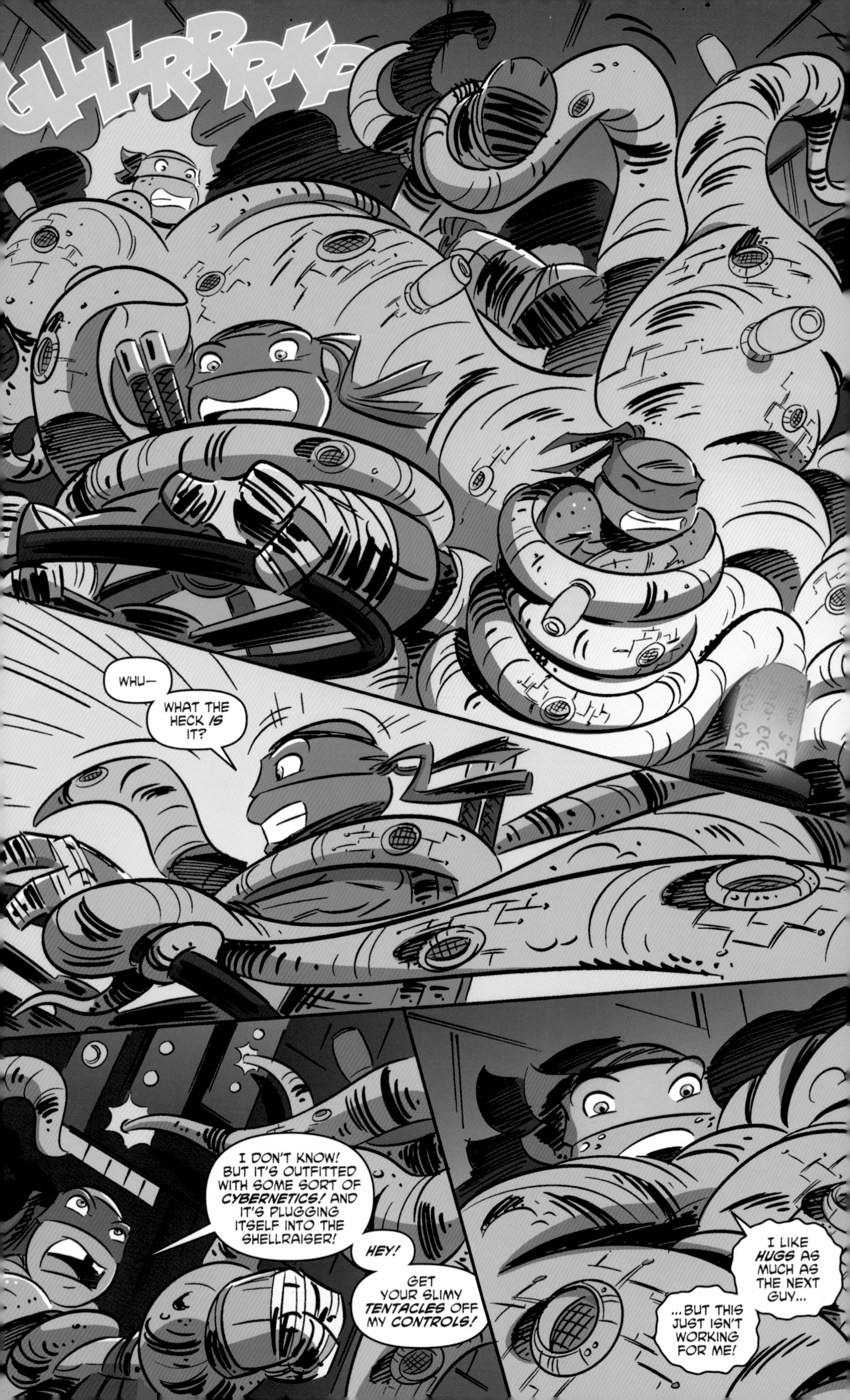
GLLLRRRRKD
WHU—
WHAT THE HECK *IS* IT?
I DON'T KNOW! BUT IT'S OUTFITTED WITH SOME SORT OF *CYBERNETICS!* AND IT'S PLUGGING ITSELF INTO THE SHELLRAISER!
HEY!
GET YOUR SLIMY *TENTACLES* OFF MY *CONTROLS!*
I LIKE *HUGS* AS MUCH AS THE NEXT GUY...
...BUT THIS JUST ISN'T WORKING FOR ME!

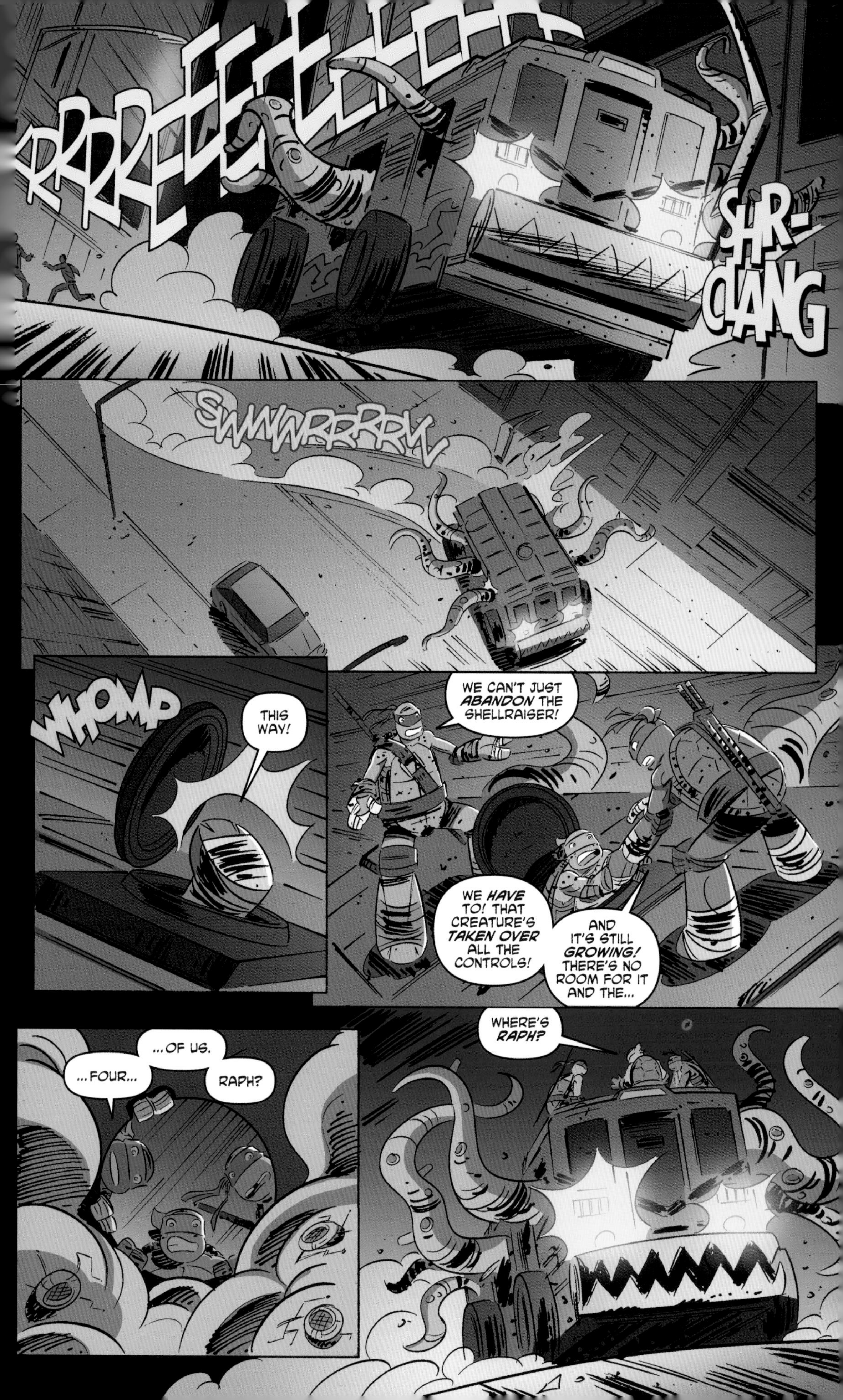

KRRRREEEEEEEEEEEEEEEE
SHR-CLANG
SWWWRRRRW
WHOMP
THIS WAY!
WE CAN'T JUST *ABANDON* THE SHELLRAISER!
WE *HAVE* TO! THAT CREATURE'S *TAKEN OVER* ALL THE CONTROLS!
AND IT'S STILL *GROWING!* THERE'S NO ROOM FOR IT AND THE...
...FOUR...
...OF US.
RAPH?
WHERE'S *RAPH?*

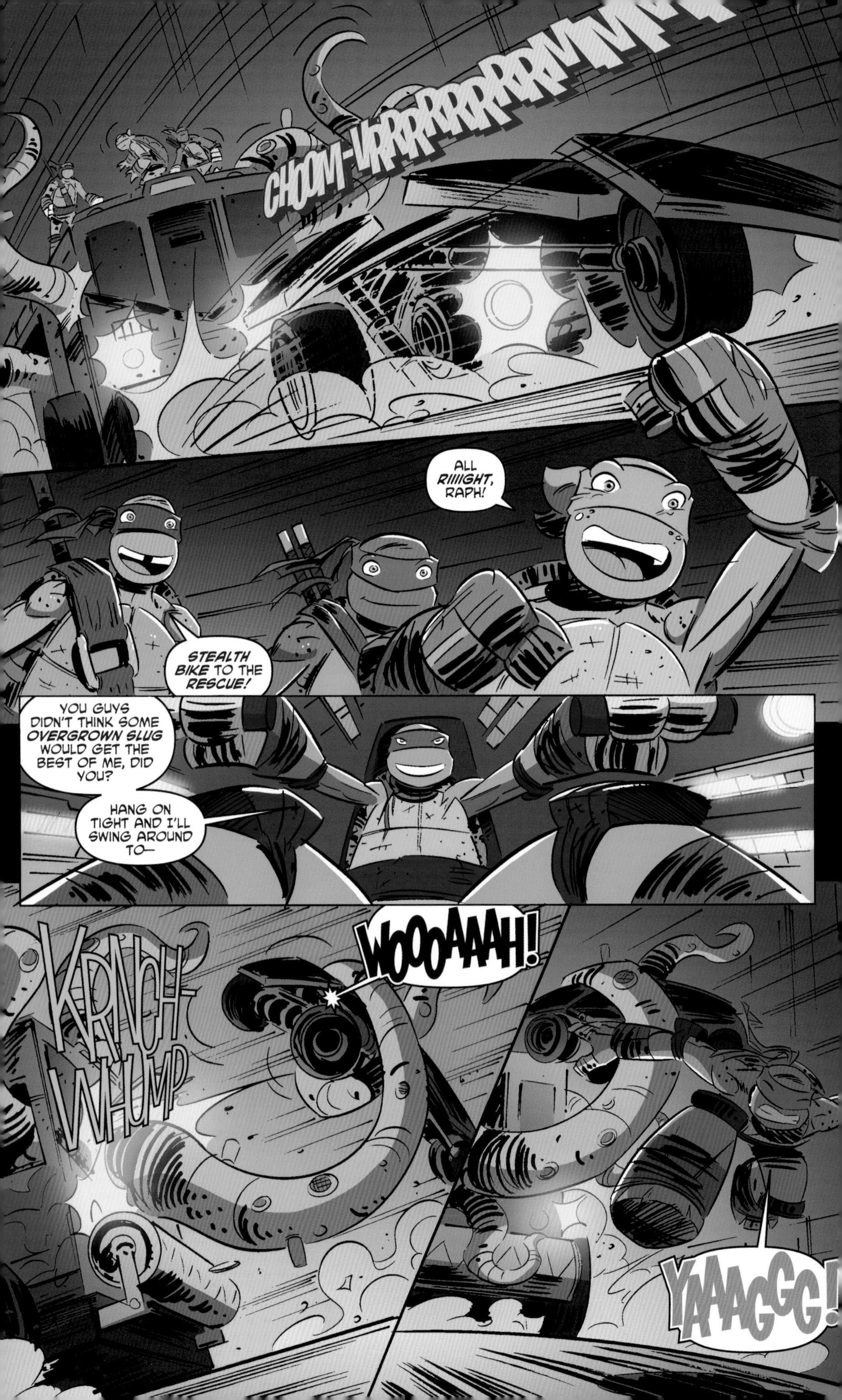

CHOOM-VRRRRRRRRRMMM
ALL RIIIIGHT, RAPH!
STEALTH BIKE TO THE RESCUE!
YOU GUYS DIDN'T THINK SOME OVERGROWN SLUG WOULD GET THE BEST OF ME, DID YOU?
HANG ON TIGHT AND I'LL SWING AROUND TO—
KRNCH-WHUMP
WOOOAAAH!
YAAAGGG!

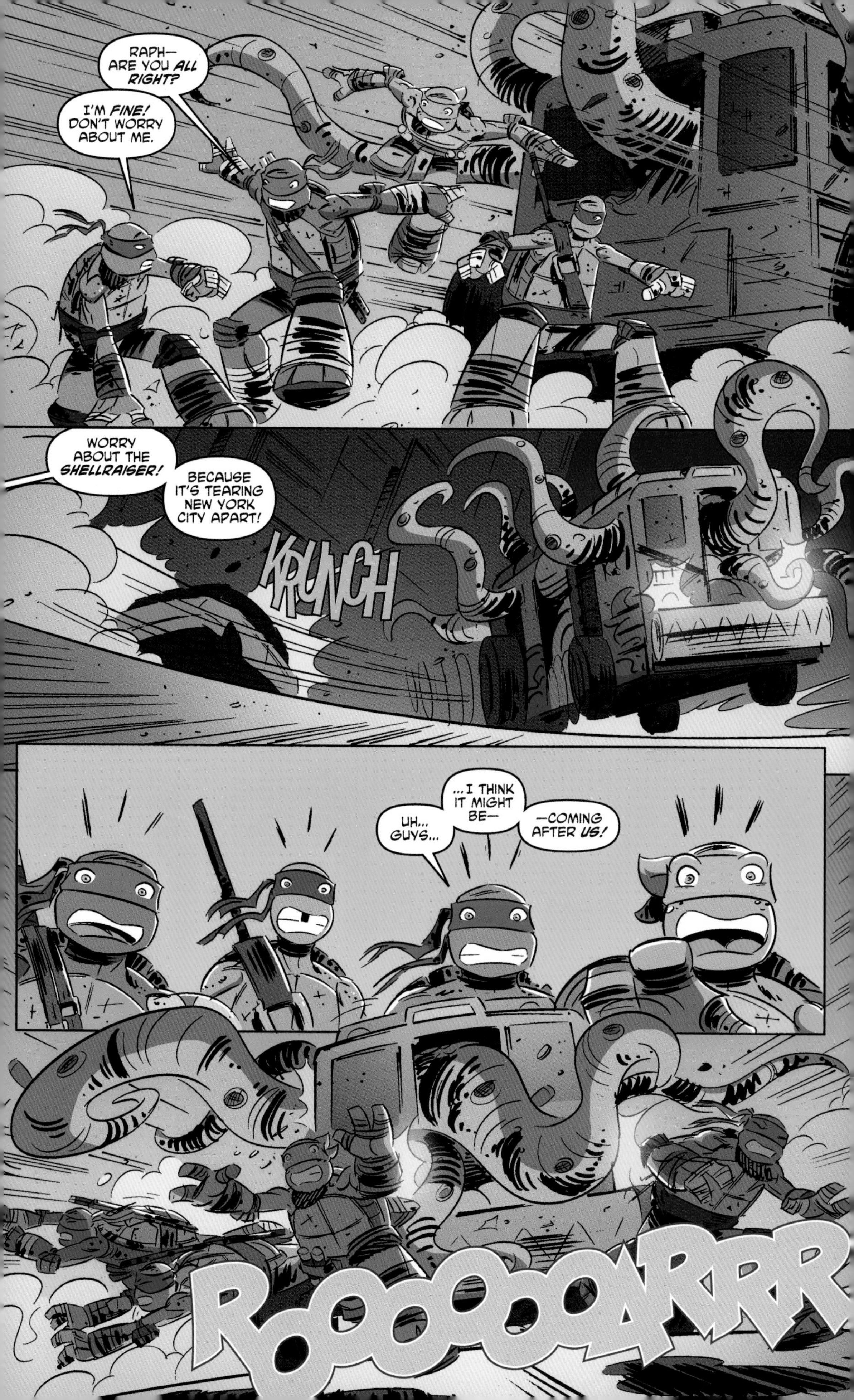
RAPH— ARE YOU ALL RIGHT?
I'M FINE! DON'T WORRY ABOUT ME.
WORRY ABOUT THE SHELLRAISER!
BECAUSE IT'S TEARING NEW YORK CITY APART!
KRUNCH
UH... GUYS...
...I THINK IT MIGHT BE—
—COMING AFTER US!
ROOOOOOARRRR

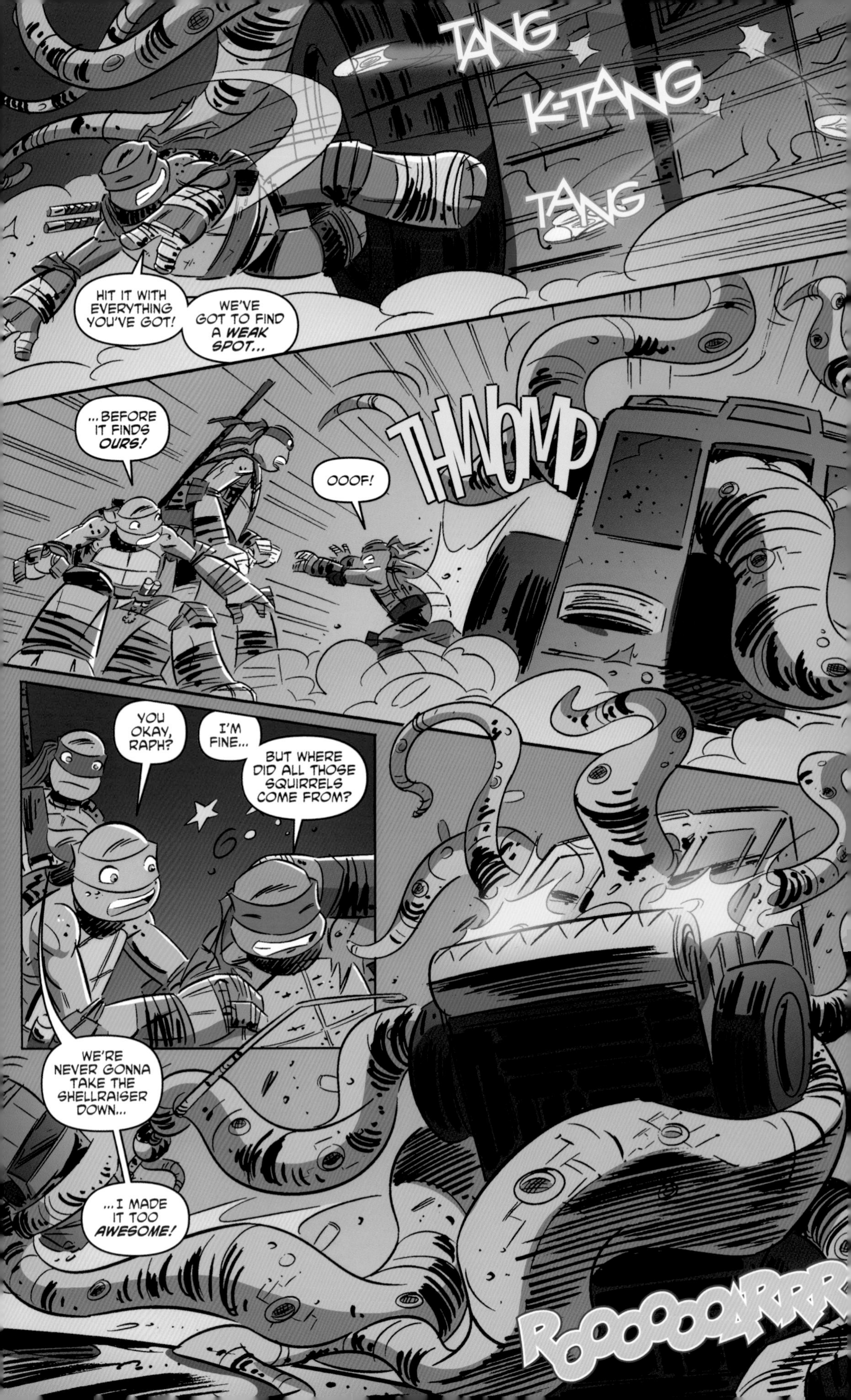
TANG
K-TANG
TANG
HIT IT WITH EVERYTHING YOU'VE GOT!
WE'VE GOT TO FIND A WEAK SPOT...
...BEFORE IT FINDS OURS!
THWOMP
OOOF!
YOU OKAY, RAPH?
I'M FINE...
BUT WHERE DID ALL THOSE SQUIRRELS COME FROM?
WE'RE NEVER GONNA TAKE THE SHELLRAISER DOWN...
...I MADE IT TOO AWESOME!
ROOOOOOARRR

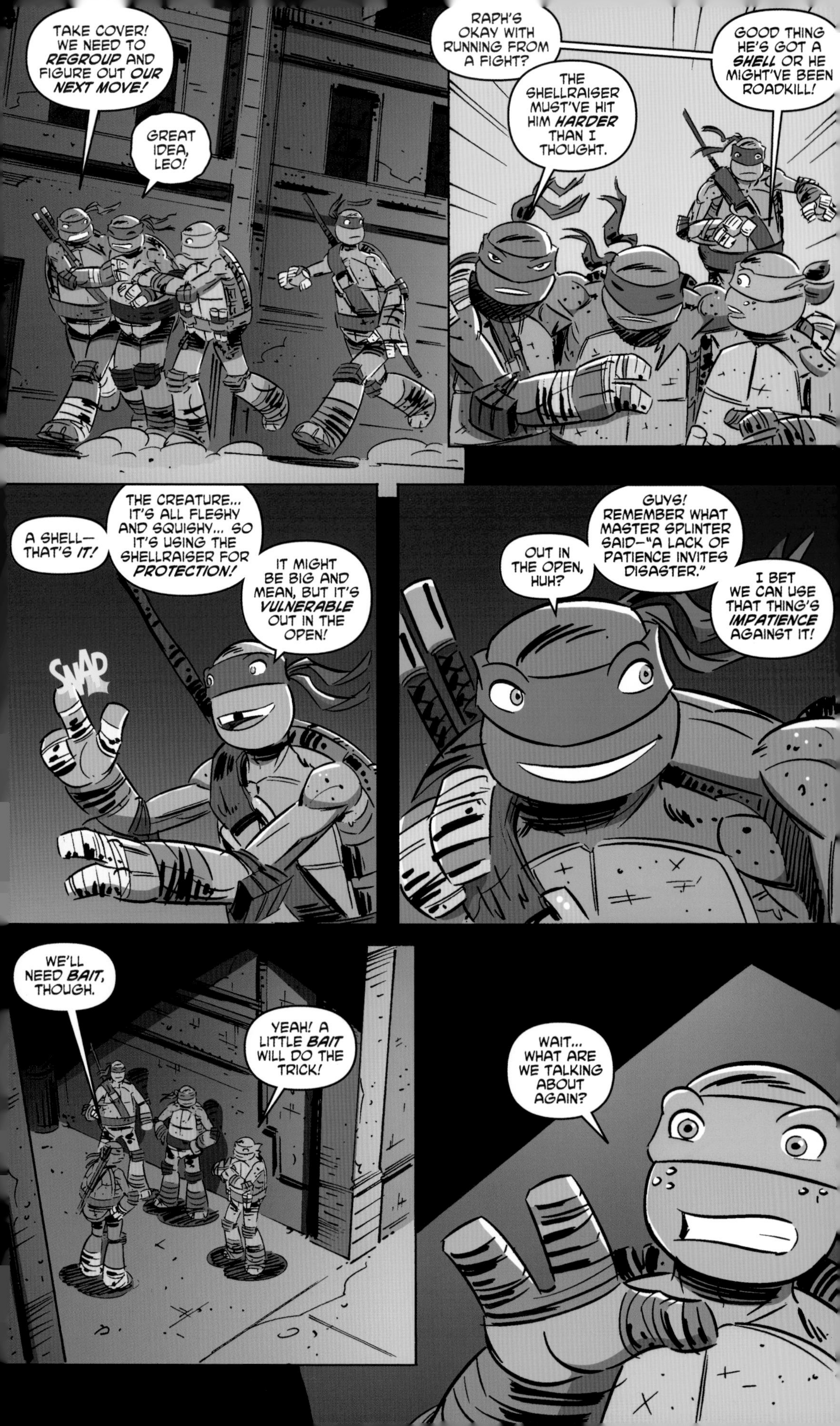

TAKE COVER! WE NEED TO REGROUP AND FIGURE OUT OUR NEXT MOVE!
GREAT IDEA, LEO!
RAPH'S OKAY WITH RUNNING FROM A FIGHT?
THE SHELLRAISER MUST'VE HIT HIM HARDER THAN I THOUGHT.
GOOD THING HE'S GOT A SHELL OR HE MIGHT'VE BEEN ROADKILL!
A SHELL— THAT'S IT!
THE CREATURE... IT'S ALL FLESHY AND SQUISHY... SO IT'S USING THE SHELLRAISER FOR PROTECTION!
IT MIGHT BE BIG AND MEAN, BUT IT'S VULNERABLE OUT IN THE OPEN!
SNAP
OUT IN THE OPEN, HUH?
GUYS! REMEMBER WHAT MASTER SPLINTER SAID—"A LACK OF PATIENCE INVITES DISASTER."
I BET WE CAN USE THAT THING'S IMPATIENCE AGAINST IT!
WE'LL NEED BAIT, THOUGH.
YEAH! A LITTLE BAIT WILL DO THE TRICK!
WAIT... WHAT ARE WE TALKING ABOUT AGAIN?

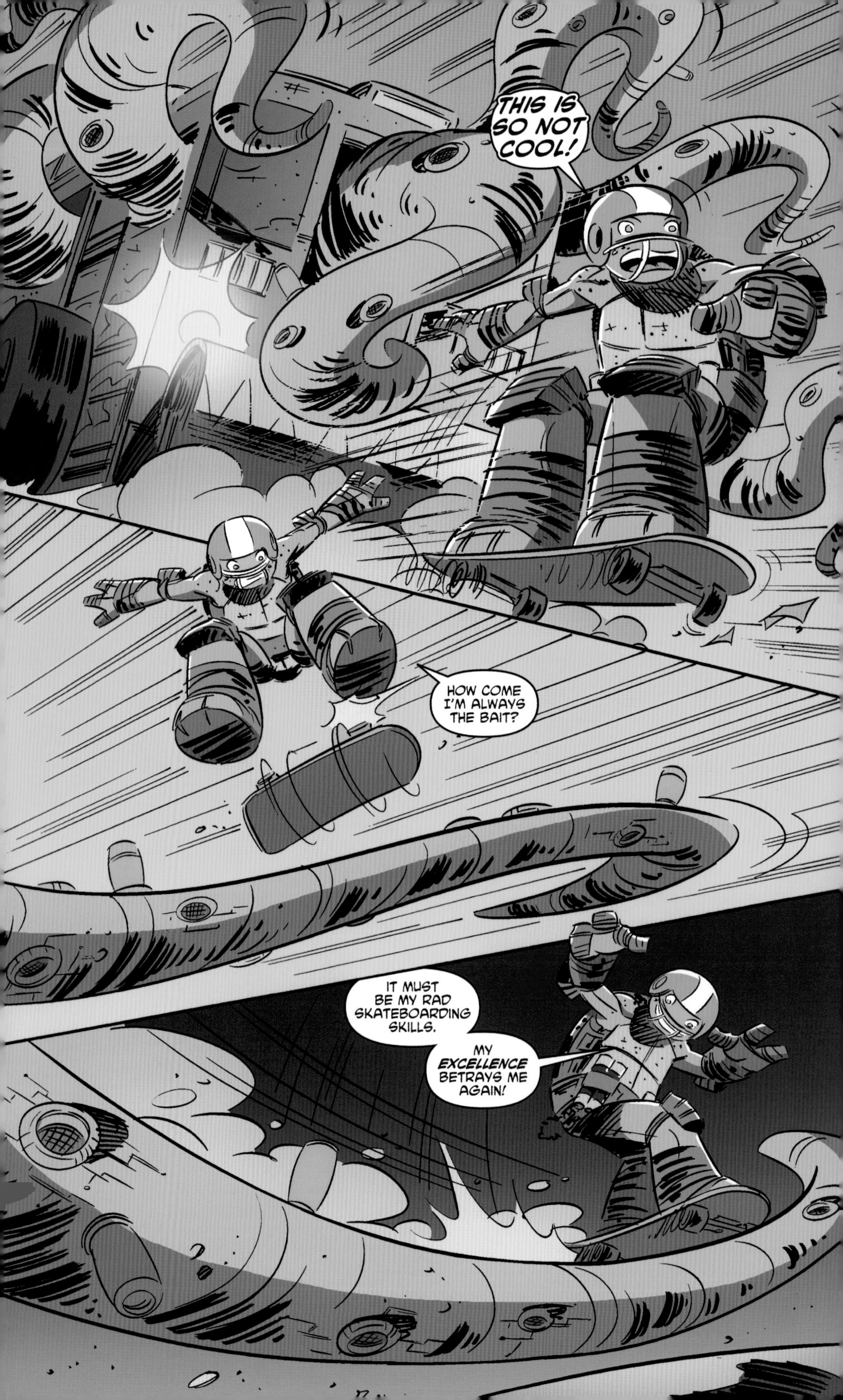
THIS IS SO NOT COOL!
HOW COME I'M ALWAYS THE BAIT?
IT MUST BE MY RAD SKATEBOARDING SKILLS.
MY *EXCELLENCE* BETRAYS ME AGAIN!

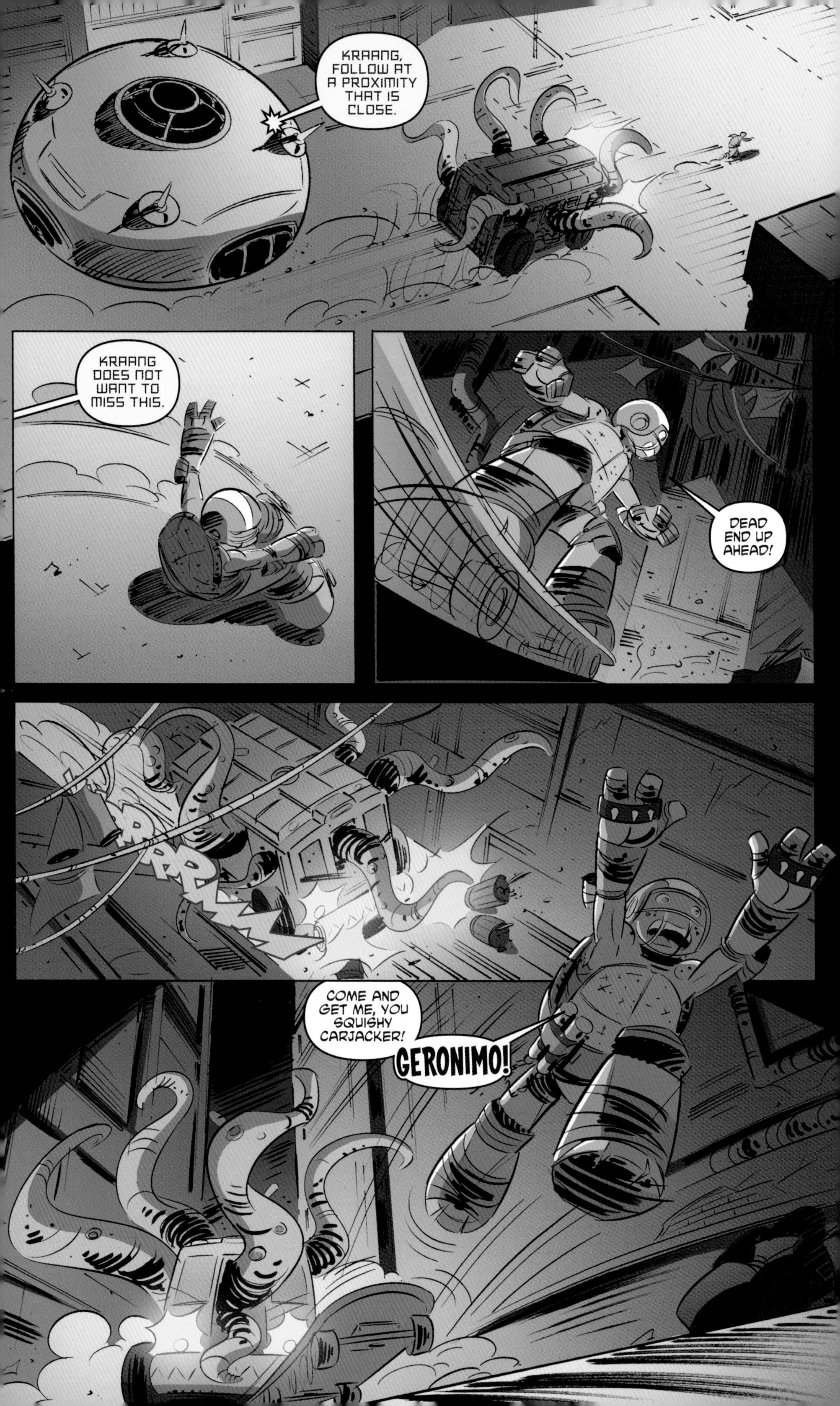

KRAANG, FOLLOW AT A PROXIMITY THAT IS CLOSE.
KRAANG DOES NOT WANT TO MISS THIS.
DEAD END UP AHEAD!
COME AND GET ME, YOU SQUISHY CARJACKER!
GERONIMO!

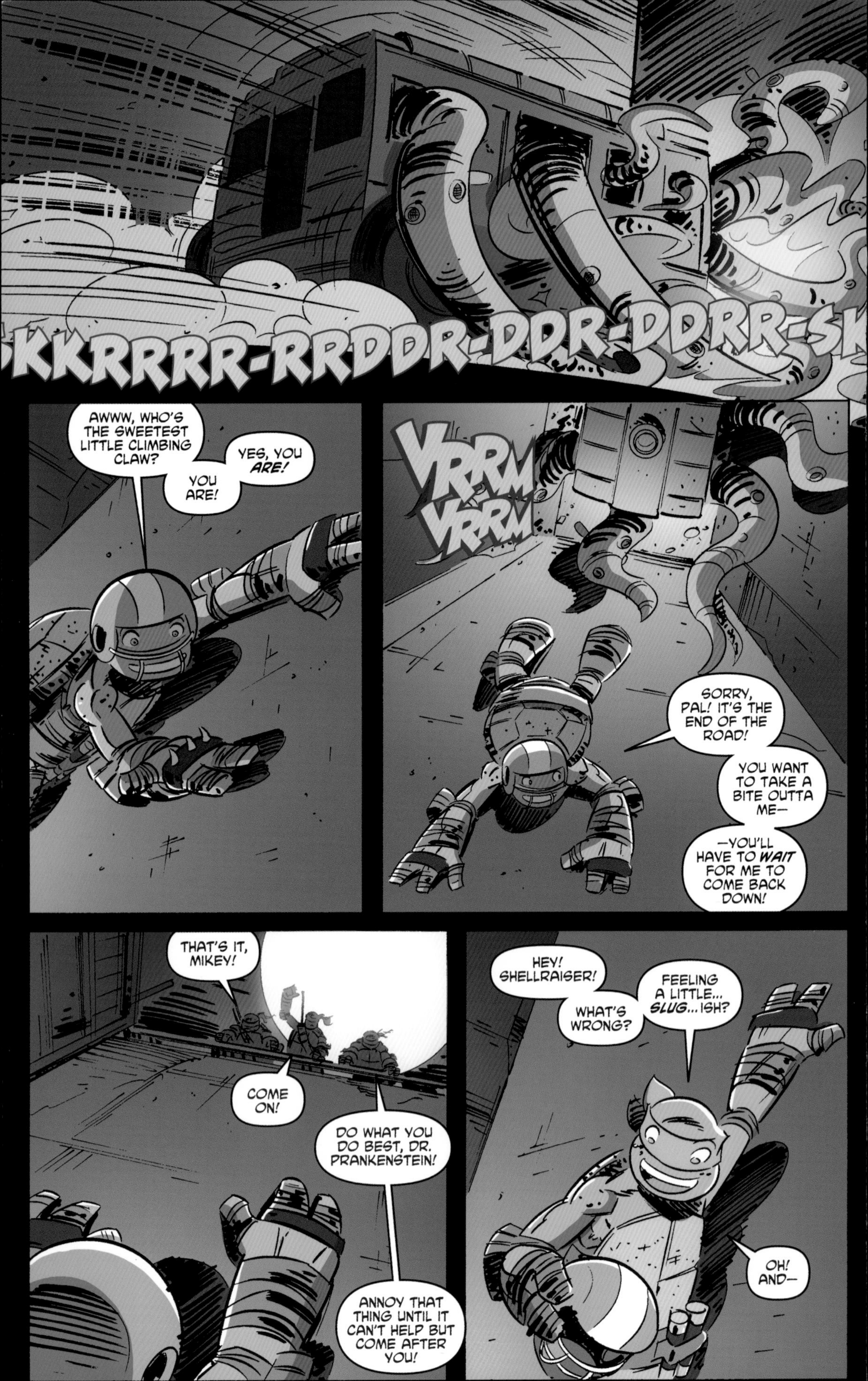
SKKRRRR-RRDDR-DDR-DDRR-SK
AWWW, WHO'S THE SWEETEST LITTLE CLIMBING CLAW?
YOU ARE!
YES, YOU ARE!
VRRM VRRM
SORRY, PAL! IT'S THE END OF THE ROAD!
YOU WANT TO TAKE A BITE OUTTA ME—
—YOU'LL HAVE TO WAIT FOR ME TO COME BACK DOWN!
THAT'S IT, MIKEY!
COME ON!
DO WHAT YOU DO BEST, DR. PRANKENSTEIN!
ANNOY THAT THING UNTIL IT CAN'T HELP BUT COME AFTER YOU!
HEY! SHELLRAISER!
WHAT'S WRONG?
FEELING A LITTLE... SLUG...ISH?
OH! AND—

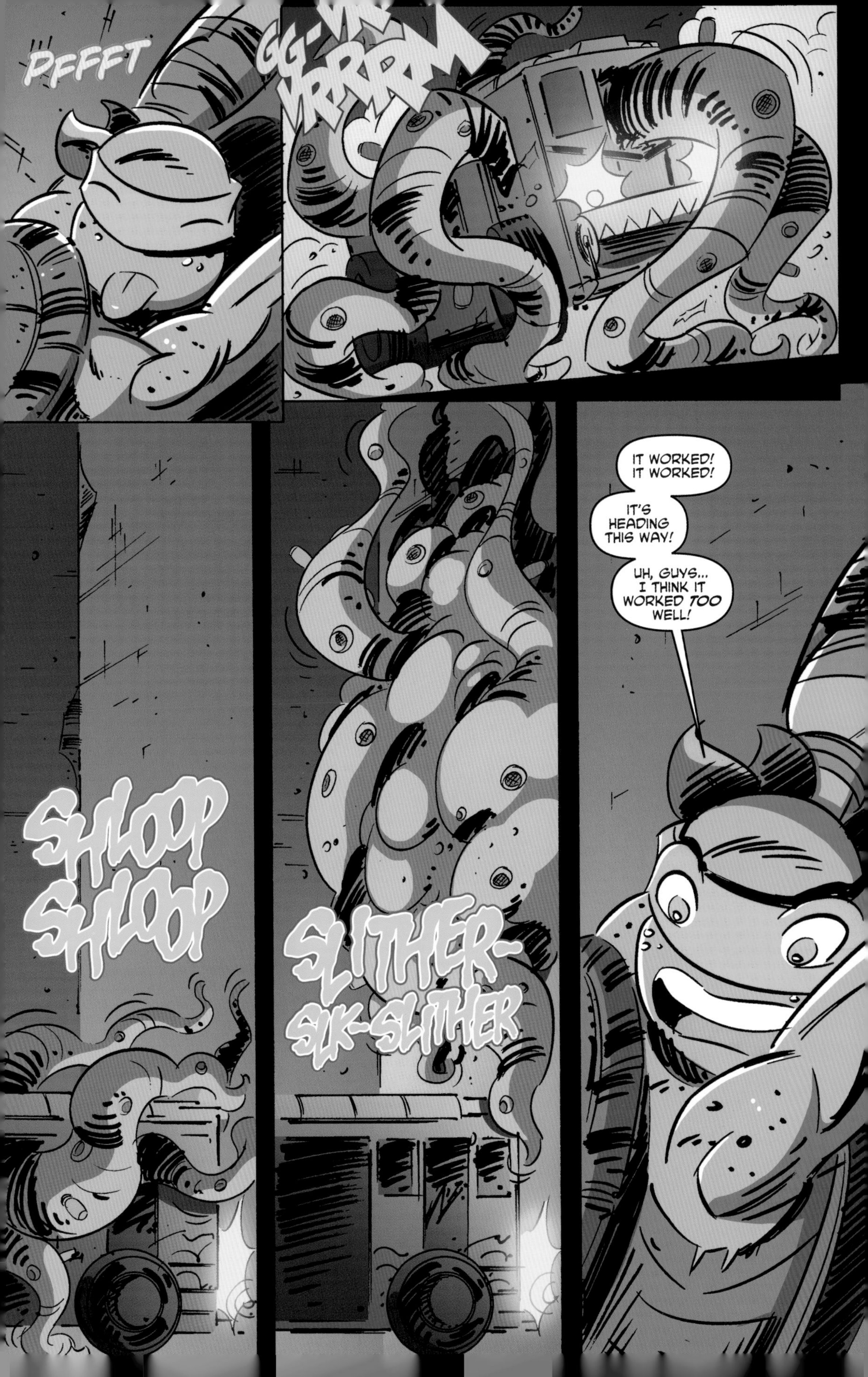
PFFFT
SHLOOP SHLOOP
SLITHER-SLK-SLITHER
IT WORKED! IT WORKED!
IT'S HEADING THIS WAY!
UH, GUYS... I THINK IT WORKED *TOO* WELL!

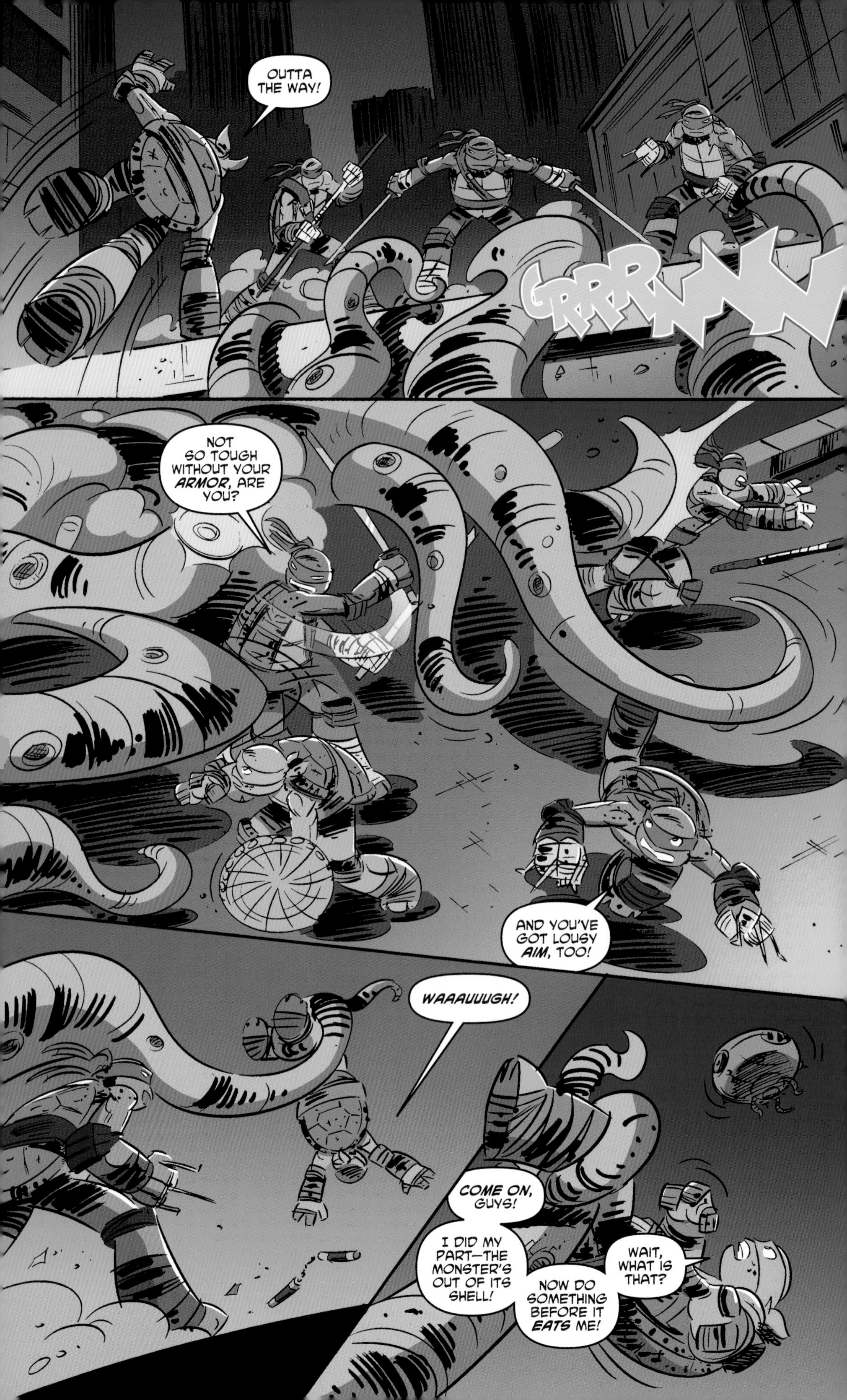
OUTTA THE WAY!
GRRRRWWNK
NOT SO TOUGH WITHOUT YOUR ARMOR, ARE YOU?
AND YOU'VE GOT LOUSY AIM, TOO!
WAAAUUUGH!
COME ON, GUYS!
I DID MY PART—THE MONSTER'S OUT OF ITS SHELL!
NOW DO SOMETHING BEFORE IT EATS ME!
WAIT, WHAT IS THAT?

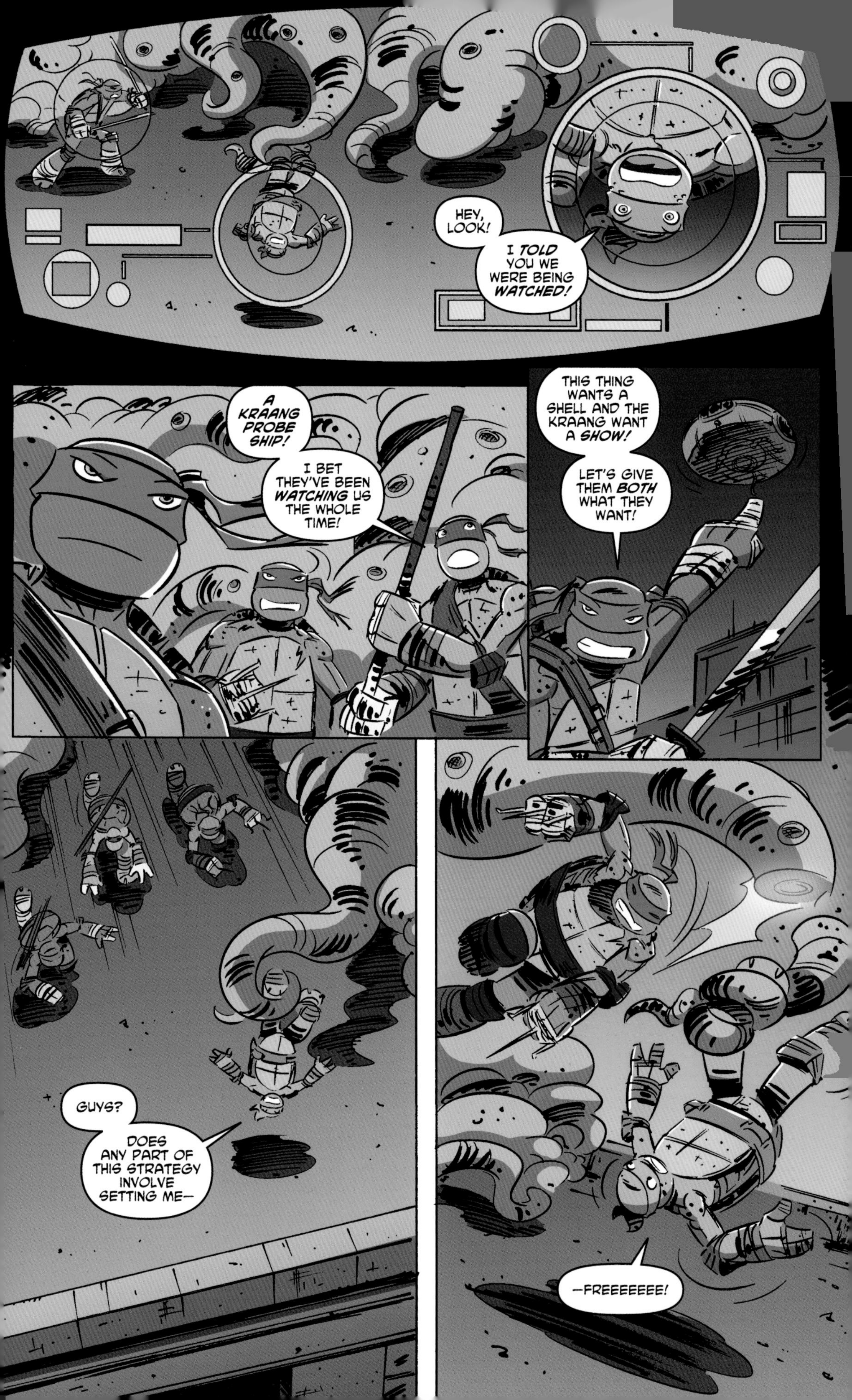
HEY, LOOK!
I TOLD YOU WE WERE BEING WATCHED!
A KRAANG PROBE SHIP!
I BET THEY'VE BEEN WATCHING US THE WHOLE TIME!
THIS THING WANTS A SHELL AND THE KRAANG WANT A SHOW!
LET'S GIVE THEM BOTH WHAT THEY WANT!
GUYS?
DOES ANY PART OF THIS STRATEGY INVOLVE SETTING ME--
--FREEEEEEE!

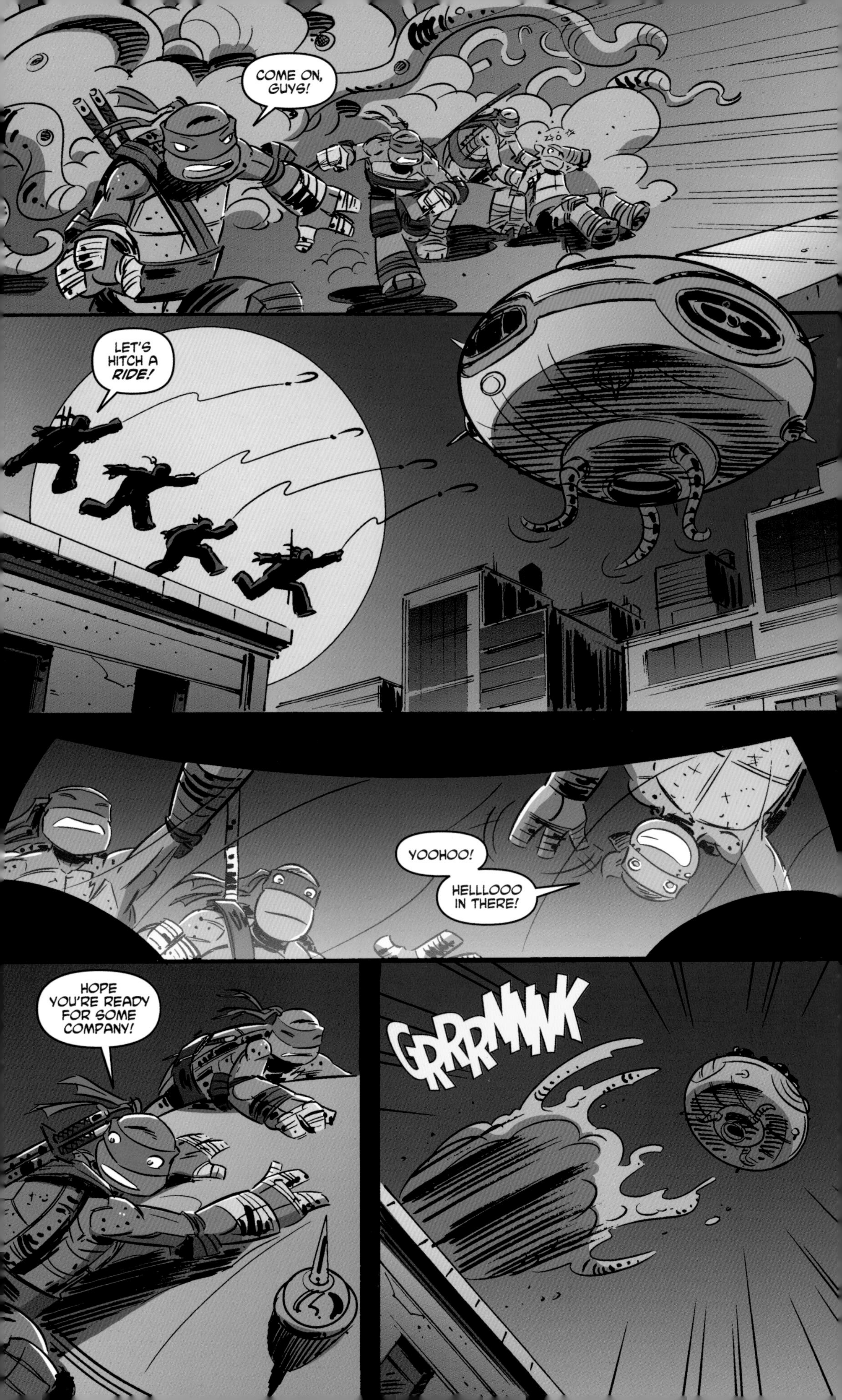
COME ON, GUYS!
LET'S HITCH A RIDE!
YOOHOO!
HELLLOOO IN THERE!
HOPE YOU'RE READY FOR SOME COMPANY!
GRRRNNNK

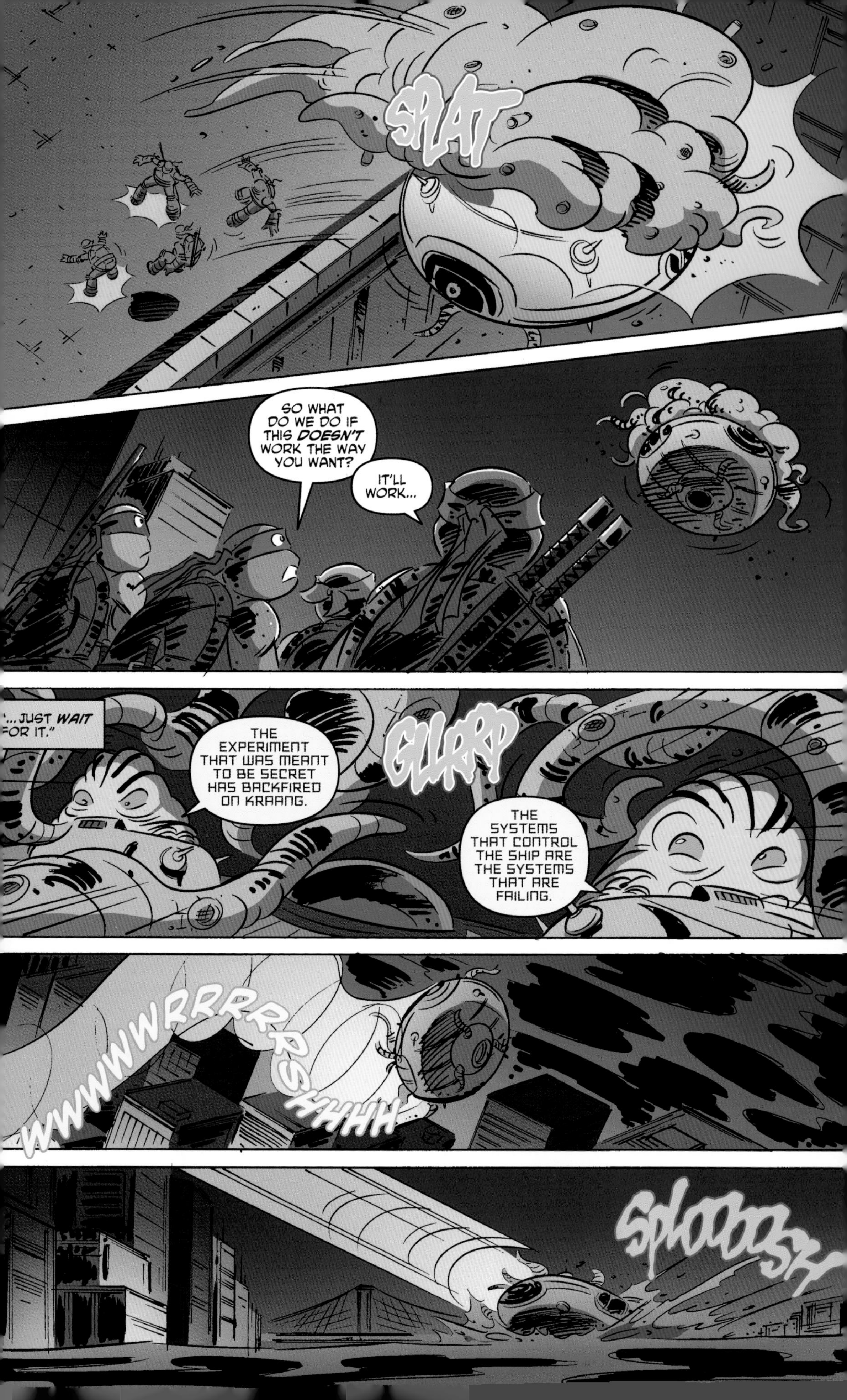
SPLAT
SO WHAT DO WE DO IF THIS DOESN'T WORK THE WAY YOU WANT?
IT'LL WORK...
"...JUST WAIT FOR IT."
THE EXPERIMENT THAT WAS MEANT TO BE SECRET HAS BACKFIRED ON KRAANG.
GLLRP
THE SYSTEMS THAT CONTROL THE SHIP ARE THE SYSTEMS THAT ARE FAILING.
WWWWWRRRRRSHHHH
SPLOOOSH

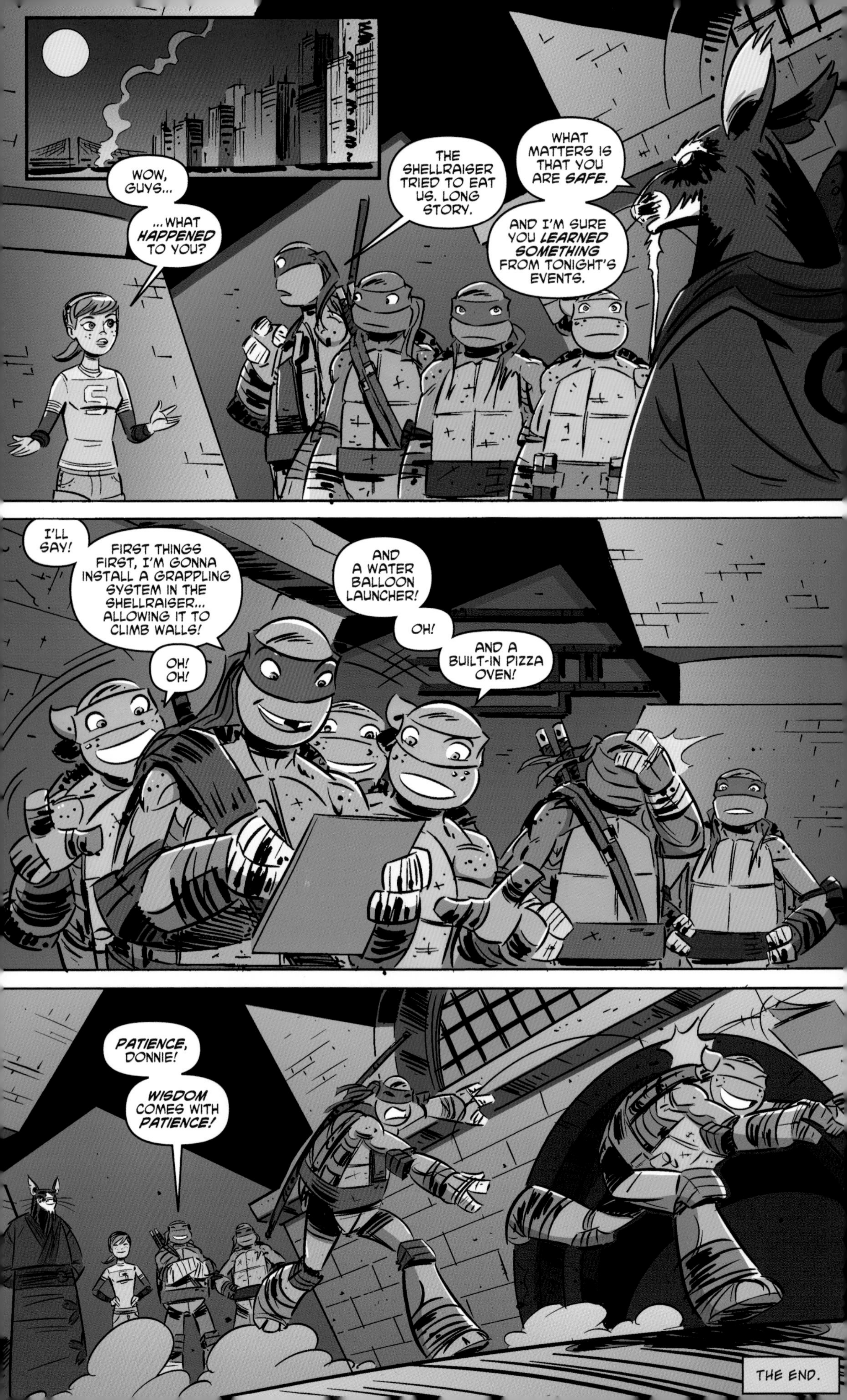
WOW, GUYS...
...WHAT HAPPENED TO YOU?
THE SHELLRAISER TRIED TO EAT US. LONG STORY.
WHAT MATTERS IS THAT YOU ARE SAFE.
AND I'M SURE YOU LEARNED SOMETHING FROM TONIGHT'S EVENTS.
I'LL SAY!
FIRST THINGS FIRST, I'M GONNA INSTALL A GRAPPLING SYSTEM IN THE SHELLRAISER... ALLOWING IT TO CLIMB WALLS!
OH! OH!
AND A WATER BALLOON LAUNCHER!
OH!
AND A BUILT-IN PIZZA OVEN!
PATIENCE, DONNIE!
WISDOM COMES WITH PATIENCE!
THE END.

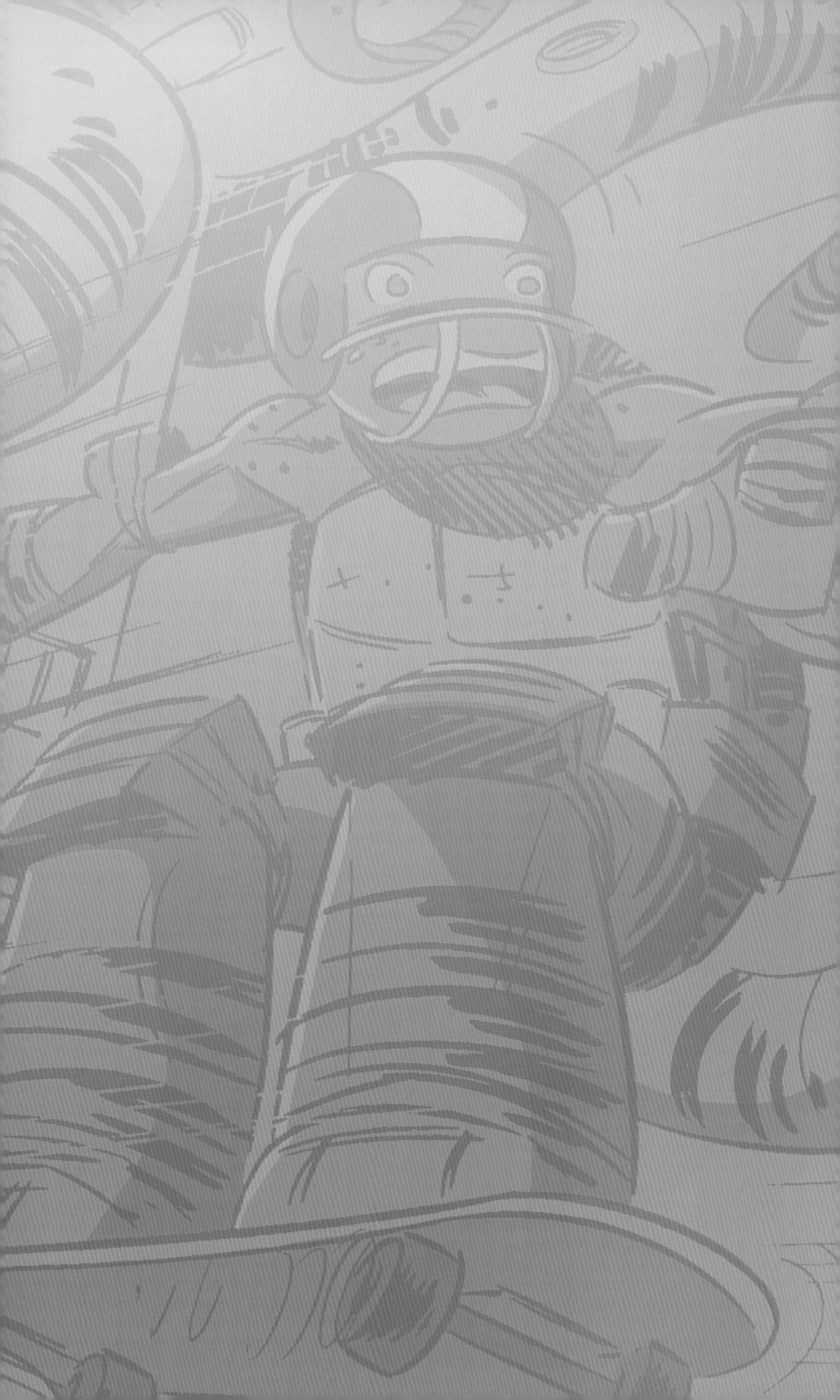

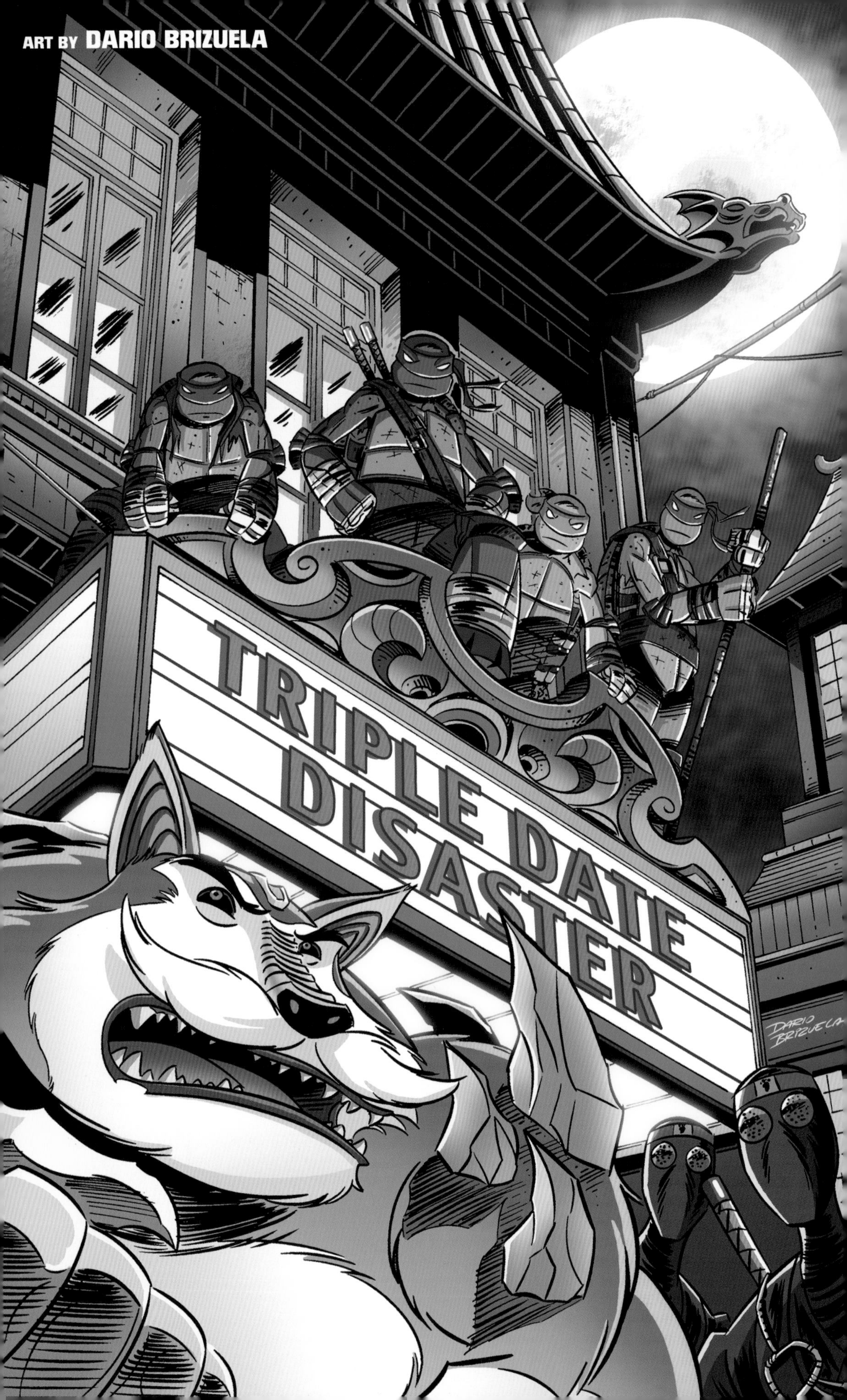
ART BY DARIO BRIZUELA
TRIPLE DATE DISASTER
DARIO BRIZUELA

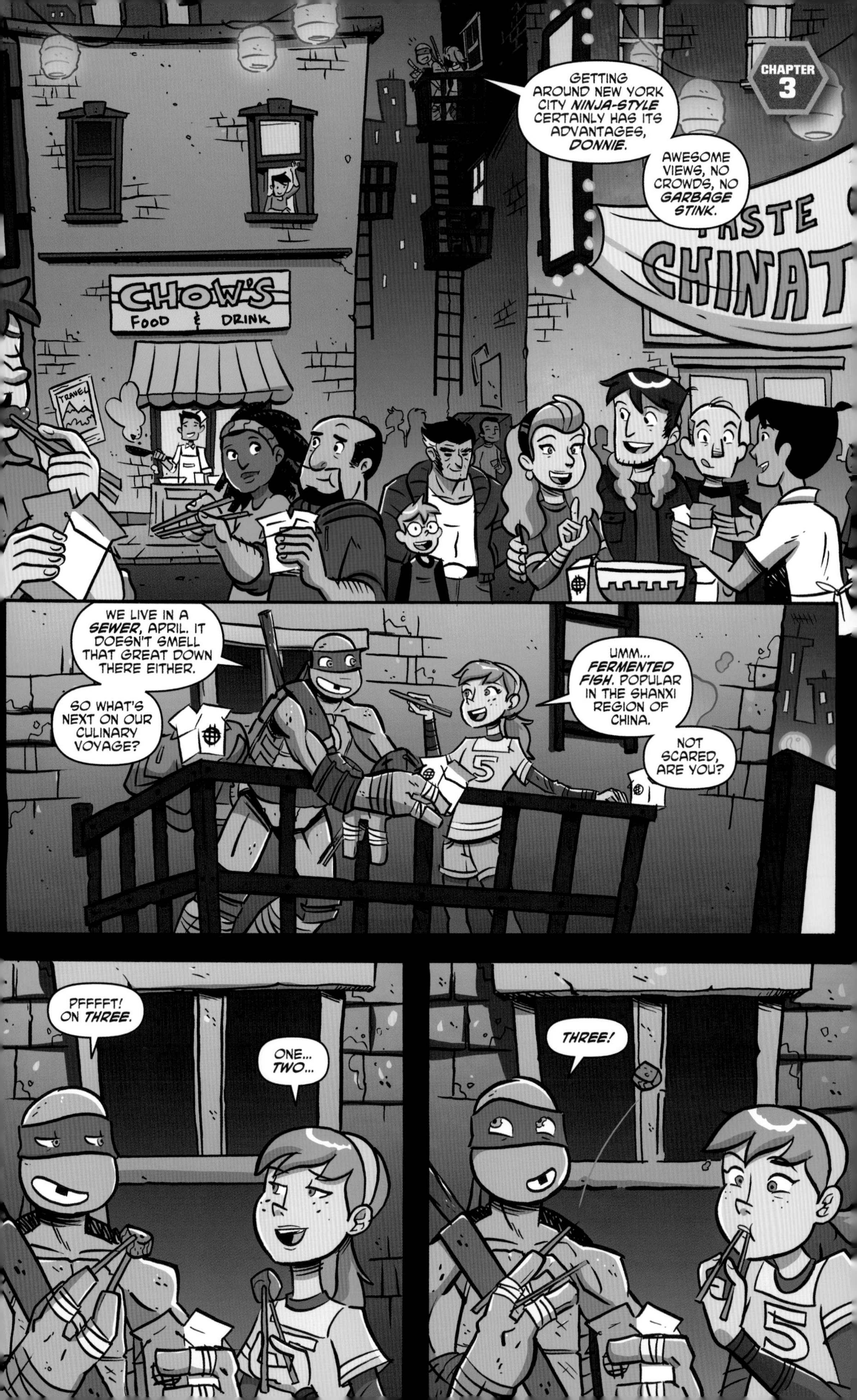
CHAPTER 3
GETTING AROUND NEW YORK CITY NINJA-STYLE CERTAINLY HAS ITS ADVANTAGES, DONNIE.
AWESOME VIEWS, NO CROWDS, NO GARBAGE STINK.
CHOW'S FOOD & DRINK
TRAVEL
TASTE CHINAT
WE LIVE IN A SEWER, APRIL. IT DOESN'T SMELL THAT GREAT DOWN THERE EITHER.
SO WHAT'S NEXT ON OUR CULINARY VOYAGE?
UMM... FERMENTED FISH. POPULAR IN THE SHANXI REGION OF CHINA.
NOT SCARED, ARE YOU?
PFFFFT! ON THREE.
ONE... TWO...
THREE!

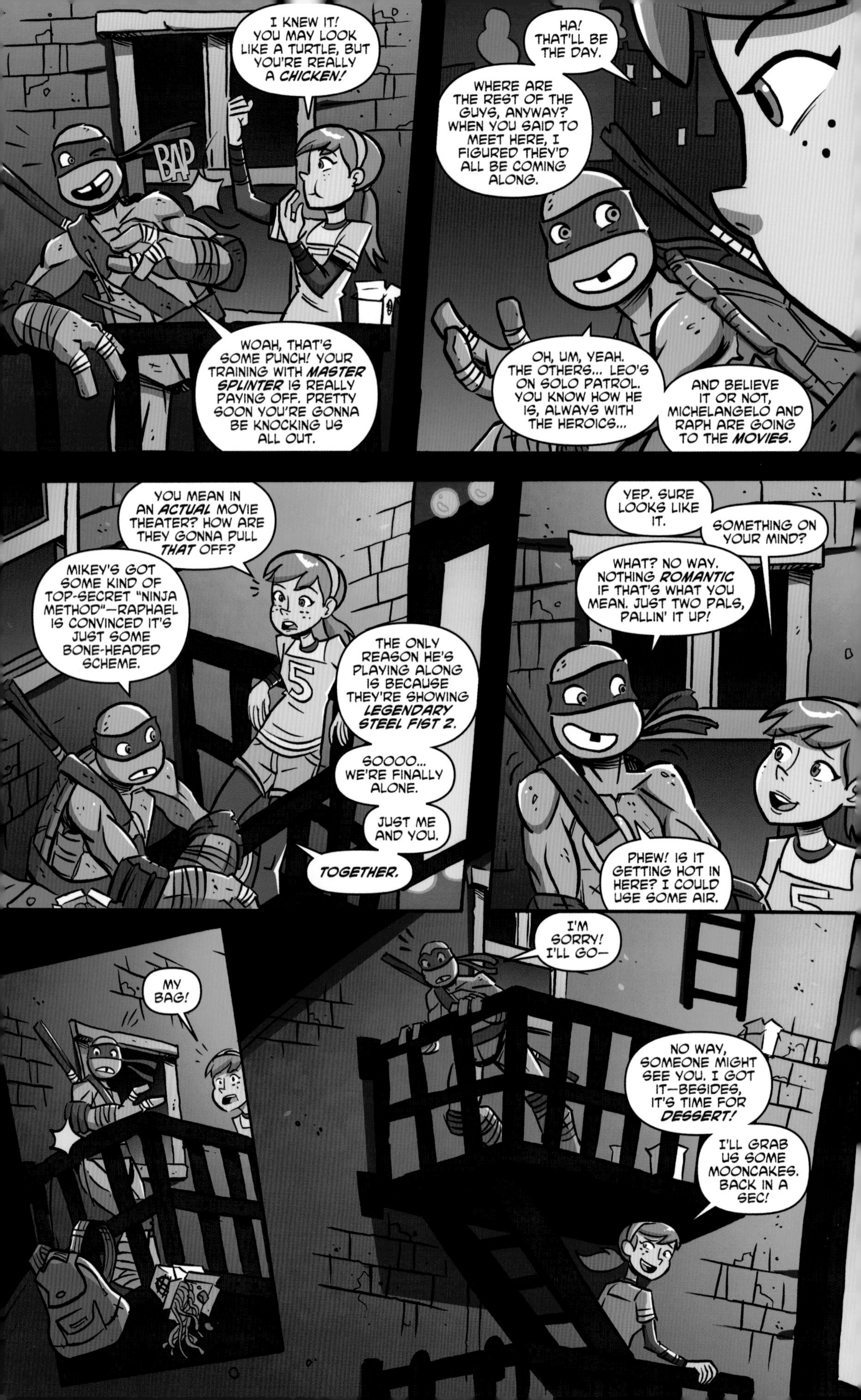
I KNEW IT! YOU MAY LOOK LIKE A TURTLE, BUT YOU'RE REALLY A CHICKEN!
BAP
WOAH, THAT'S SOME PUNCH! YOUR TRAINING WITH MASTER SPLINTER IS REALLY PAYING OFF. PRETTY SOON YOU'RE GONNA BE KNOCKING US ALL OUT.
HA! THAT'LL BE THE DAY.
WHERE ARE THE REST OF THE GUYS, ANYWAY? WHEN YOU SAID TO MEET HERE, I FIGURED THEY'D ALL BE COMING ALONG.
OH, UM, YEAH. THE OTHERS... LEO'S ON SOLO PATROL. YOU KNOW HOW HE IS, ALWAYS WITH THE HEROICS...
AND BELIEVE IT OR NOT, MICHELANGELO AND RAPH ARE GOING TO THE MOVIES.
YOU MEAN IN AN ACTUAL MOVIE THEATER? HOW ARE THEY GONNA PULL THAT OFF?
MIKEY'S GOT SOME KIND OF TOP-SECRET "NINJA METHOD"—RAPHAEL IS CONVINCED IT'S JUST SOME BONE-HEADED SCHEME.
THE ONLY REASON HE'S PLAYING ALONG IS BECAUSE THEY'RE SHOWING LEGENDARY STEEL FIST 2.
SOOOO... WE'RE FINALLY ALONE.
JUST ME AND YOU.
TOGETHER.
YEP. SURE LOOKS LIKE IT.
SOMETHING ON YOUR MIND?
WHAT? NO WAY. NOTHING ROMANTIC IF THAT'S WHAT YOU MEAN. JUST TWO PALS, PALLIN' IT UP!
PHEW! IS IT GETTING HOT IN HERE? I COULD USE SOME AIR.
MY BAG!
I'M SORRY! I'LL GO—
NO WAY, SOMEONE MIGHT SEE YOU. I GOT IT—BESIDES, IT'S TIME FOR DESSERT!
I'LL GRAB US SOME MOONCAKES. BACK IN A SEC!

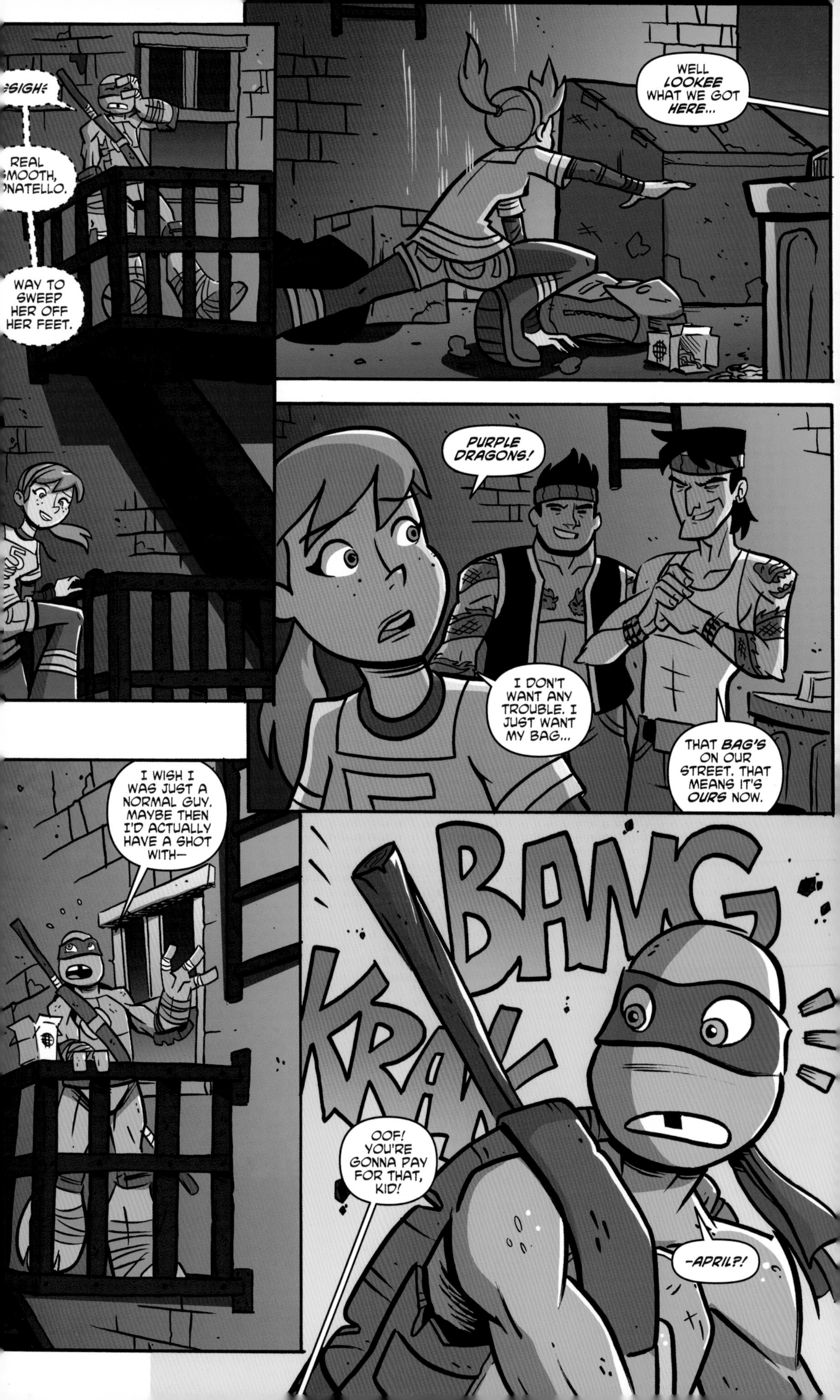
⸗SIGH⸗
REAL SMOOTH, ONATELLO.
WAY TO SWEEP HER OFF HER FEET.
WELL LOOKEE WHAT WE GOT HERE...
PURPLE DRAGONS!
I DON'T WANT ANY TROUBLE. I JUST WANT MY BAG...
THAT BAG'S ON OUR STREET. THAT MEANS IT'S OURS NOW.
I WISH I WAS JUST A NORMAL GUY. MAYBE THEN I'D ACTUALLY HAVE A SHOT WITH—
BAMG
KRAK
OOF! YOU'RE GONNA PAY FOR THAT, KID!
-APRIL?!

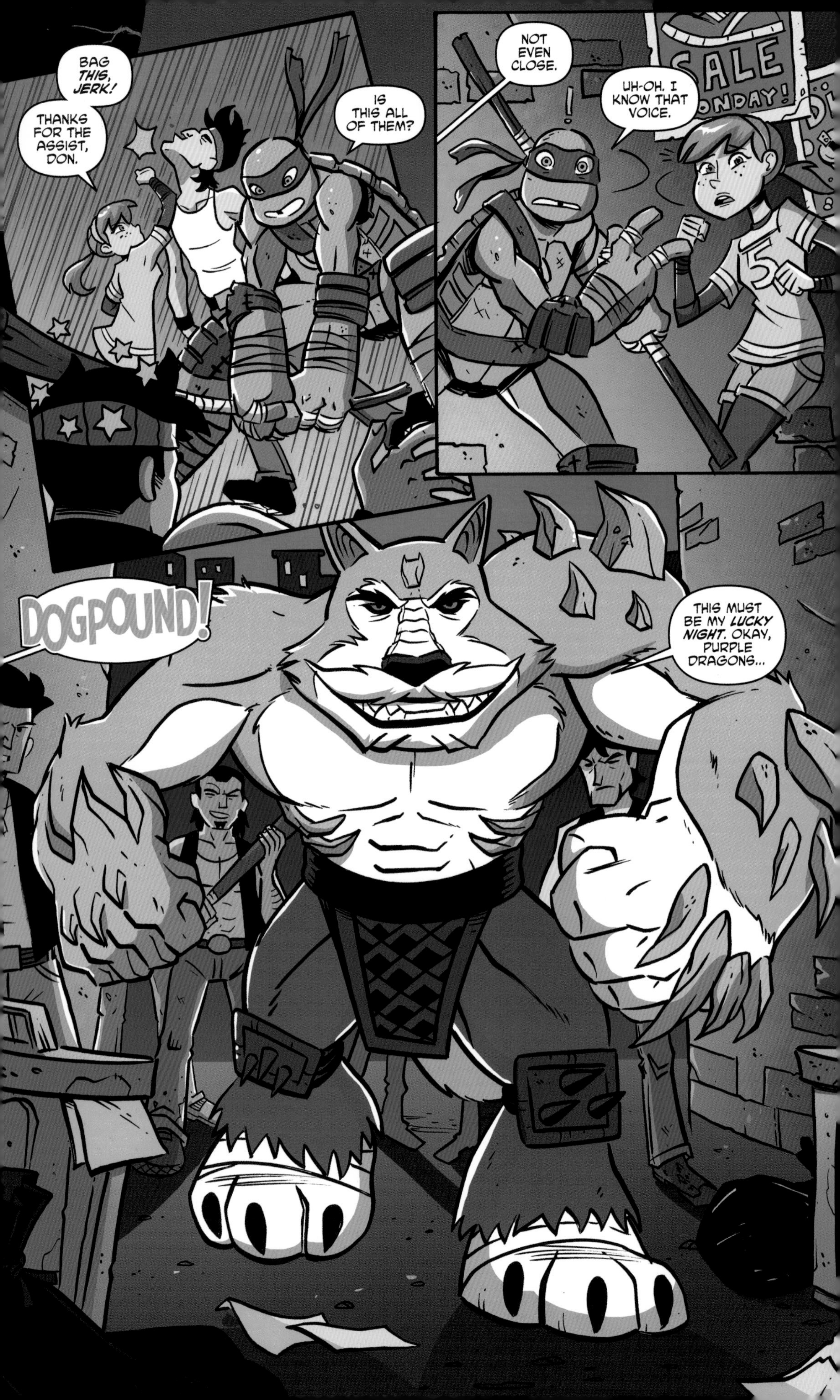
BAG *THIS*, *JERK!*
THANKS FOR THE ASSIST, DON.
IS THIS ALL OF THEM?
NOT EVEN CLOSE.
!
UH-OH. I KNOW THAT VOICE.
SALE
ONDAY!
DOGPOUND!
THIS MUST BE MY *LUCKY NIGHT*. OKAY, PURPLE DRAGONS...

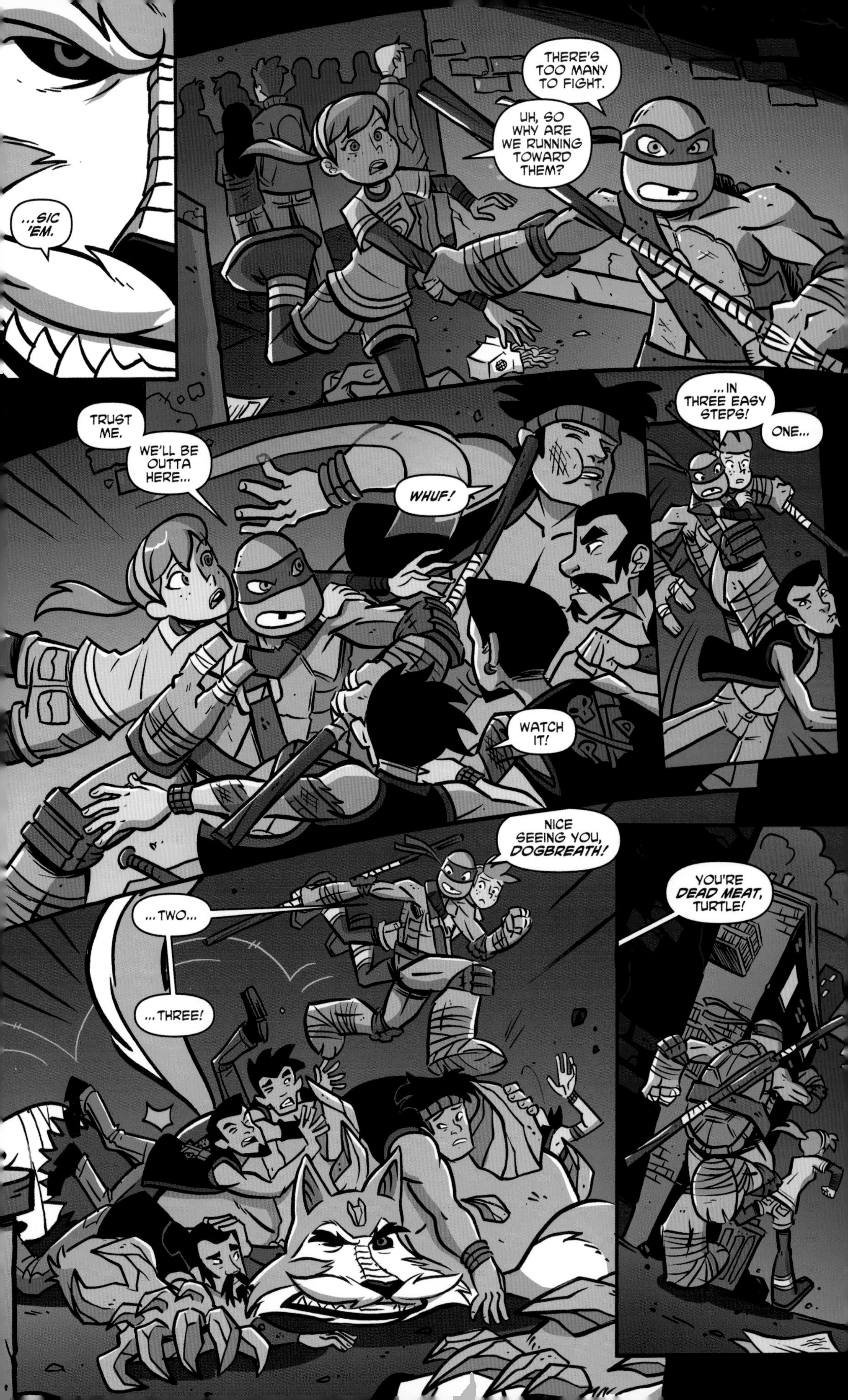
...SIC 'EM.
THERE'S TOO MANY TO FIGHT.
UH, SO WHY ARE WE RUNNING TOWARD THEM?
TRUST ME.
WE'LL BE OUTTA HERE...
WHUF!
WATCH IT!
...IN THREE EASY STEPS!
ONE...
NICE SEEING YOU, *DOGBREATH!*
...TWO...
...THREE!
YOU'RE *DEAD MEAT,* TURTLE!

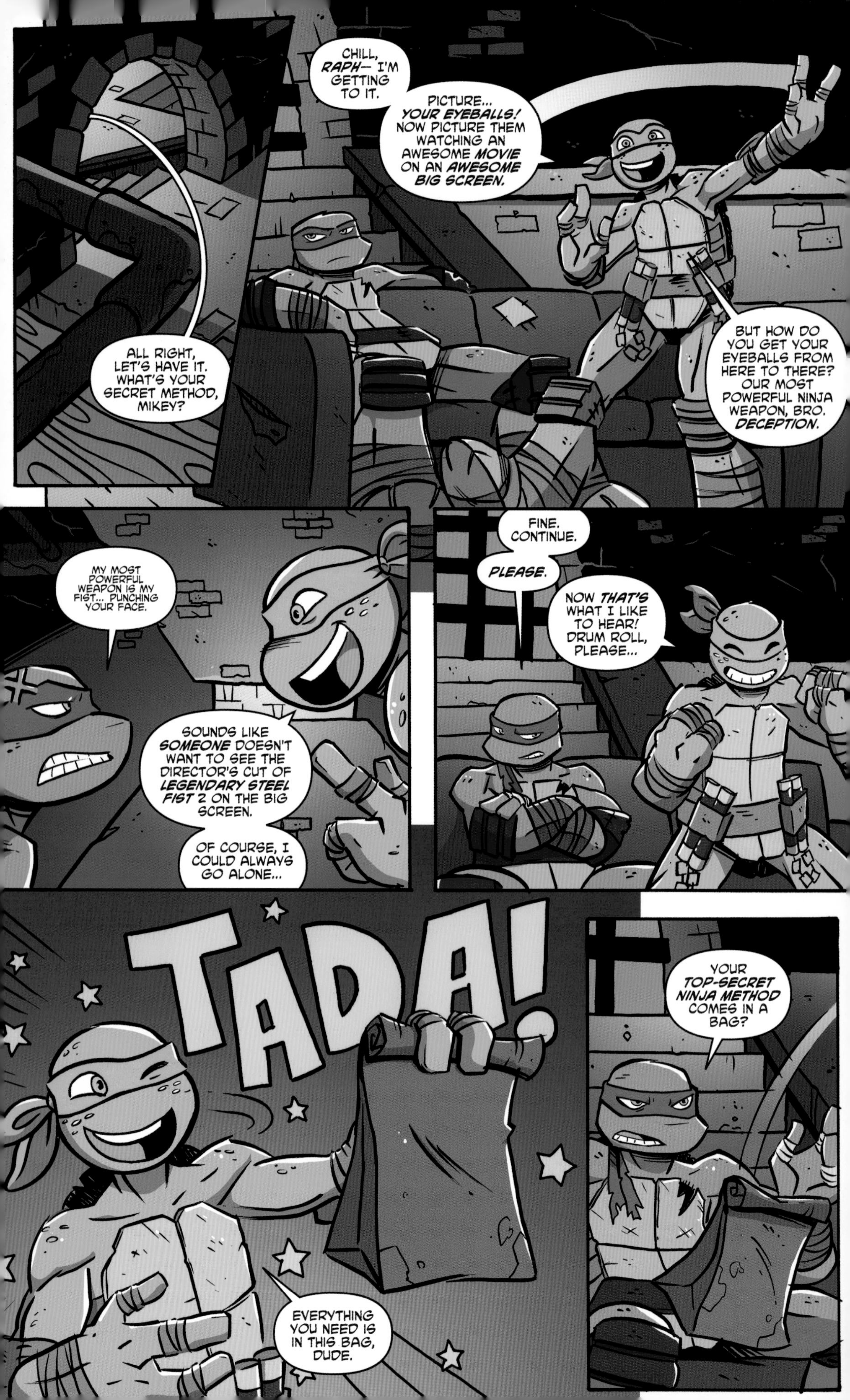
CHILL, RAPH— I'M GETTING TO IT.
PICTURE... YOUR EYEBALLS! NOW PICTURE THEM WATCHING AN AWESOME MOVIE ON AN AWESOME BIG SCREEN.
ALL RIGHT, LET'S HAVE IT. WHAT'S YOUR SECRET METHOD, MIKEY?
BUT HOW DO YOU GET YOUR EYEBALLS FROM HERE TO THERE? OUR MOST POWERFUL NINJA WEAPON, BRO. DECEPTION.
MY MOST POWERFUL WEAPON IS MY FIST... PUNCHING YOUR FACE.
SOUNDS LIKE SOMEONE DOESN'T WANT TO SEE THE DIRECTOR'S CUT OF LEGENDARY STEEL FIST 2 ON THE BIG SCREEN.
OF COURSE, I COULD ALWAYS GO ALONE...
FINE. CONTINUE.
PLEASE.
NOW THAT'S WHAT I LIKE TO HEAR! DRUM ROLL, PLEASE...
TADA!
EVERYTHING YOU NEED IS IN THIS BAG, DUDE.
YOUR TOP-SECRET NINJA METHOD COMES IN A BAG?

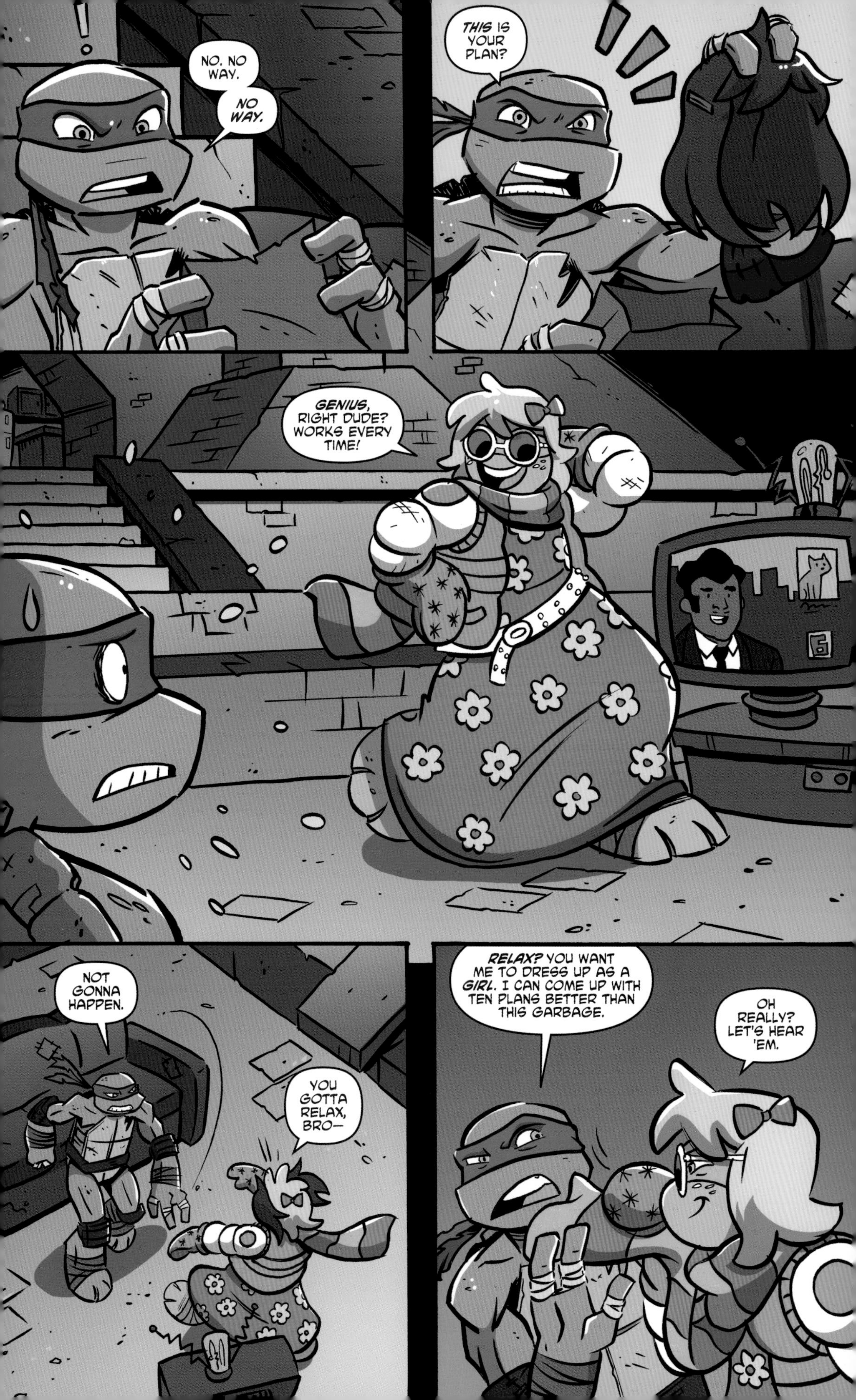
NO. NO WAY.
NO WAY.
THIS IS YOUR PLAN?
GENIUS, RIGHT DUDE? WORKS EVERY TIME!
NOT GONNA HAPPEN.
YOU GOTTA RELAX, BRO—
RELAX? YOU WANT ME TO DRESS UP AS A GIRL. I CAN COME UP WITH TEN PLANS BETTER THAN THIS GARBAGE.
OH REALLY? LET'S HEAR 'EM.

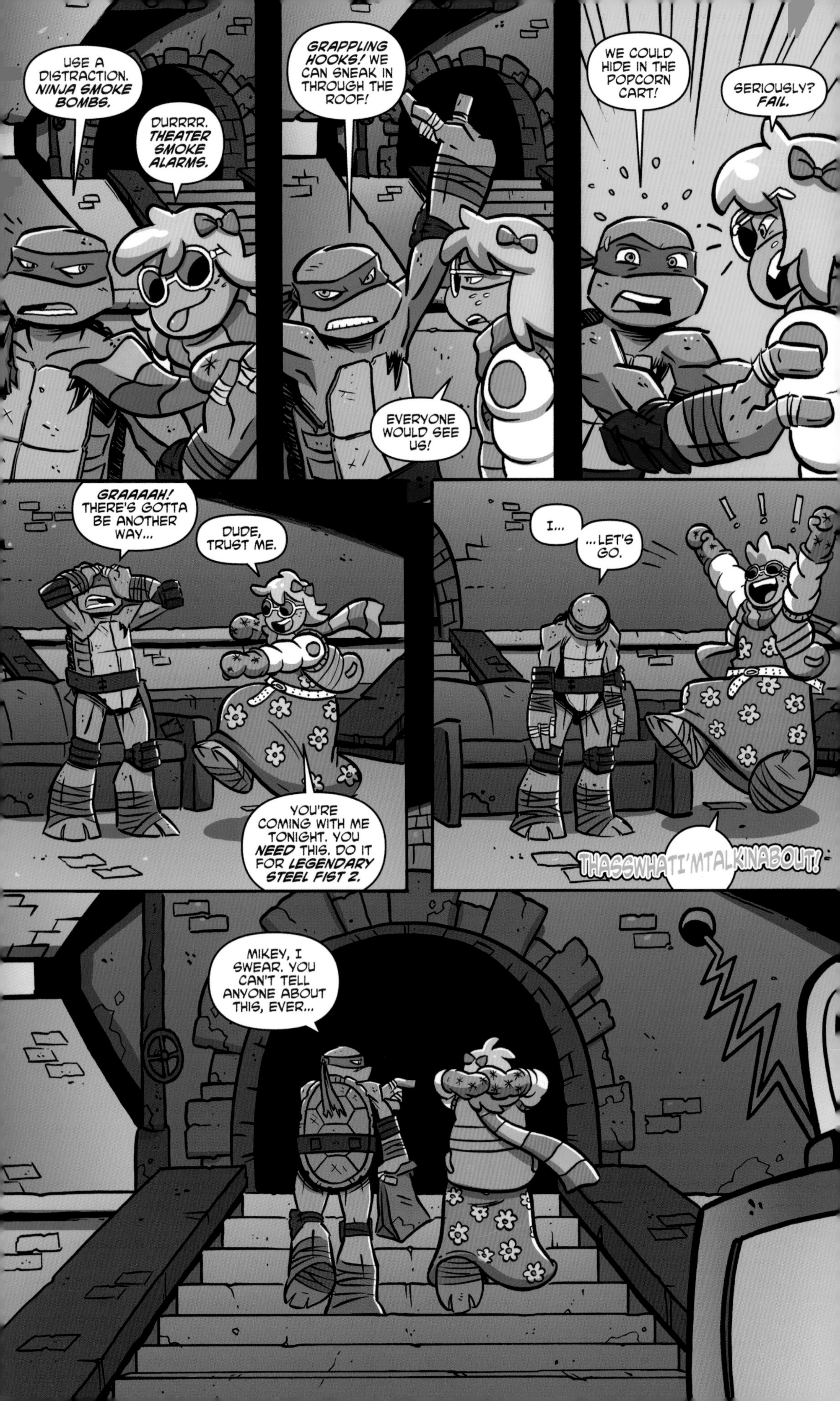
USE A DISTRACTION. *NINJA SMOKE BOMBS.*
DURRRR. *THEATER SMOKE ALARMS.*
GRAPPLING HOOKS! WE CAN SNEAK IN THROUGH THE ROOF!
EVERYONE WOULD SEE US!
WE COULD HIDE IN THE POPCORN CART!
SERIOUSLY? *FAIL.*
GRAAAAH! THERE'S GOTTA BE ANOTHER WAY...
DUDE, TRUST ME.
YOU'RE COMING WITH ME TONIGHT. YOU *NEED* THIS. DO IT FOR *LEGENDARY STEEL FIST 2.*
I...
...LET'S GO.
! ! !
THASSWHATI'MTALKINABOUT!
MIKEY, I SWEAR. YOU CAN'T TELL ANYONE ABOUT THIS, EVER...

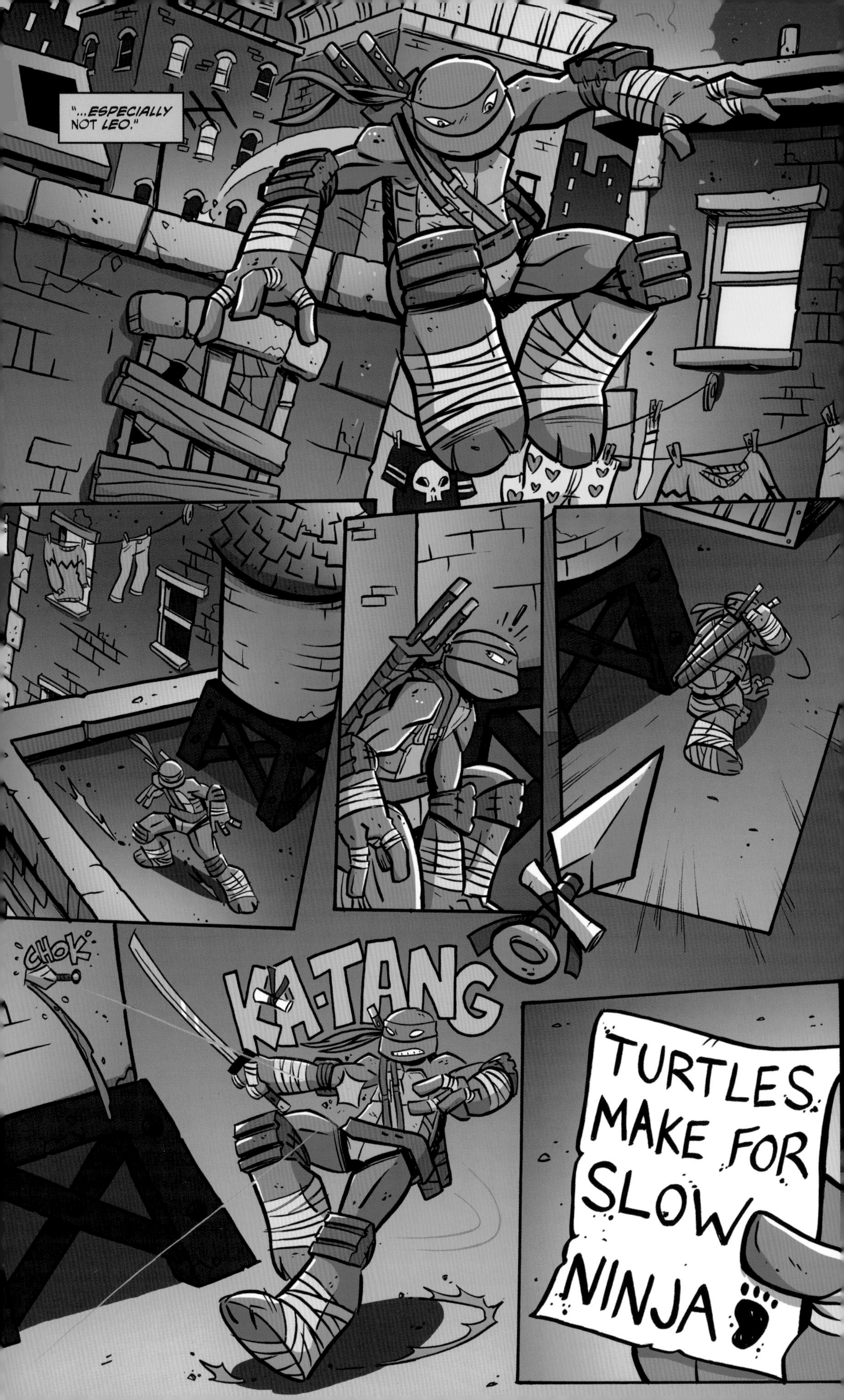
"...ESPECIALLY NOT LEO."
CHOK
KA-TANG
TURTLES MAKE FOR SLOW NINJA

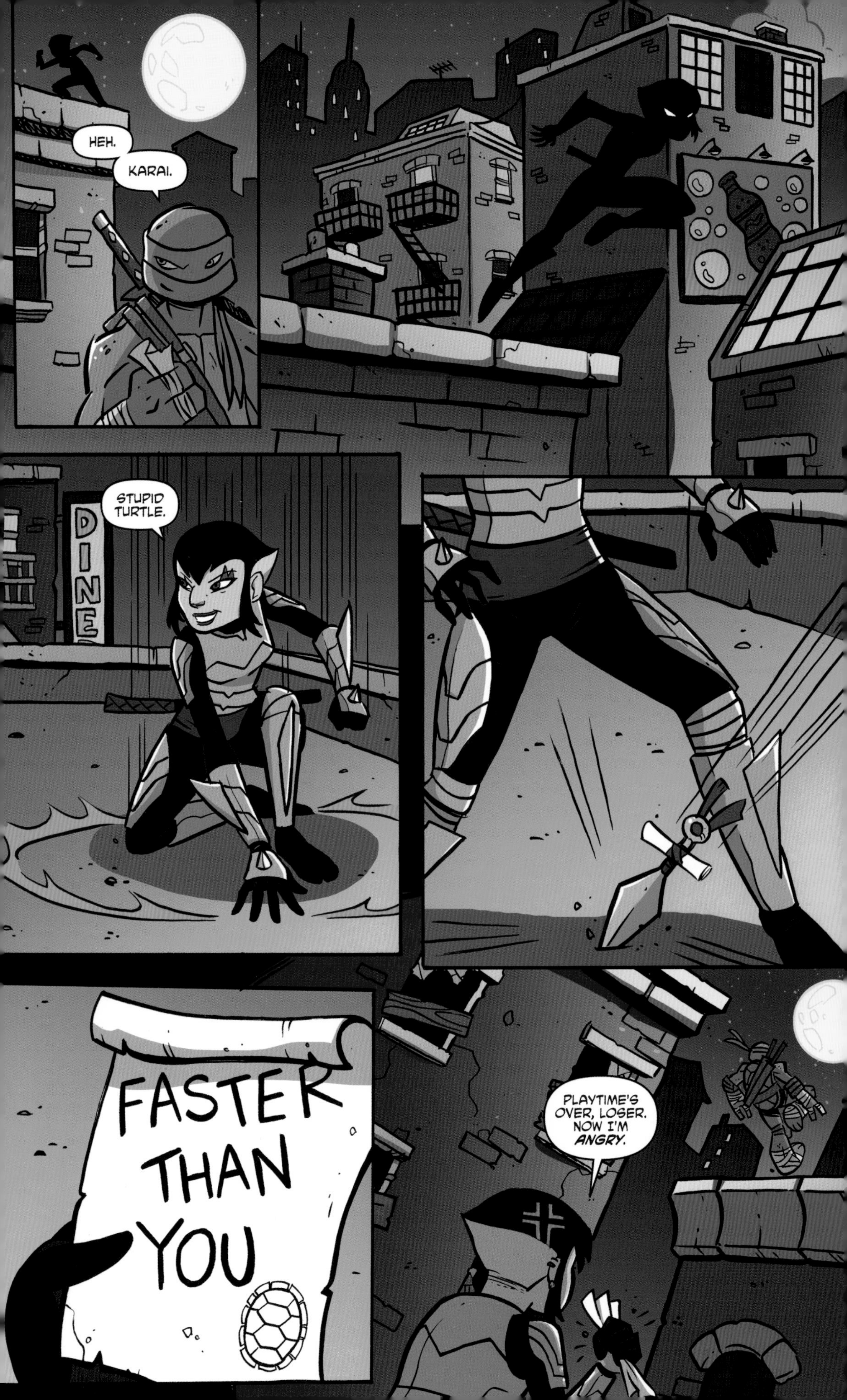
HEH.
KARAI.
STUPID TURTLE.
DINE
FASTER THAN YOU
PLAYTIME'S OVER, LOSER. NOW I'M *ANGRY*.

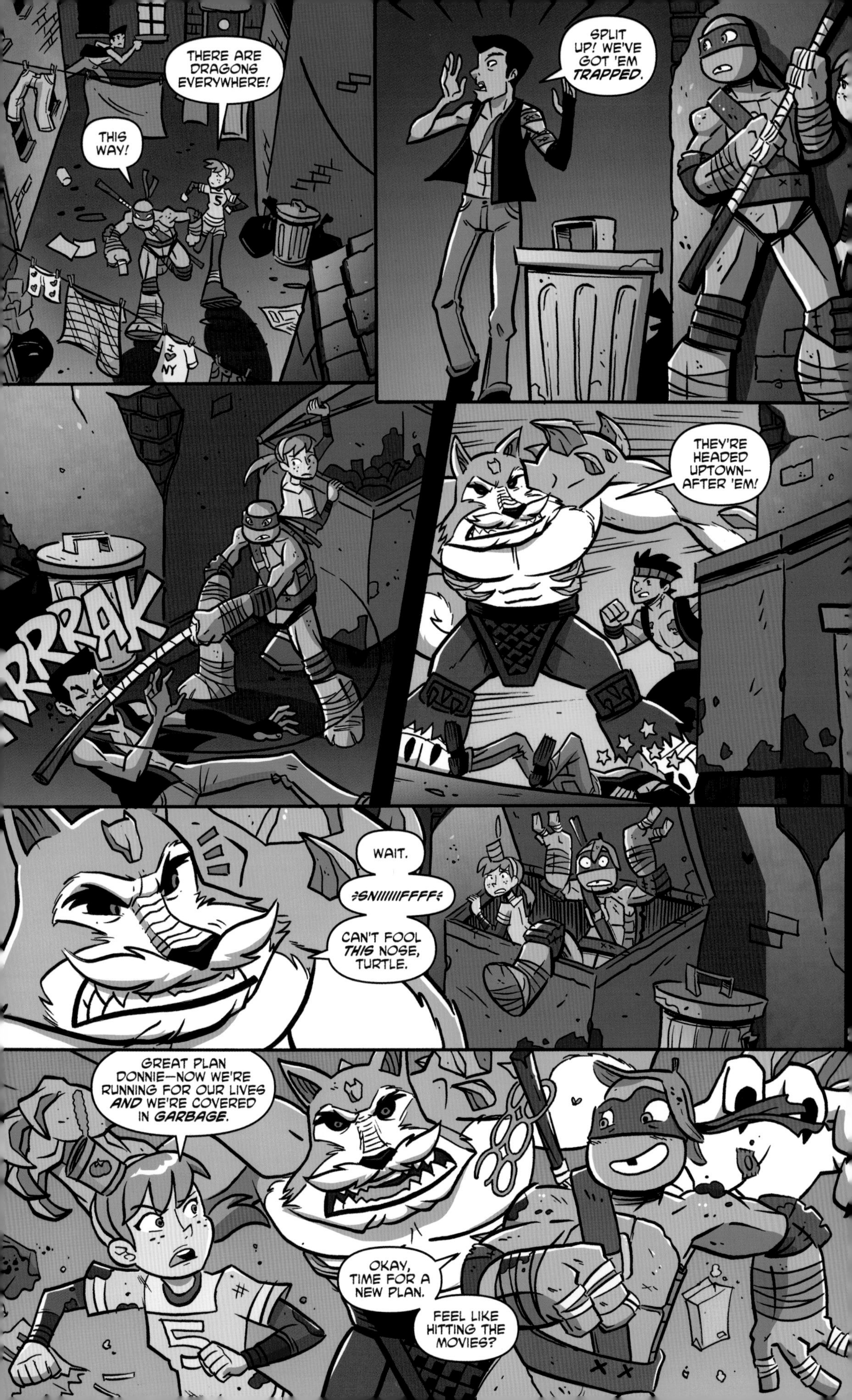
THERE ARE DRAGONS EVERYWHERE!
THIS WAY!
SPLIT UP! WE'VE GOT 'EM TRAPPED.
RRRAK
THEY'RE HEADED UPTOWN— AFTER 'EM!
WAIT.
SNIIIIIFFFF
CAN'T FOOL THIS NOSE, TURTLE.
GREAT PLAN DONNIE—NOW WE'RE RUNNING FOR OUR LIVES AND WE'RE COVERED IN GARBAGE.
OKAY, TIME FOR A NEW PLAN.
FEEL LIKE HITTING THE MOVIES?

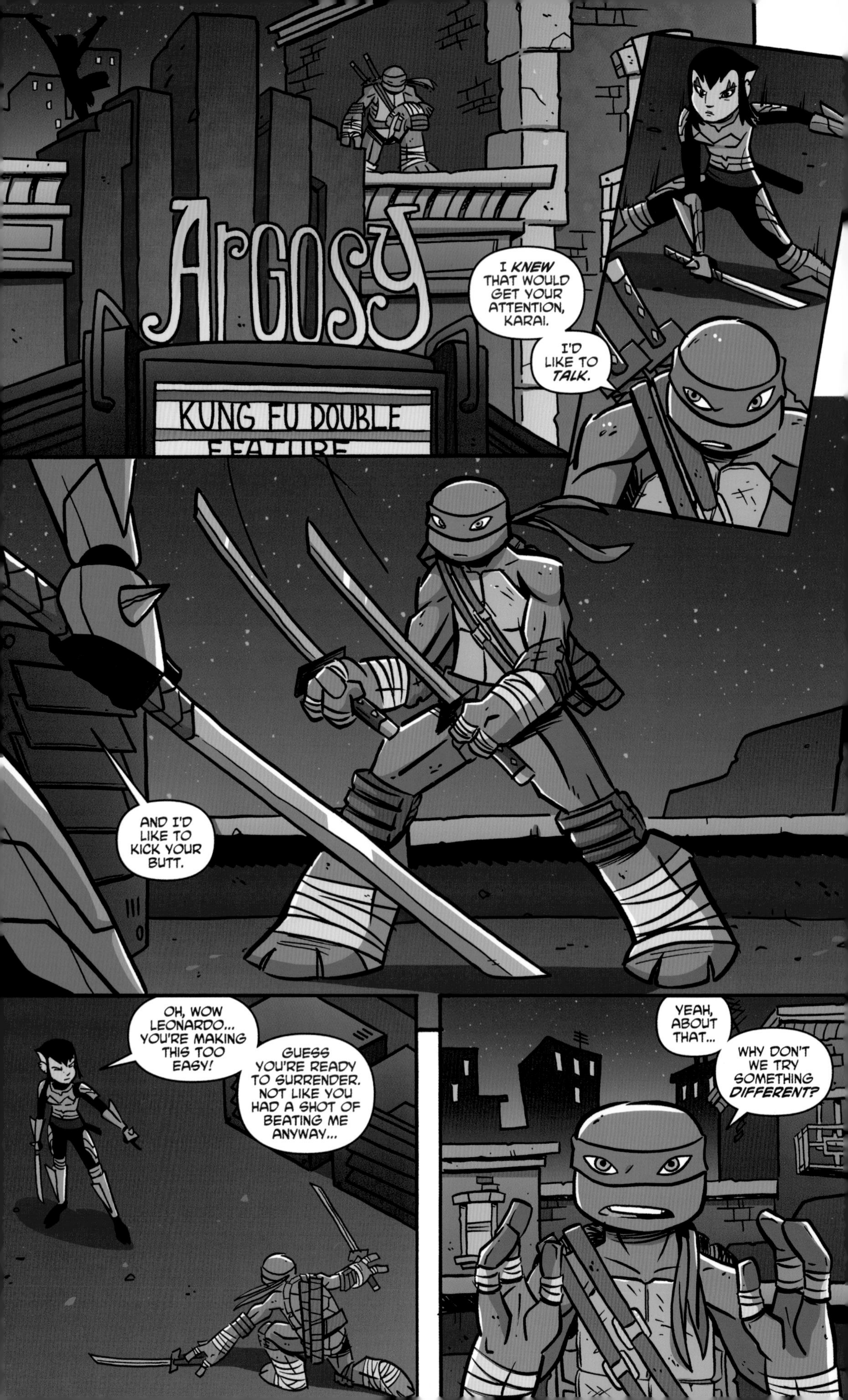
ArGOSY
KUNG FU DOUBLE
FEATURE
I KNEW THAT WOULD GET YOUR ATTENTION, KARAI.
I'D LIKE TO TALK.
AND I'D LIKE TO KICK YOUR BUTT.
OH, WOW LEONARDO... YOU'RE MAKING THIS TOO EASY!
GUESS YOU'RE READY TO SURRENDER. NOT LIKE YOU HAD A SHOT OF BEATING ME ANYWAY...
YEAH, ABOUT THAT...
WHY DON'T WE TRY SOMETHING DIFFERENT?

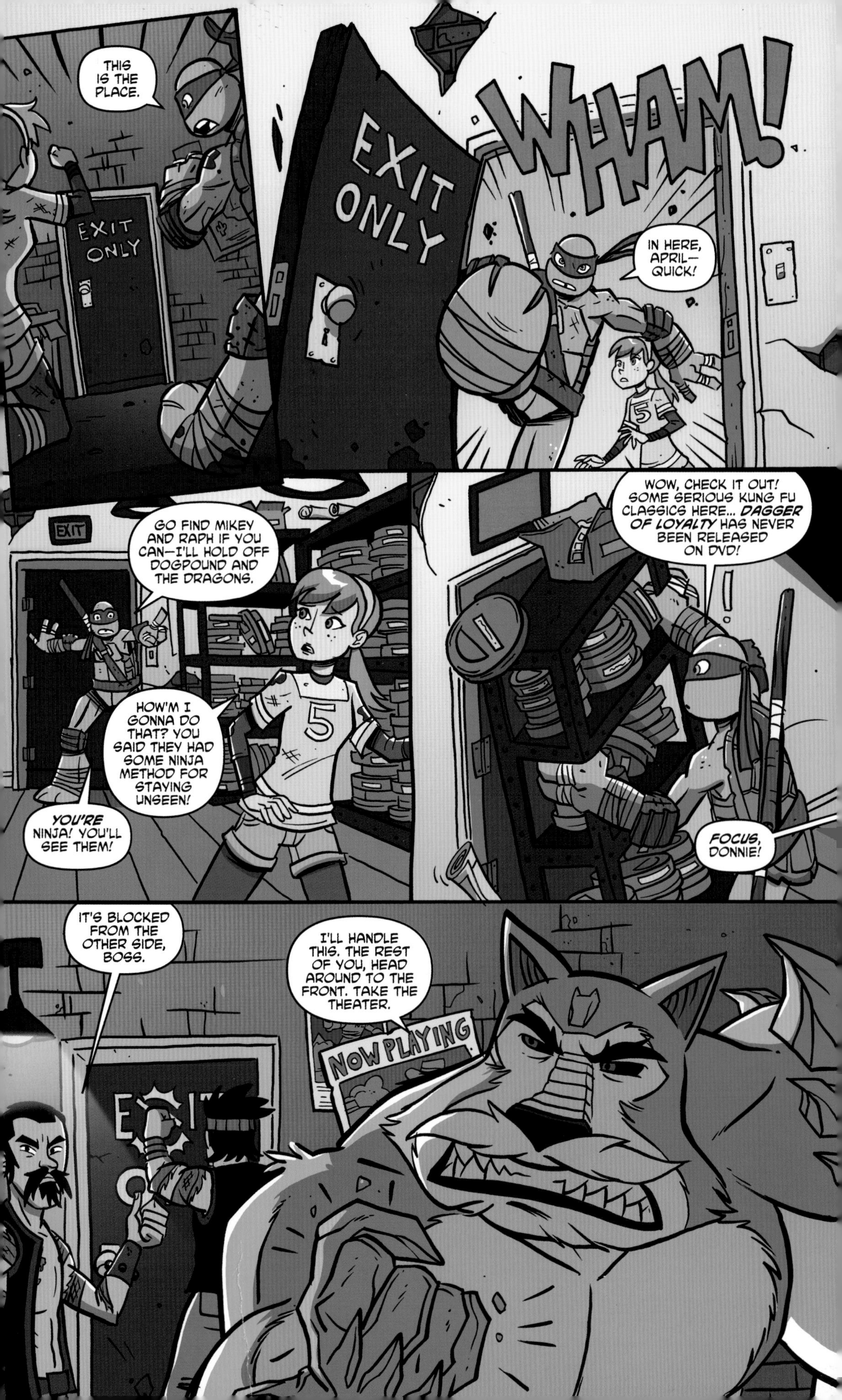
THIS IS THE PLACE.
EXIT ONLY
EXIT ONLY
WHAM!
IN HERE, APRIL—QUICK!
EXIT
GO FIND MIKEY AND RAPH IF YOU CAN—I'LL HOLD OFF DOGPOUND AND THE DRAGONS.
HOW'M I GONNA DO THAT? YOU SAID THEY HAD SOME NINJA METHOD FOR STAYING UNSEEN!
YOU'RE NINJA! YOU'LL SEE THEM!
WOW, CHECK IT OUT! SOME SERIOUS KUNG FU CLASSICS HERE... ***DAGGER OF LOYALTY*** HAS NEVER BEEN RELEASED ON DVD!
FOCUS, DONNIE!
IT'S BLOCKED FROM THE OTHER SIDE, BOSS.
I'LL HANDLE THIS. THE REST OF YOU, HEAD AROUND TO THE FRONT. TAKE THE THEATER.
NOW PLAYING

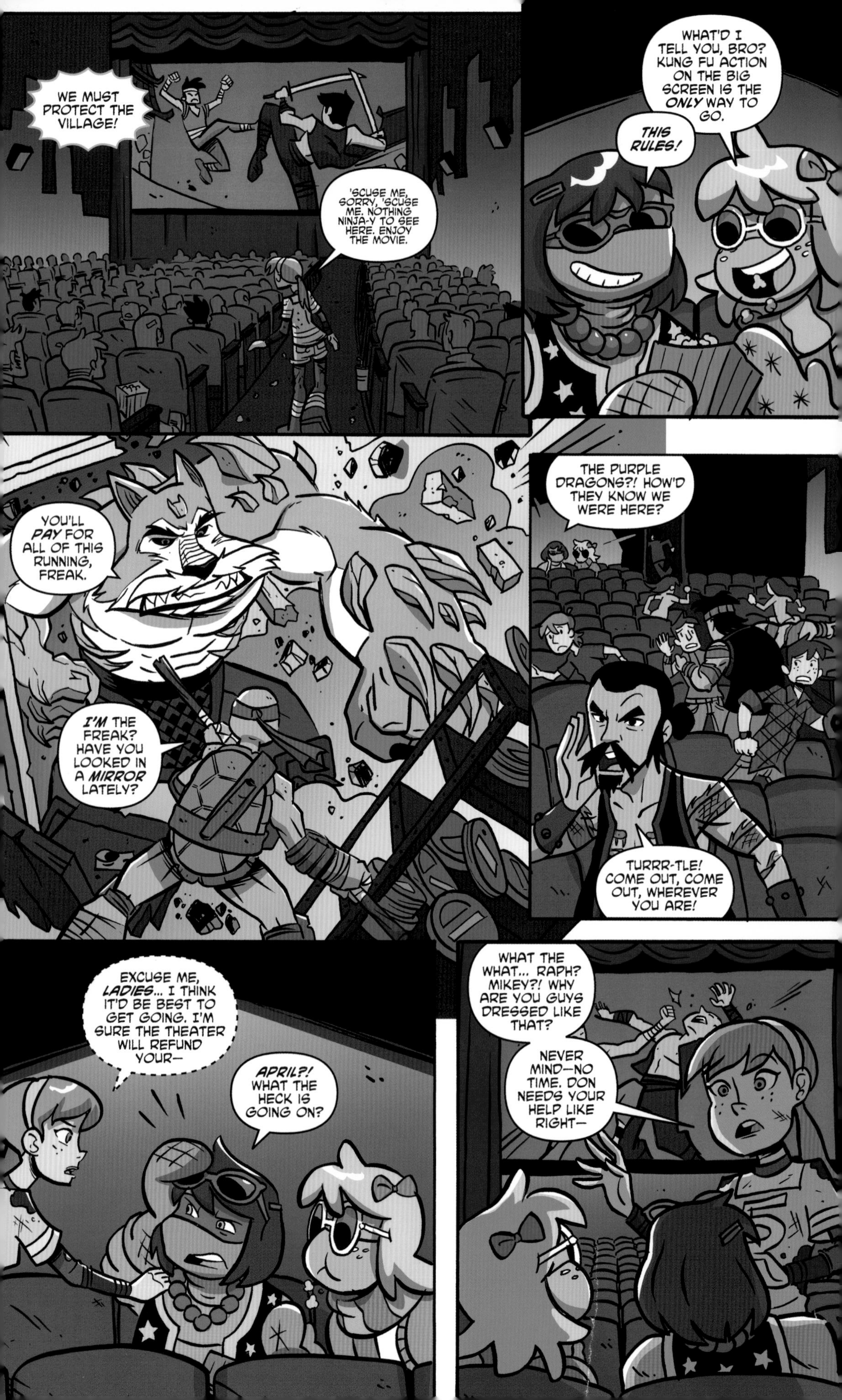

WE MUST PROTECT THE VILLAGE!
'SCUSE ME, SORRY, 'SCUSE ME. NOTHING NINJA-Y TO SEE HERE. ENJOY THE MOVIE.
WHAT'D I TELL YOU, BRO? KUNG FU ACTION ON THE BIG SCREEN IS THE ONLY WAY TO GO.
THIS RULES!
YOU'LL PAY FOR ALL OF THIS RUNNING, FREAK.
I'M THE FREAK? HAVE YOU LOOKED IN A MIRROR LATELY?
THE PURPLE DRAGONS?! HOW'D THEY KNOW WE WERE HERE?
TURRR-TLE! COME OUT, COME OUT, WHEREVER YOU ARE!
EXCUSE ME, LADIES... I THINK IT'D BE BEST TO GET GOING. I'M SURE THE THEATER WILL REFUND YOUR—
APRIL?! WHAT THE HECK IS GOING ON?
WHAT THE WHAT... RAPH? MIKEY?! WHY ARE YOU GUYS DRESSED LIKE THAT?
NEVER MIND—NO TIME. DON NEEDS YOUR HELP LIKE RIGHT—

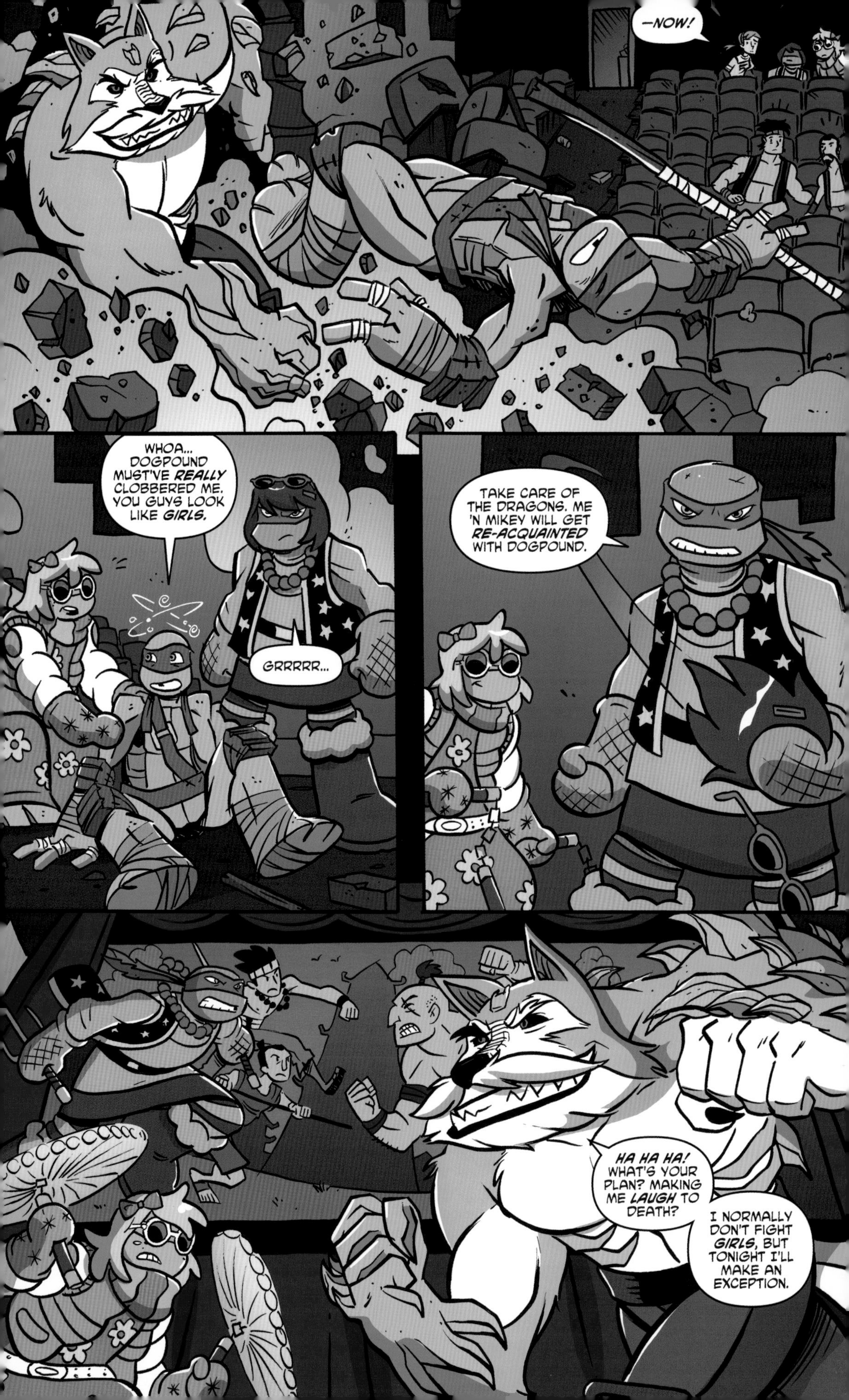
—NOW!
WHOA... DOGPOUND MUST'VE REALLY CLOBBERED ME. YOU GUYS LOOK LIKE GIRLS.
GRRRRR...
TAKE CARE OF THE DRAGONS. ME 'N MIKEY WILL GET RE-ACQUAINTED WITH DOGPOUND.
HA HA HA! WHAT'S YOUR PLAN? MAKING ME LAUGH TO DEATH?
I NORMALLY DON'T FIGHT GIRLS, BUT TONIGHT I'LL MAKE AN EXCEPTION.

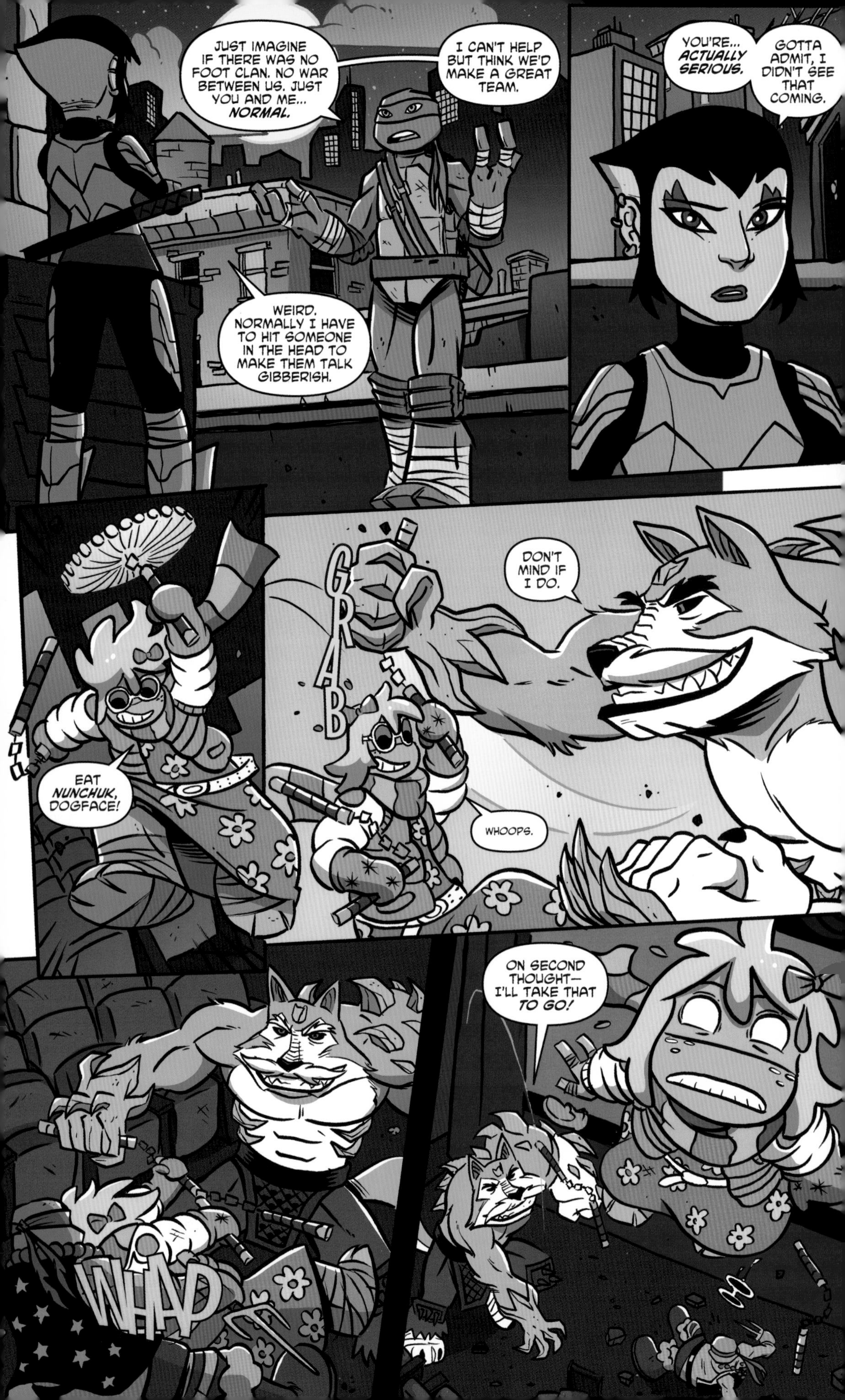
JUST IMAGINE IF THERE WAS NO FOOT CLAN. NO WAR BETWEEN US. JUST YOU AND ME... NORMAL.
I CAN'T HELP BUT THINK WE'D MAKE A GREAT TEAM.
WEIRD. NORMALLY I HAVE TO HIT SOMEONE IN THE HEAD TO MAKE THEM TALK GIBBERISH.
YOU'RE... ACTUALLY SERIOUS.
GOTTA ADMIT, I DIDN'T SEE THAT COMING.
EAT NUNCHUK, DOGFACE!
GRAB
DON'T MIND IF I DO.
WHOOPS.
WHAP
ON SECOND THOUGHT— I'LL TAKE THAT TO GO!

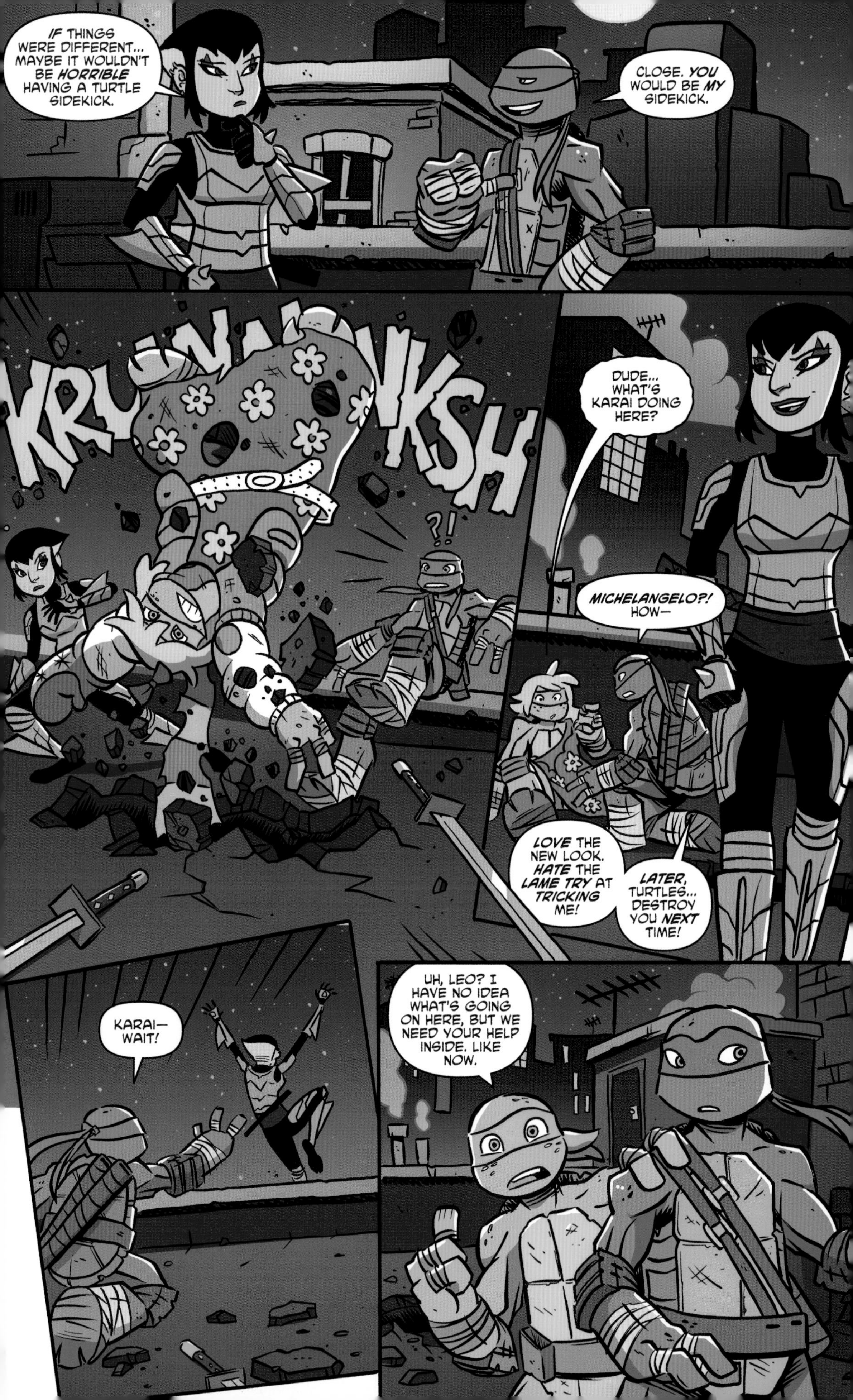
IF THINGS WERE DIFFERENT... MAYBE IT WOULDN'T BE HORRIBLE HAVING A TURTLE SIDEKICK.
CLOSE. YOU WOULD BE MY SIDEKICK.
KRUNNNNKSH
?!
DUDE... WHAT'S KARAI DOING HERE?
MICHELANGELO?! HOW—
LOVE THE NEW LOOK. HATE THE LAME TRY AT TRICKING ME!
LATER, TURTLES... DESTROY YOU NEXT TIME!
KARAI— WAIT!
UH, LEO? I HAVE NO IDEA WHAT'S GOING ON HERE, BUT WE NEED YOUR HELP INSIDE. LIKE NOW.

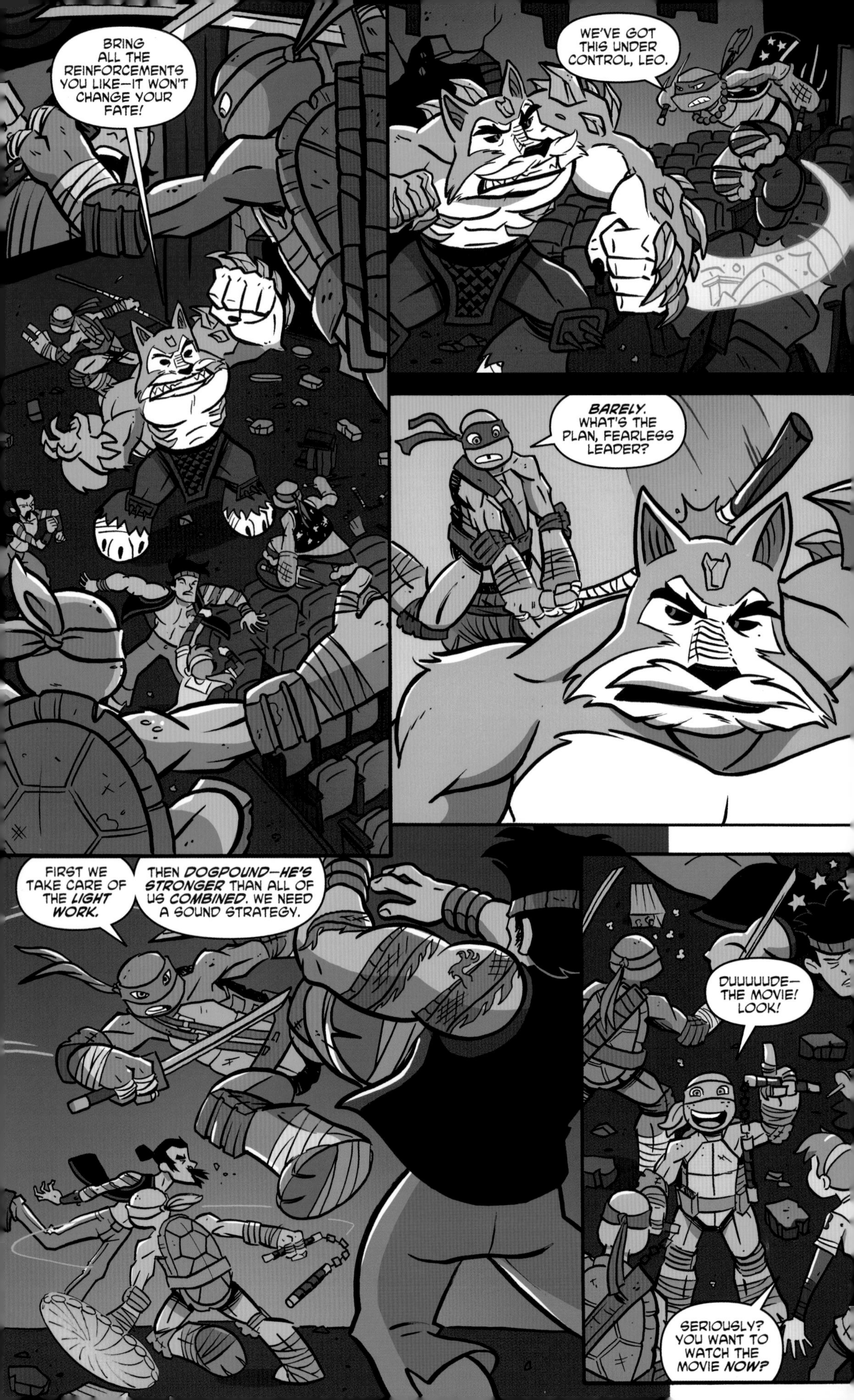
BRING ALL THE REINFORCEMENTS YOU LIKE—IT WON'T CHANGE YOUR FATE!
WE'VE GOT THIS UNDER CONTROL, LEO.
BARELY. WHAT'S THE PLAN, FEARLESS LEADER?
FIRST WE TAKE CARE OF THE *LIGHT WORK.*
THEN *DOGPOUND*—*HE'S STRONGER* THAN ALL OF US *COMBINED*. WE NEED A SOUND STRATEGY.
DUUUUUDE— THE MOVIE! LOOK!
SERIOUSLY? YOU WANT TO WATCH THE MOVIE *NOW?*

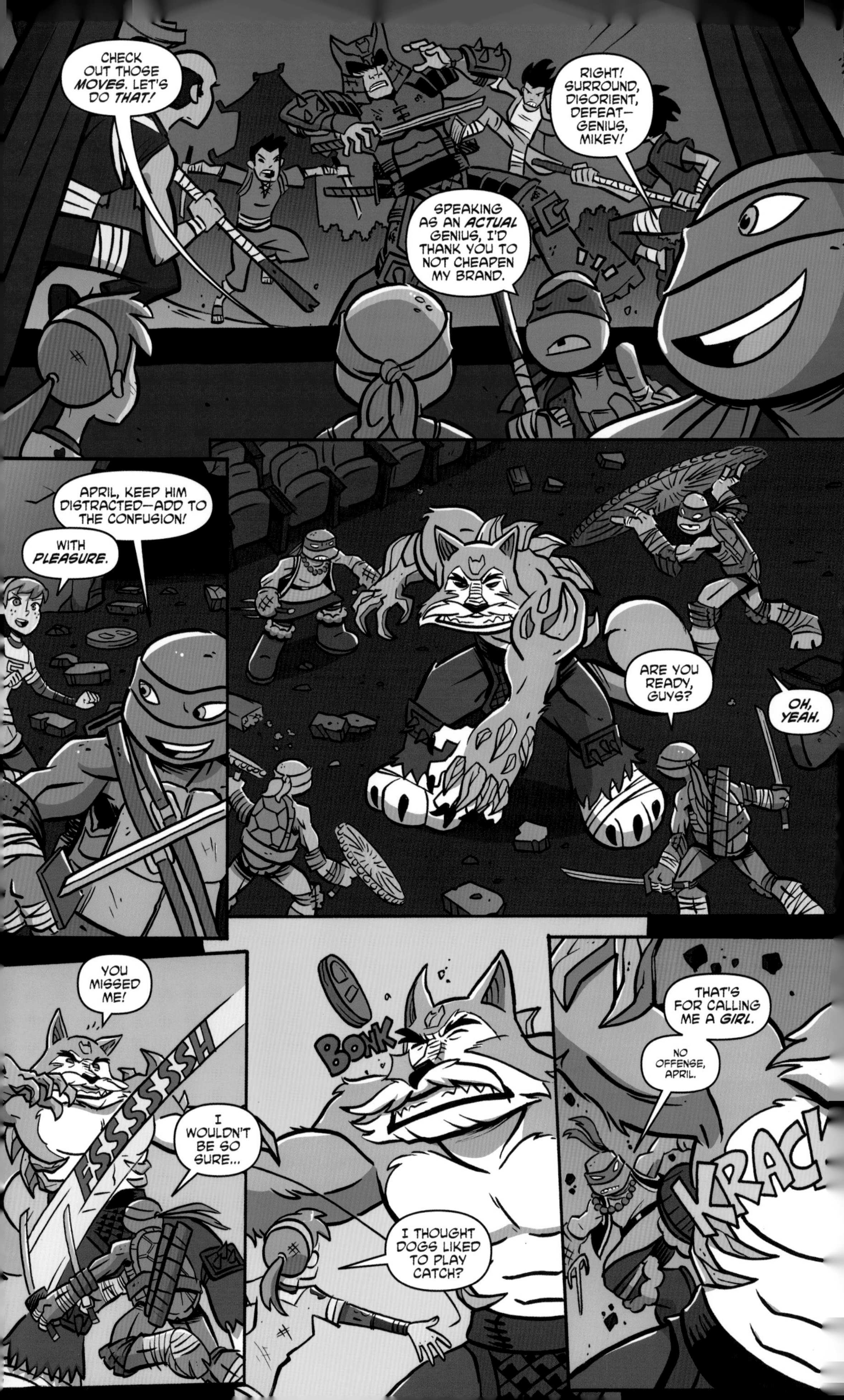
CHECK OUT THOSE MOVES. LET'S DO THAT!
RIGHT! SURROUND, DISORIENT, DEFEAT— GENIUS, MIKEY!
SPEAKING AS AN ACTUAL GENIUS, I'D THANK YOU TO NOT CHEAPEN MY BRAND.
APRIL, KEEP HIM DISTRACTED—ADD TO THE CONFUSION!
WITH PLEASURE.
ARE YOU READY, GUYS?
OH, YEAH.
YOU MISSED ME!
FSSSSSSSH
I WOULDN'T BE SO SURE...
BONK
I THOUGHT DOGS LIKED TO PLAY CATCH?
THAT'S FOR CALLING ME A GIRL.
NO OFFENSE, APRIL.
KRACK

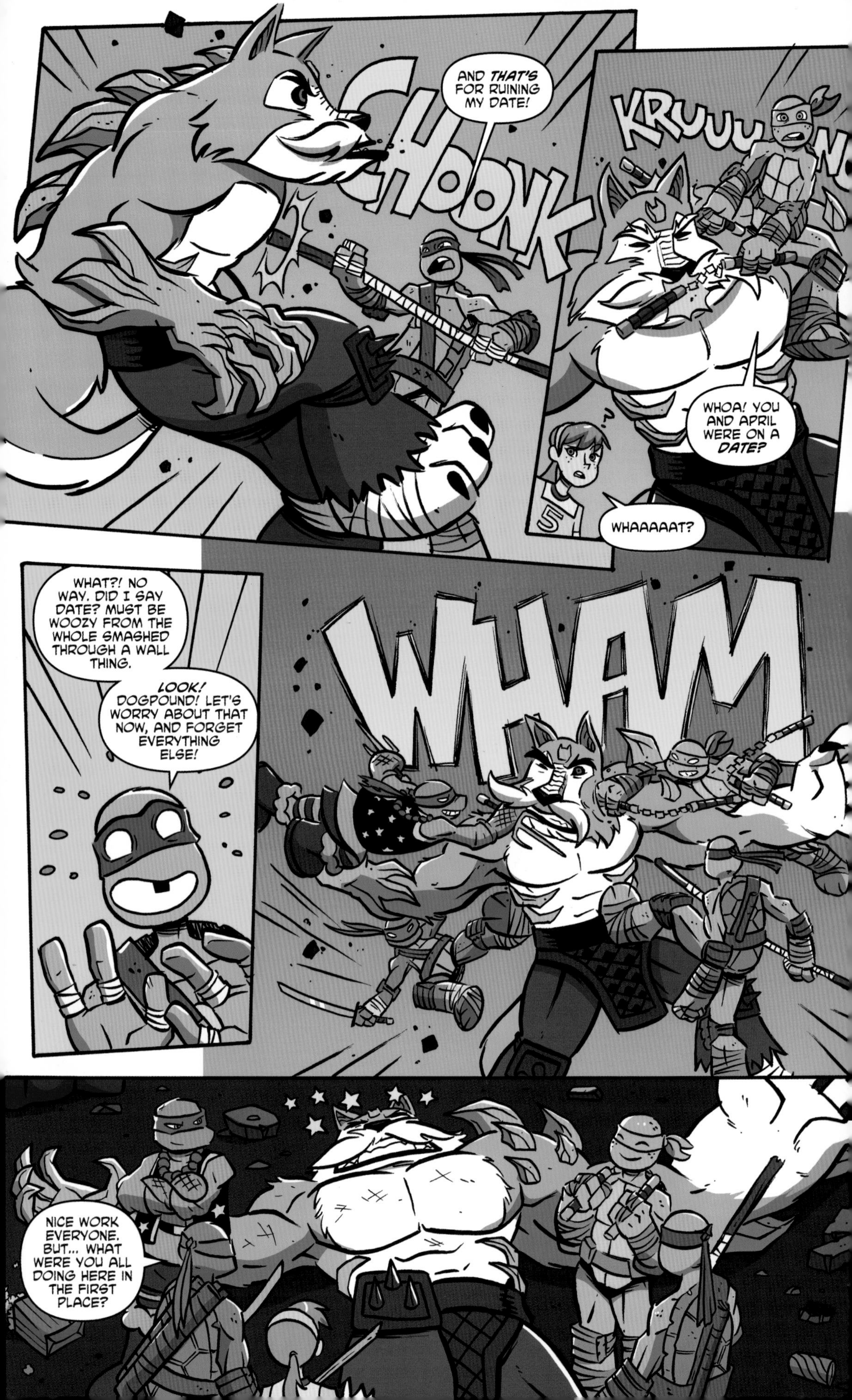

CHOONK
AND THAT'S FOR RUINING MY DATE!
KRUUUUNCH
WHOA! YOU AND APRIL WERE ON A DATE?
WHAAAAAT?
WHAT?! NO WAY. DID I SAY DATE? MUST BE WOOZY FROM THE WHOLE SMASHED THROUGH A WALL THING.
LOOK! DOGPOUND! LET'S WORRY ABOUT THAT NOW, AND FORGET EVERYTHING ELSE!
WHAM
NICE WORK EVERYONE. BUT... WHAT WERE YOU ALL DOING HERE IN THE FIRST PLACE?

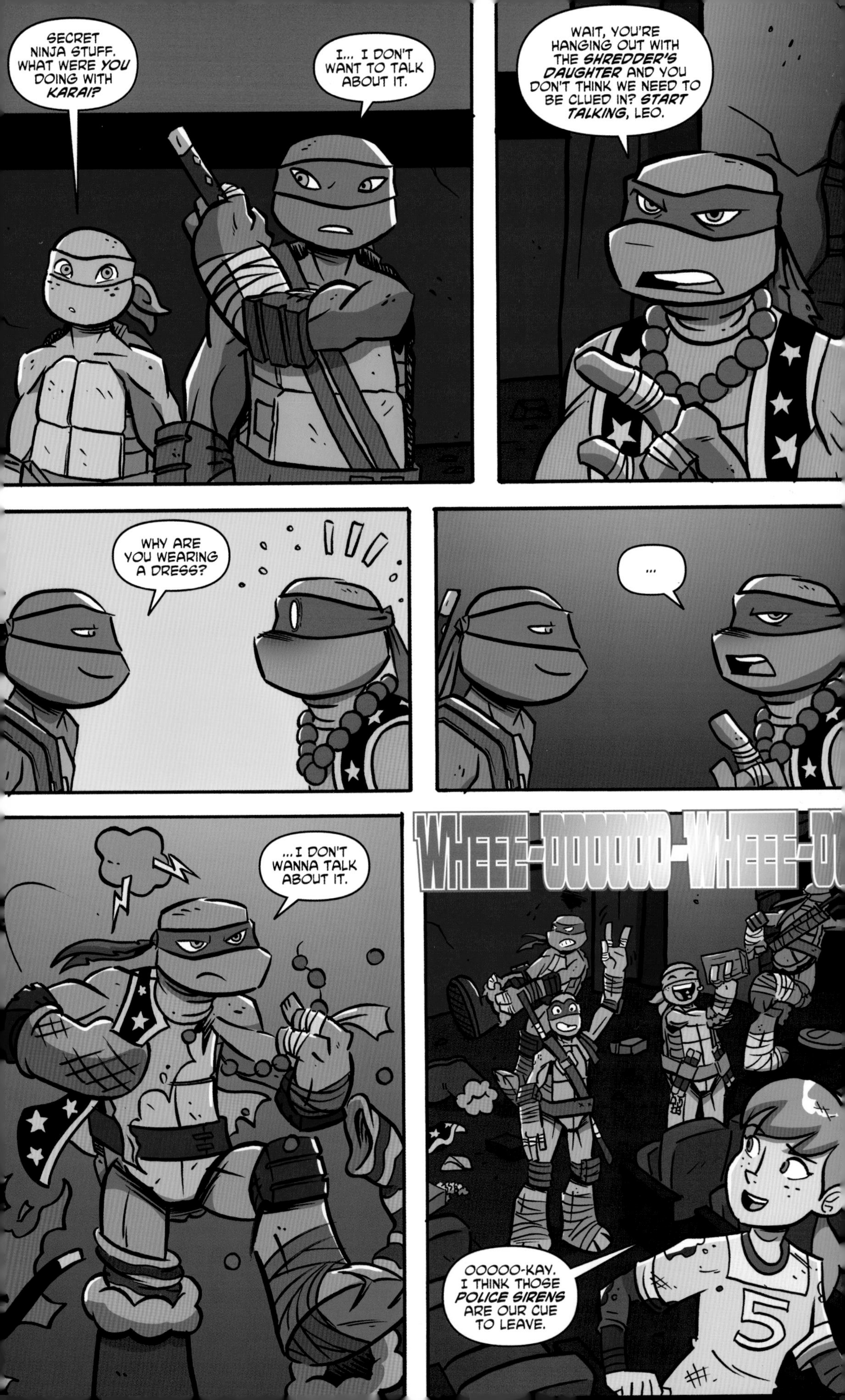
SECRET NINJA STUFF. WHAT WERE *YOU* DOING WITH *KARAI?*
I... I DON'T WANT TO TALK ABOUT IT.
WAIT, YOU'RE HANGING OUT WITH THE *SHREDDER'S DAUGHTER* AND YOU DON'T THINK WE NEED TO BE CLUED IN? *START TALKING*, LEO.
WHY ARE YOU WEARING A DRESS?
...
...I DON'T WANNA TALK ABOUT IT.
WHEEE-OOOOOO-WHEEE-OO
OOOOO-KAY. I THINK THOSE *POLICE SIRENS* ARE OUR CUE TO LEAVE.

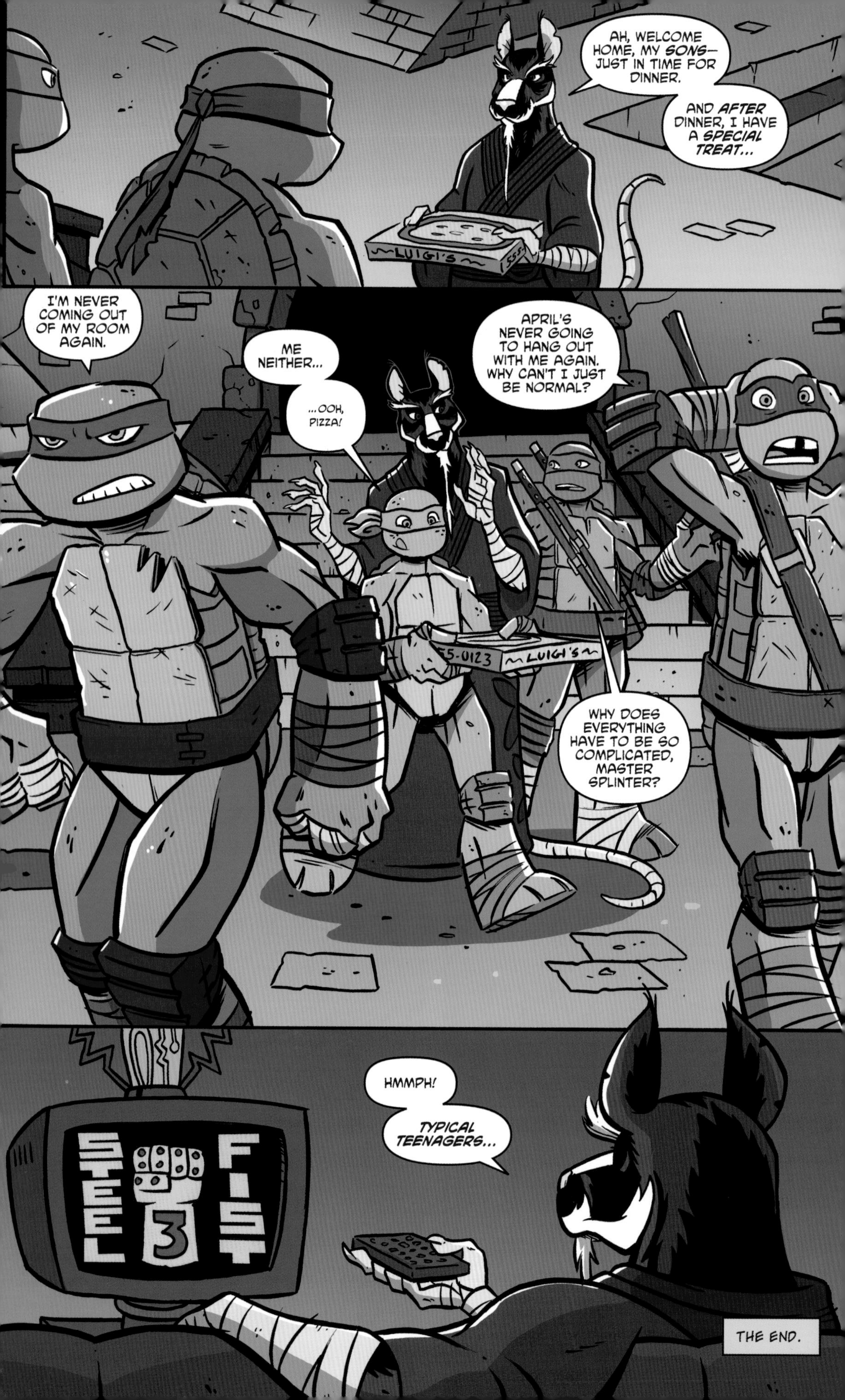
AH, WELCOME HOME, MY SONS— JUST IN TIME FOR DINNER.
AND AFTER DINNER, I HAVE A SPECIAL TREAT...
LUIGI'S
I'M NEVER COMING OUT OF MY ROOM AGAIN.
ME NEITHER...
...OOH, PIZZA!
APRIL'S NEVER GOING TO HANG OUT WITH ME AGAIN. WHY CAN'T I JUST BE NORMAL?
LUIGI'S
WHY DOES EVERYTHING HAVE TO BE SO COMPLICATED, MASTER SPLINTER?
HMMPH!
TYPICAL TEENAGERS...
STEEL FIST 3
THE END.

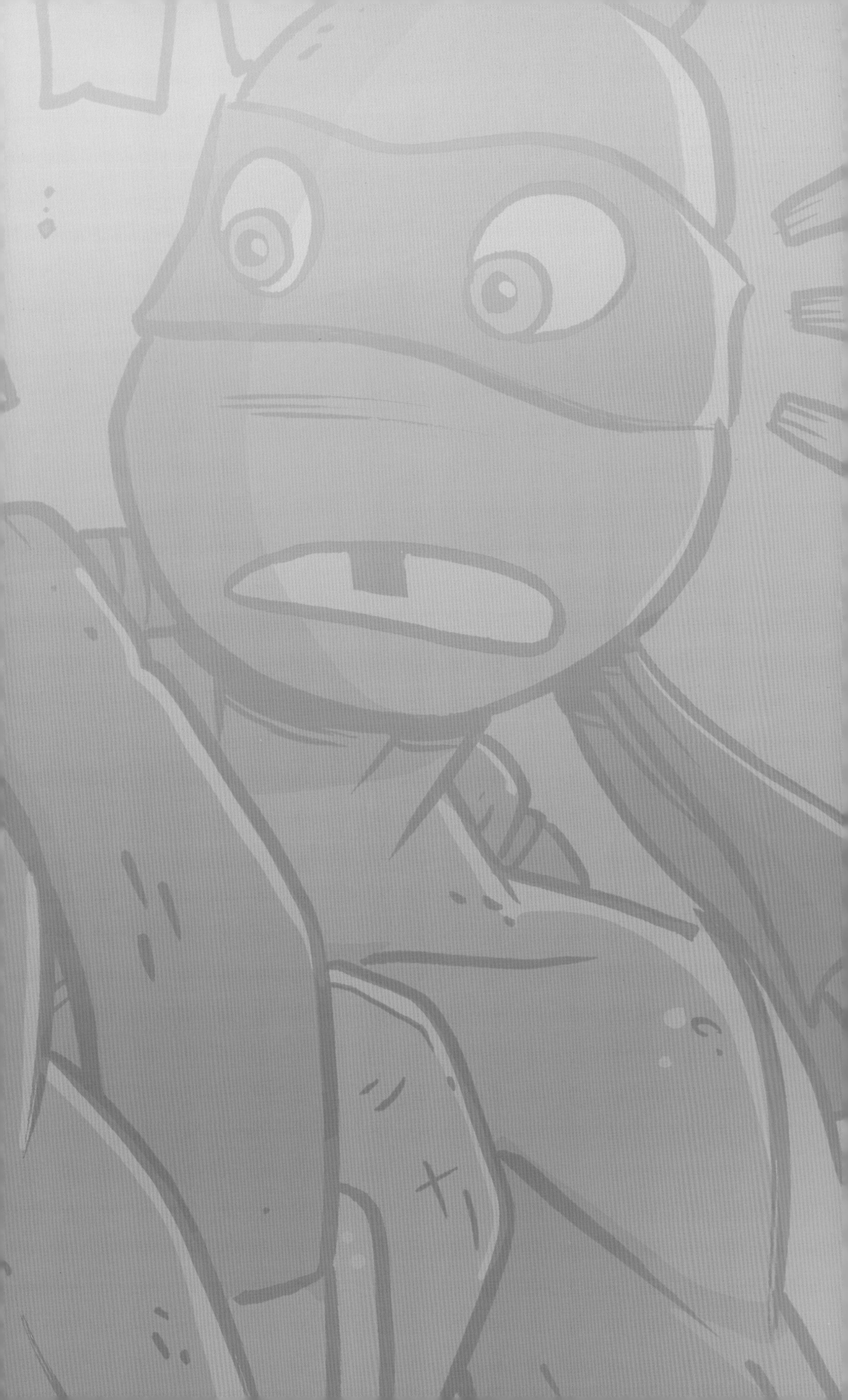

ART BY **DARIO BRIZUELA**

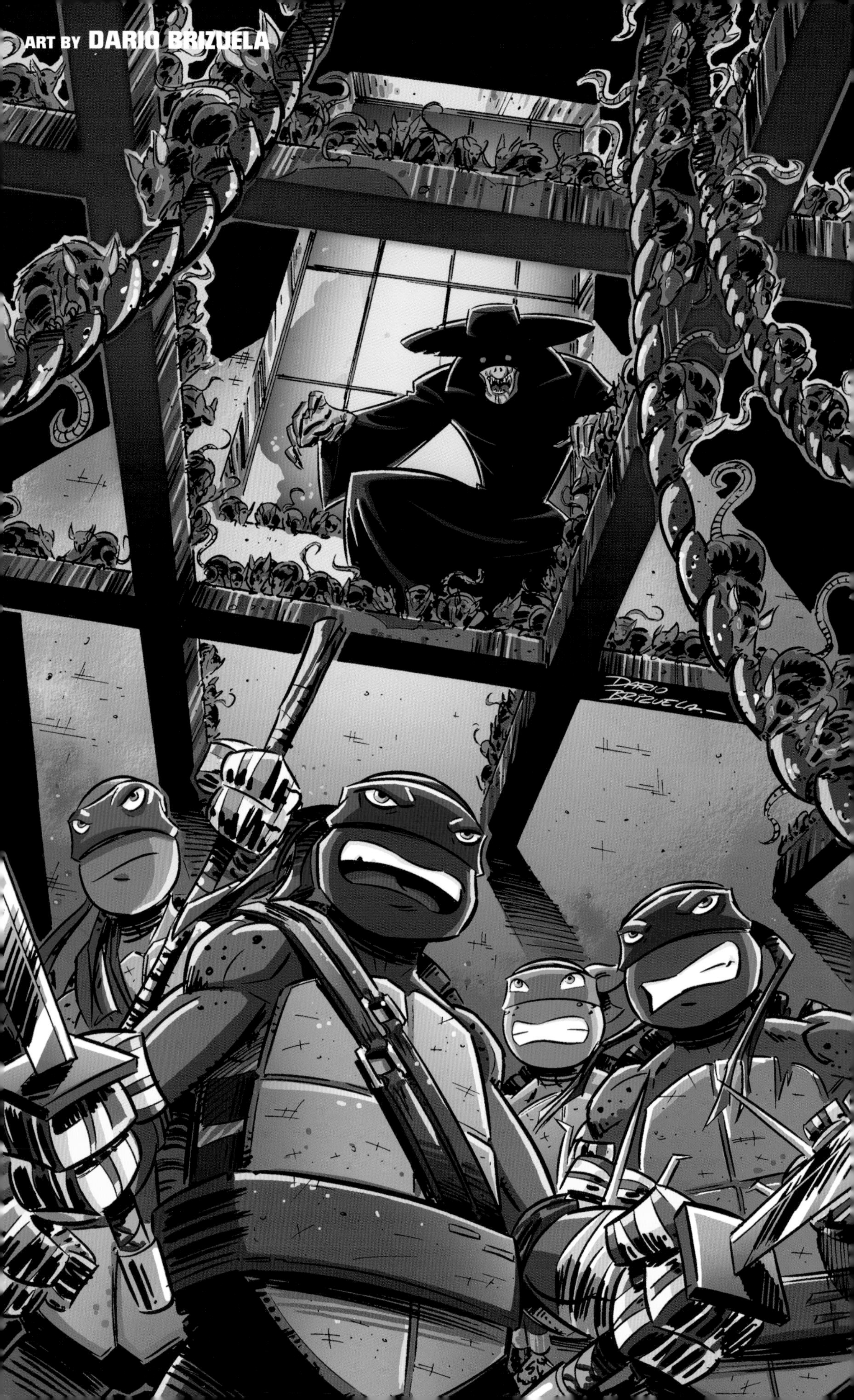
DARIO
BRIZUELA

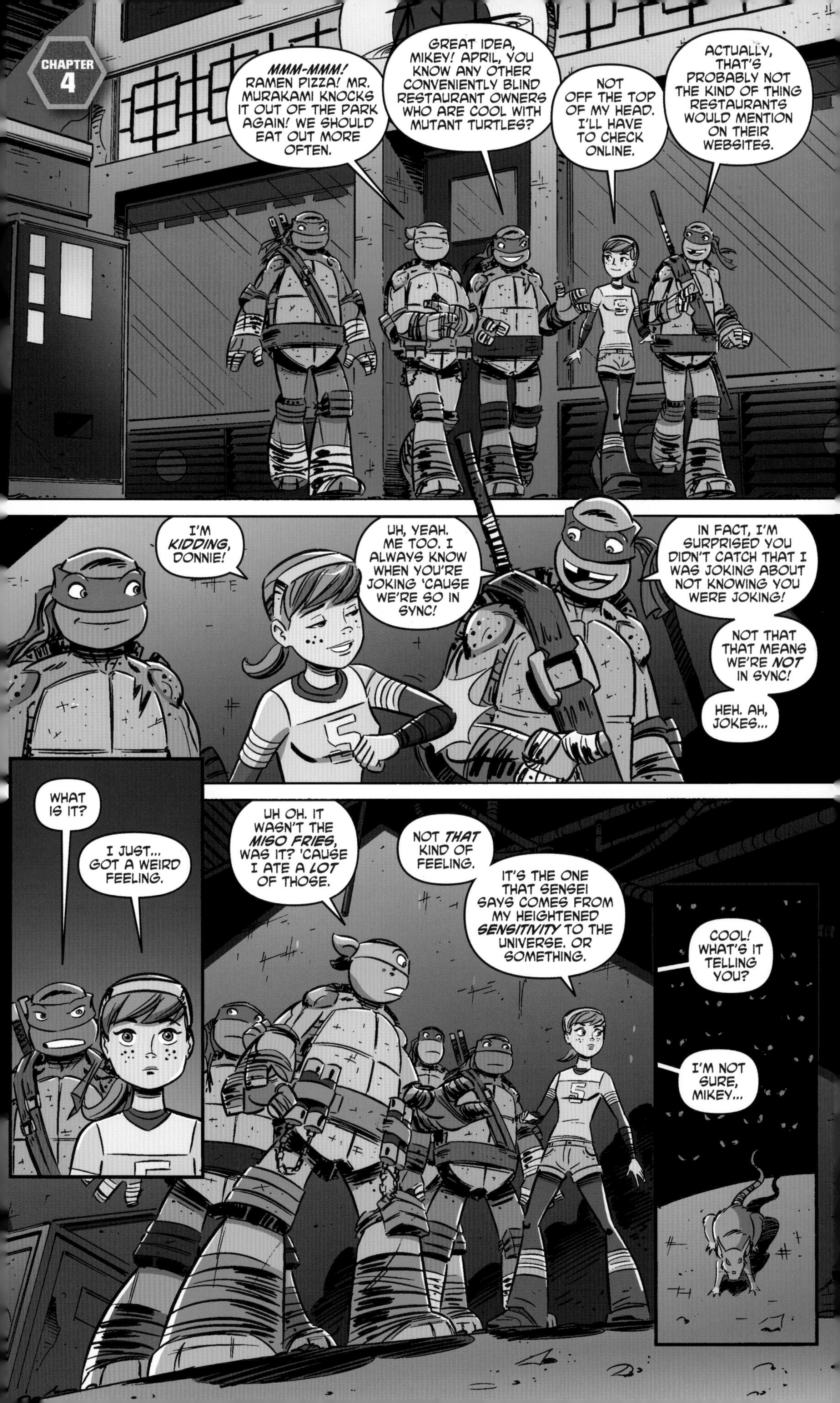
CHAPTER 4
MMM-MMM! RAMEN PIZZA! MR. MURAKAMI KNOCKS IT OUT OF THE PARK AGAIN! WE SHOULD EAT OUT MORE OFTEN.
GREAT IDEA, MIKEY! APRIL, YOU KNOW ANY OTHER CONVENIENTLY BLIND RESTAURANT OWNERS WHO ARE COOL WITH MUTANT TURTLES?
NOT OFF THE TOP OF MY HEAD. I'LL HAVE TO CHECK ONLINE.
ACTUALLY, THAT'S PROBABLY NOT THE KIND OF THING RESTAURANTS WOULD MENTION ON THEIR WEBSITES.
I'M KIDDING, DONNIE!
UH, YEAH. ME TOO. I ALWAYS KNOW WHEN YOU'RE JOKING 'CAUSE WE'RE SO IN SYNC!
IN FACT, I'M SURPRISED YOU DIDN'T CATCH THAT I WAS JOKING ABOUT NOT KNOWING YOU WERE JOKING!
NOT THAT THAT MEANS WE'RE NOT IN SYNC!
HEH. AH, JOKES...
WHAT IS IT?
I JUST... GOT A WEIRD FEELING.
UH OH. IT WASN'T THE MISO FRIES, WAS IT? 'CAUSE I ATE A LOT OF THOSE.
NOT THAT KIND OF FEELING.
IT'S THE ONE THAT SENSEI SAYS COMES FROM MY HEIGHTENED SENSITIVITY TO THE UNIVERSE. OR SOMETHING.
COOL! WHAT'S IT TELLING YOU?
I'M NOT SURE, MIKEY...

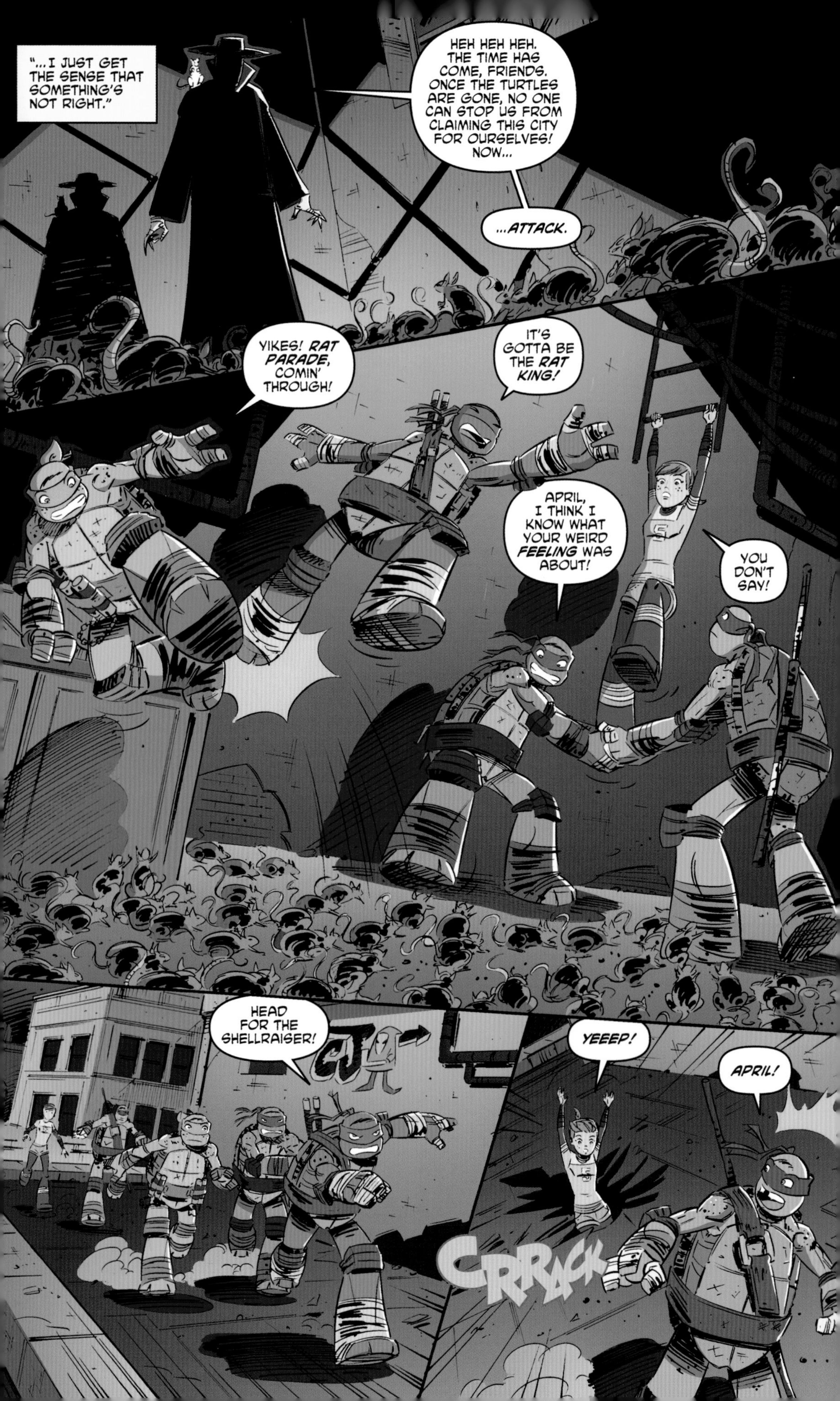
"...I JUST GET THE SENSE THAT SOMETHING'S NOT RIGHT."
HEH HEH HEH. THE TIME HAS COME, FRIENDS. ONCE THE TURTLES ARE GONE, NO ONE CAN STOP US FROM CLAIMING THIS CITY FOR OURSELVES! NOW...
...ATTACK.
YIKES! RAT PARADE, COMIN' THROUGH!
IT'S GOTTA BE THE RAT KING!
APRIL, I THINK I KNOW WHAT YOUR WEIRD FEELING WAS ABOUT!
YOU DON'T SAY!
HEAD FOR THE SHELLRAISER!
YEEEP!
APRIL!
CRRACK

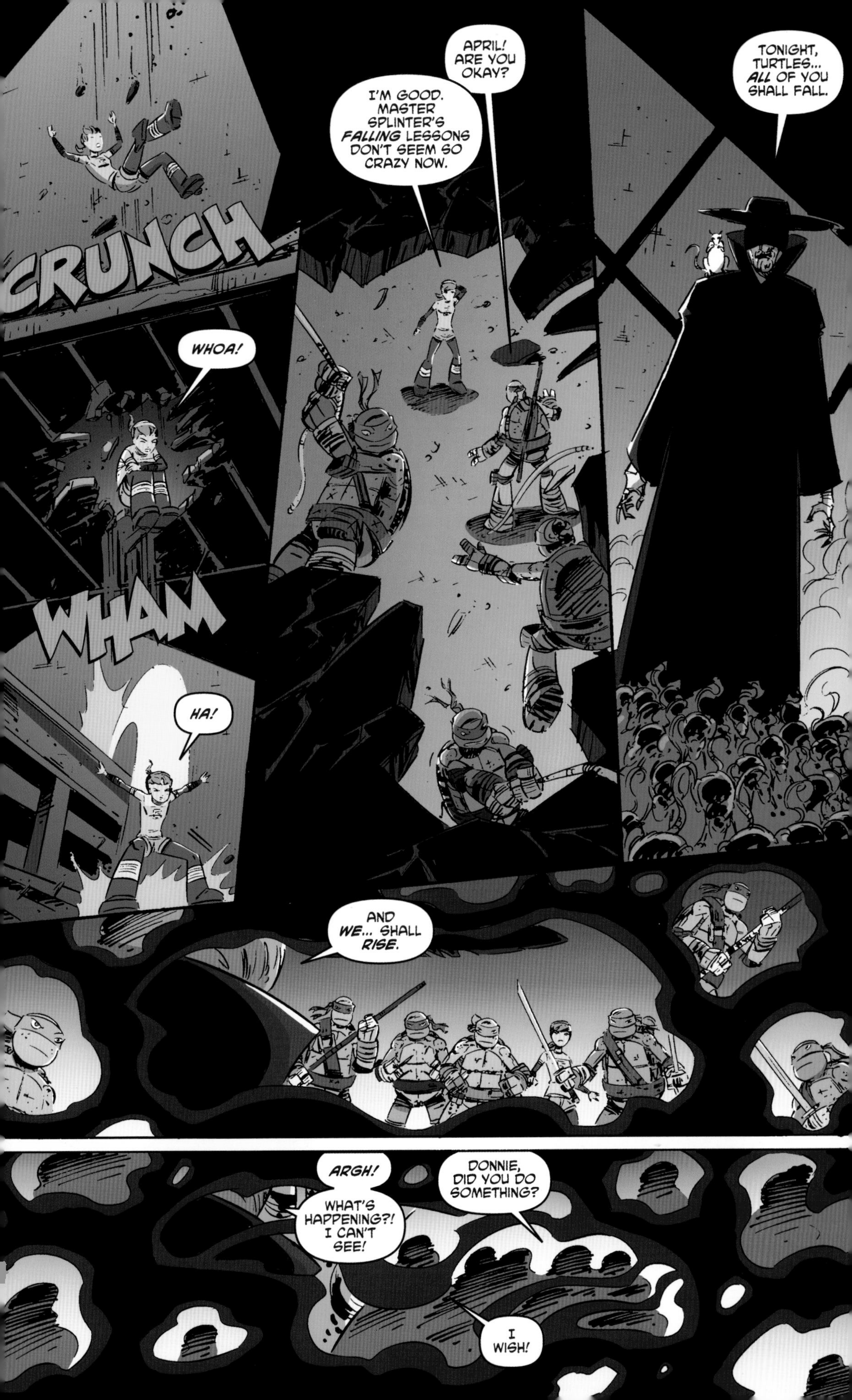

CRUNCH
WHOA!
WHAM
HA!
APRIL! ARE YOU OKAY?
I'M GOOD. MASTER SPLINTER'S *FALLING* LESSONS DON'T SEEM SO CRAZY NOW.
TONIGHT, TURTLES... *ALL* OF YOU SHALL FALL.
AND *WE*... SHALL *RISE*.
ARGH!
WHAT'S HAPPENING?! I CAN'T SEE!
DONNIE, DID YOU DO SOMETHING?
I WISH!

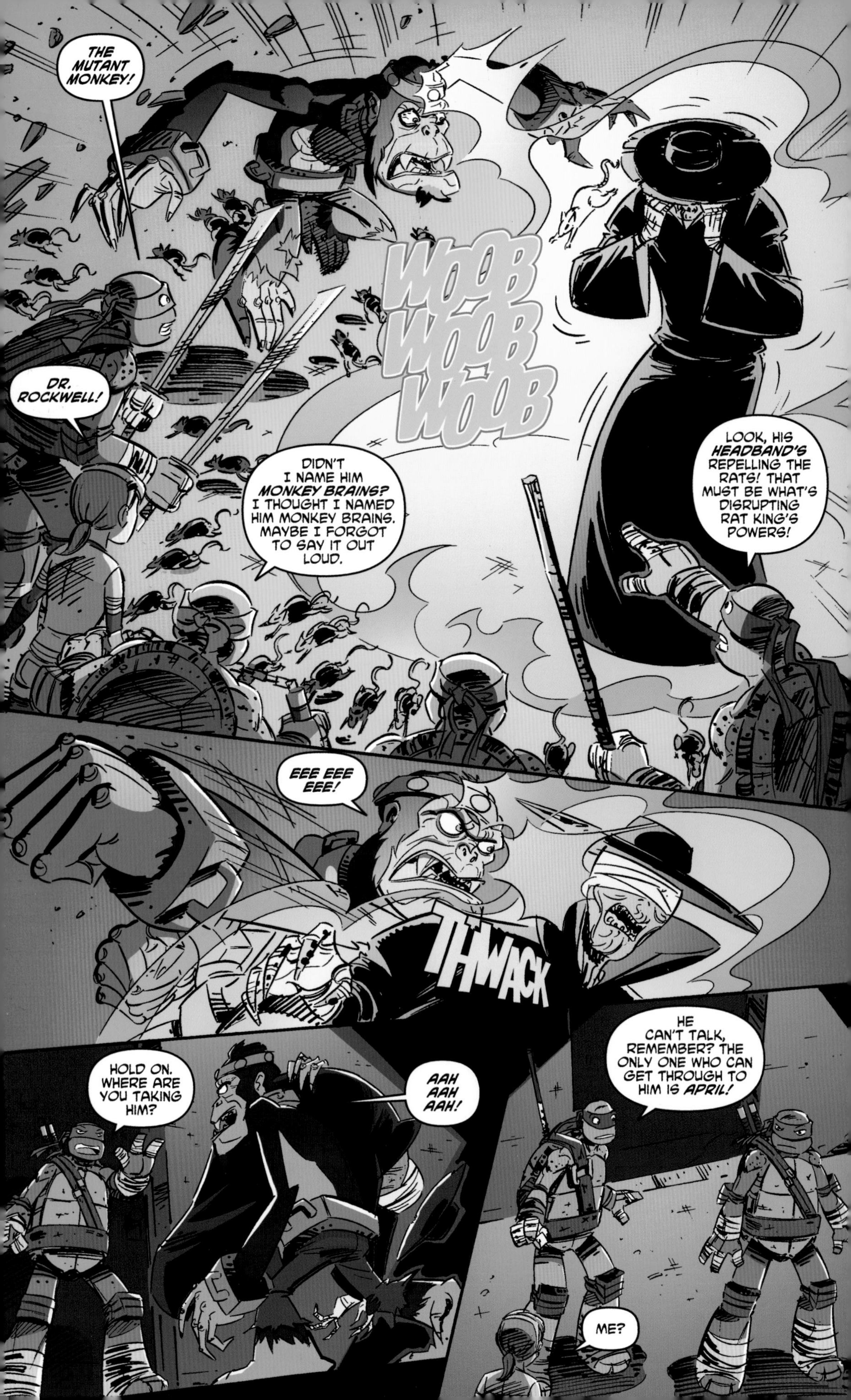
THE MUTANT MONKEY!
DR. ROCKWELL!
WOOB WOOB WOOB
DIDN'T I NAME HIM MONKEY BRAINS? I THOUGHT I NAMED HIM MONKEY BRAINS. MAYBE I FORGOT TO SAY IT OUT LOUD.
LOOK, HIS HEADBAND'S REPELLING THE RATS! THAT MUST BE WHAT'S DISRUPTING RAT KING'S POWERS!
EEE EEE EEE!
THWACK
HOLD ON. WHERE ARE YOU TAKING HIM?
AAH AAH AAH!
HE CAN'T TALK, REMEMBER? THE ONLY ONE WHO CAN GET THROUGH TO HIM IS APRIL!
ME?

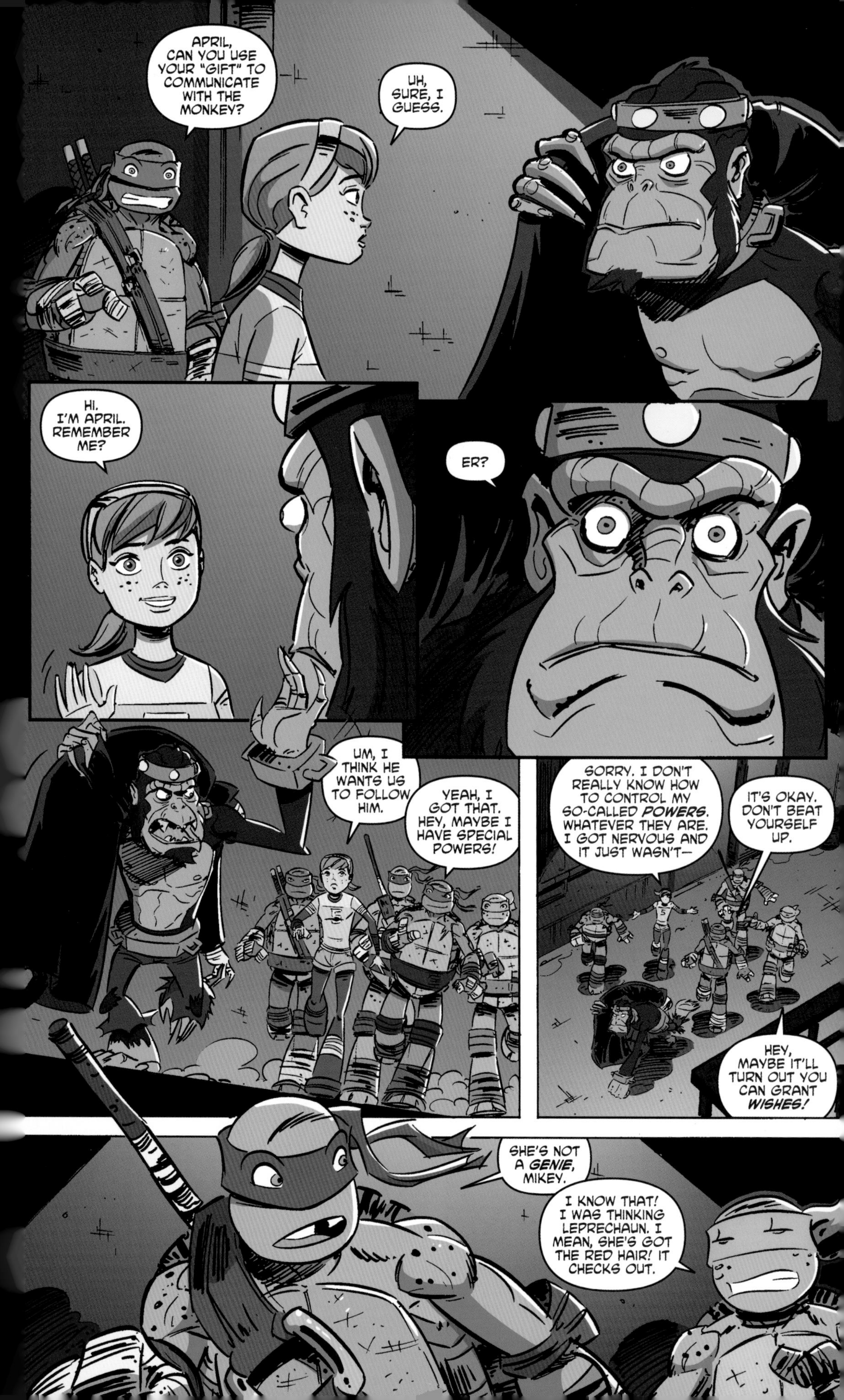
APRIL, CAN YOU USE YOUR "GIFT" TO COMMUNICATE WITH THE MONKEY?
UH, SURE, I GUESS.
HI. I'M APRIL. REMEMBER ME?
ER?
UM, I THINK HE WANTS US TO FOLLOW HIM.
YEAH, I GOT THAT. HEY, MAYBE I HAVE SPECIAL POWERS!
SORRY. I DON'T REALLY KNOW HOW TO CONTROL MY SO-CALLED *POWERS*. WHATEVER THEY ARE. I GOT NERVOUS AND IT JUST WASN'T—
IT'S OKAY. DON'T BEAT YOURSELF UP.
HEY, MAYBE IT'LL TURN OUT YOU CAN GRANT *WISHES!*
SHE'S NOT A *GENIE*, MIKEY.
I KNOW THAT! I WAS THINKING LEPRECHAUN. I MEAN, SHE'S GOT THE RED HAIR! IT CHECKS OUT.

"WOW! THAT MONKEY BUILT THIS LAB ALL THIS BY HIMSELF?"

I MEAN, IT'S NOT AS IMPRESSIVE AS MINE, BUT IT'S DARN GOOD.

IT'S NOT THAT SURPRISING. DR. ROCKWELL *WAS* A SUCCESSFUL NEUROCHEMIST.

LOOK AT ALL THESE *PROTOTYPES!* THIS MUST BE WHERE HE BUILT THAT HEADBAND THING.

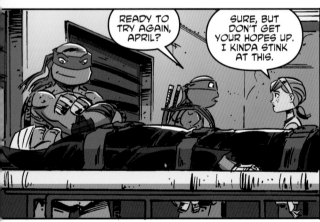

READY TO TRY AGAIN, APRIL?

SURE, BUT DON'T GET YOUR HOPES UP. I KINDA STINK AT THIS.

DR. ROCKWELL.

WHAT'S GOING ON? THEY'RE NOT *SAYING* ANYTHING!

SHH! THEY'RE COMMUNICATING PSYCHICALLY! I THINK.

WELL, IF THEY'RE TALKING WITH THEIR *MINDS,* THEN WHY DO I NEED TO BE *QUIET?*

HUH. I GUESS I DON'T KNOW.

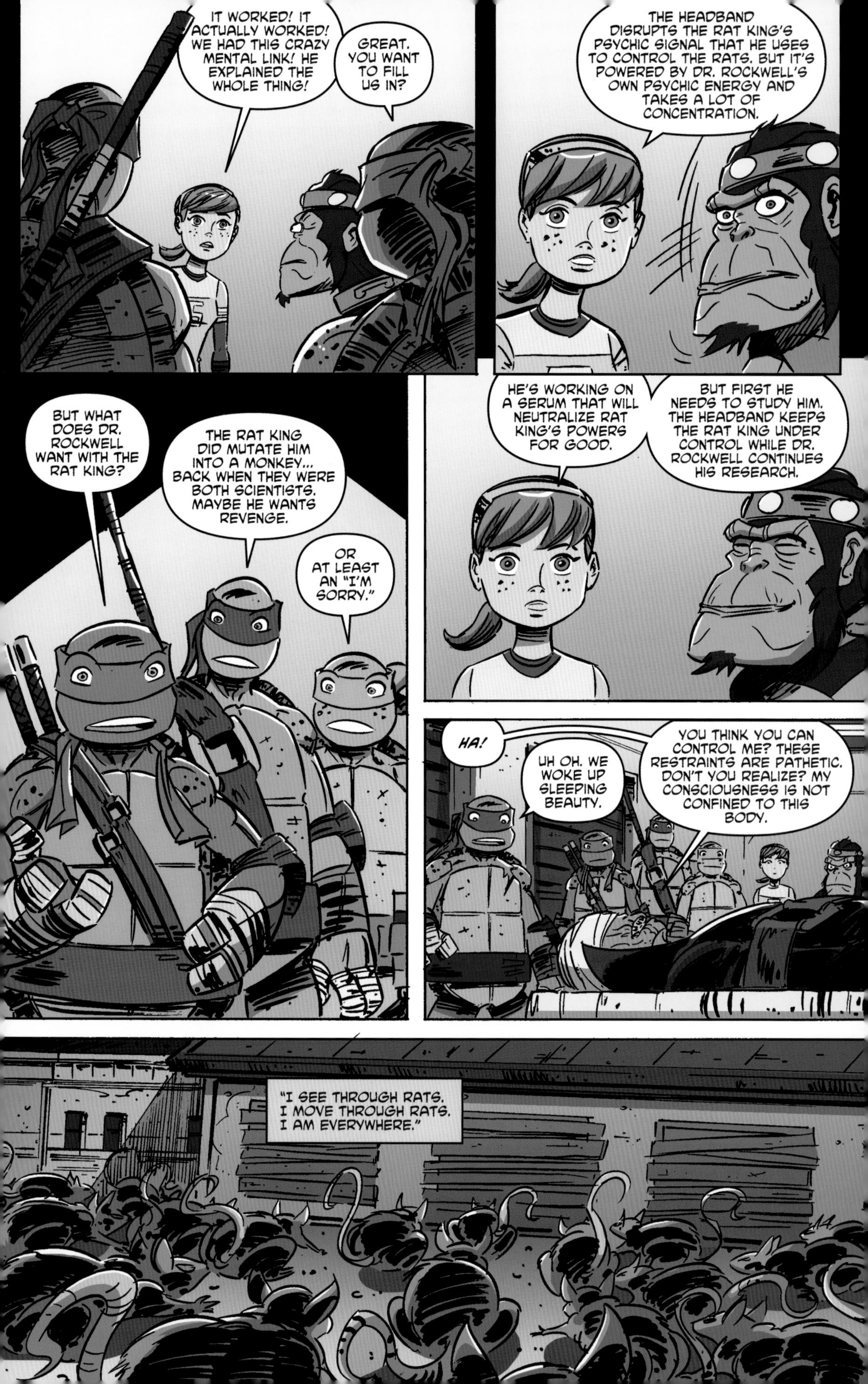
IT WORKED! IT ACTUALLY WORKED! WE HAD THIS CRAZY MENTAL LINK! HE EXPLAINED THE WHOLE THING!
GREAT. YOU WANT TO FILL US IN?
THE HEADBAND DISRUPTS THE RAT KING'S PSYCHIC SIGNAL THAT HE USES TO CONTROL THE RATS. BUT IT'S POWERED BY DR. ROCKWELL'S OWN PSYCHIC ENERGY AND TAKES A LOT OF CONCENTRATION.
BUT WHAT DOES DR. ROCKWELL WANT WITH THE RAT KING?
THE RAT KING DID MUTATE HIM INTO A MONKEY... BACK WHEN THEY WERE BOTH SCIENTISTS. MAYBE HE WANTS REVENGE.
OR AT LEAST AN "I'M SORRY."
HE'S WORKING ON A SERUM THAT WILL NEUTRALIZE RAT KING'S POWERS FOR GOOD.
BUT FIRST HE NEEDS TO STUDY HIM. THE HEADBAND KEEPS THE RAT KING UNDER CONTROL WHILE DR. ROCKWELL CONTINUES HIS RESEARCH.
HA!
UH OH. WE WOKE UP SLEEPING BEAUTY.
YOU THINK YOU CAN CONTROL ME? THESE RESTRAINTS ARE PATHETIC. DON'T YOU REALIZE? MY CONSCIOUSNESS IS NOT CONFINED TO THIS BODY.
"I SEE THROUGH RATS. I MOVE THROUGH RATS. I AM EVERYWHERE."

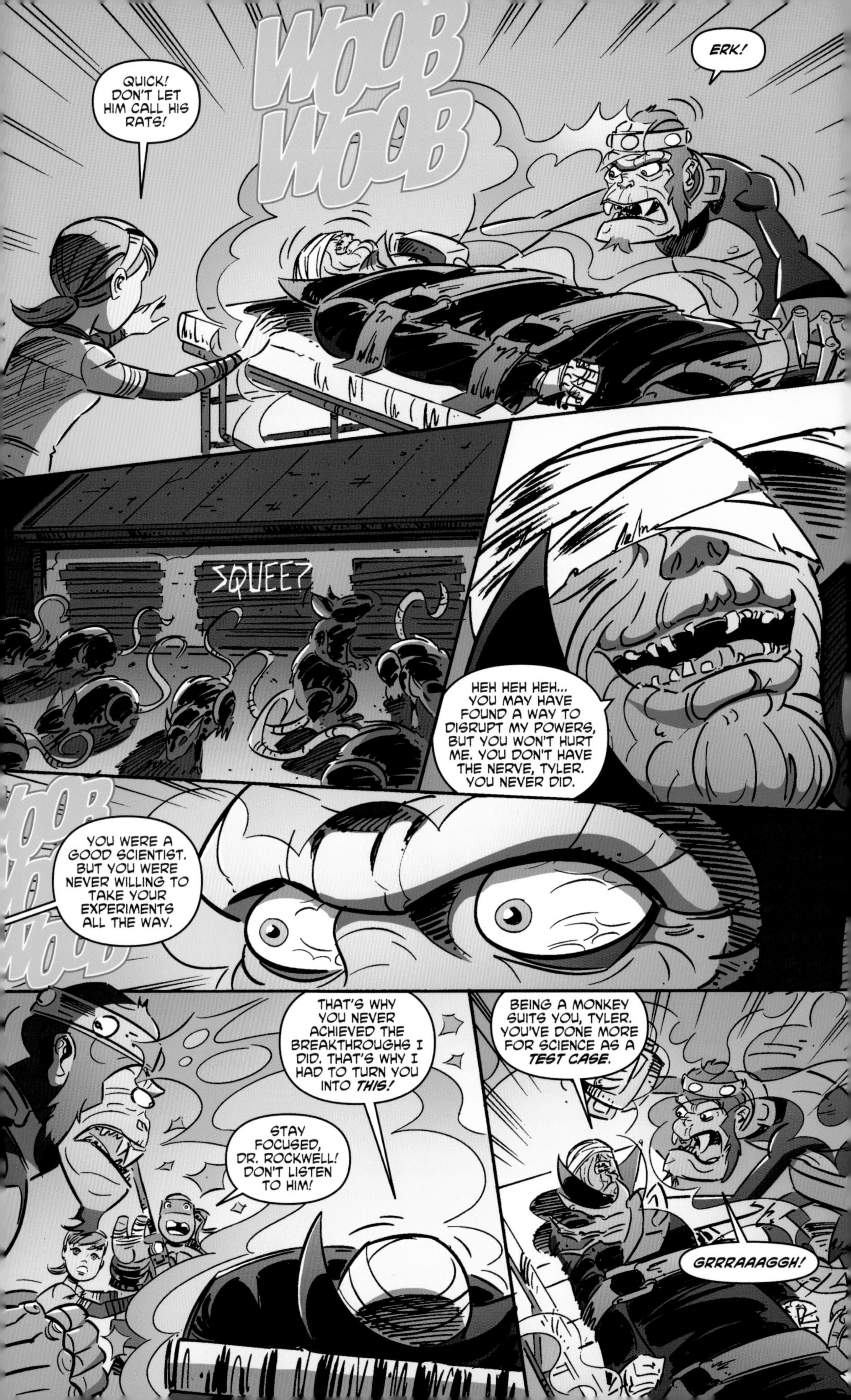
WOOB WOOB
QUICK! DON'T LET HIM CALL HIS RATS!
ERK!
SQUEE?
HEH HEH HEH... YOU MAY HAVE FOUND A WAY TO DISRUPT MY POWERS, BUT YOU WON'T HURT ME. YOU DON'T HAVE THE NERVE, TYLER. YOU NEVER DID.
YOU WERE A GOOD SCIENTIST. BUT YOU WERE NEVER WILLING TO TAKE YOUR EXPERIMENTS ALL THE WAY.
THAT'S WHY YOU NEVER ACHIEVED THE BREAKTHROUGHS I DID. THAT'S WHY I HAD TO TURN YOU INTO *THIS!*
STAY FOCUSED, DR. ROCKWELL! DON'T LISTEN TO HIM!
BEING A MONKEY SUITS YOU, TYLER. YOU'VE DONE MORE FOR SCIENCE AS A *TEST CASE*.
GRRRAAAGGH!

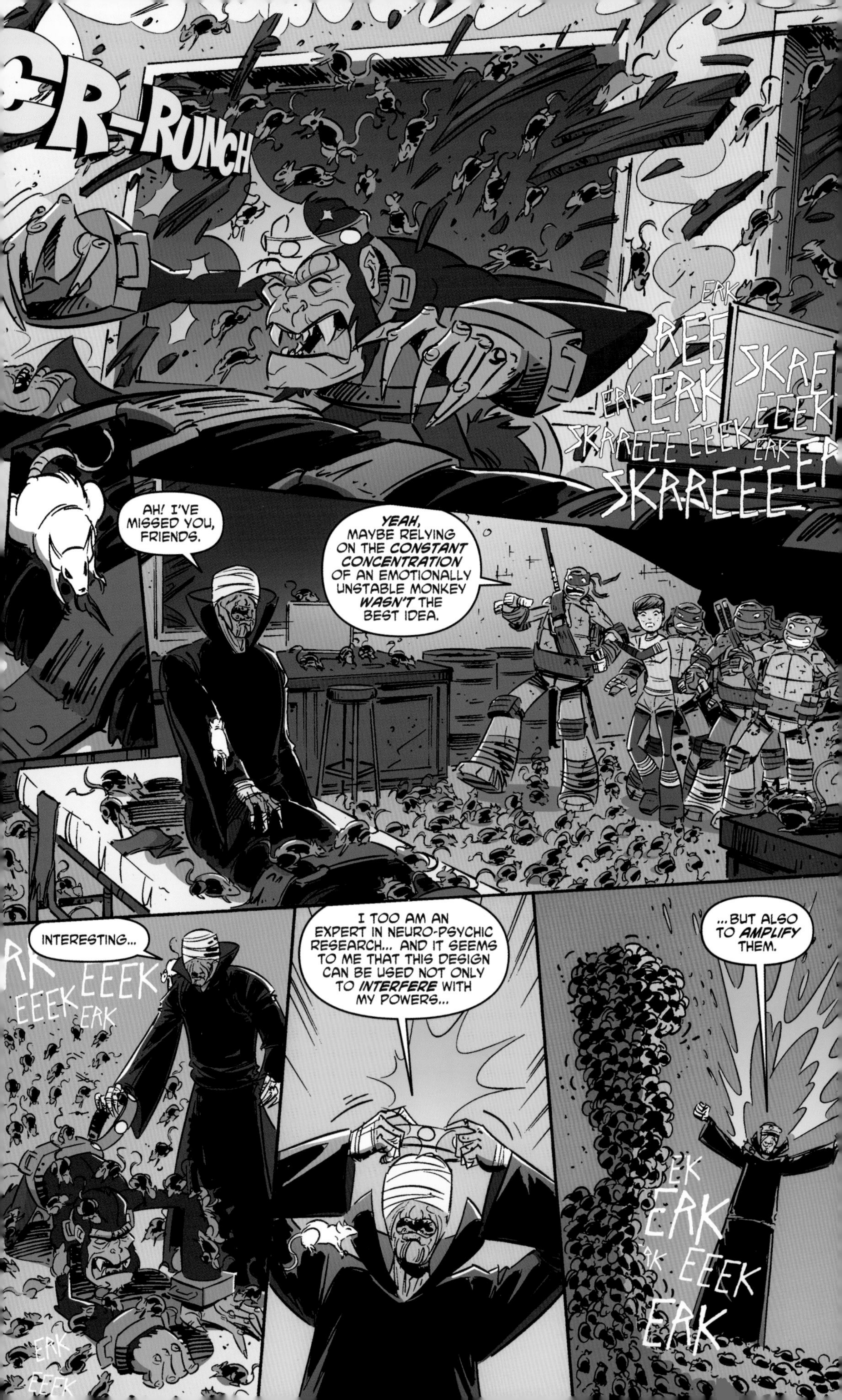
CR-RUNCH
ERK
SKREE
SKREE
ERK
ERK
EEEK
SKREEE EEEK
ERK
SKREEEE
AH! I'VE MISSED YOU, FRIENDS.
YEAH, MAYBE RELYING ON THE ***CONSTANT CONCENTRATION*** OF AN EMOTIONALLY UNSTABLE MONKEY ***WASN'T*** THE BEST IDEA.
INTERESTING...
EEEK
EEEK
ERK
I TOO AM AN EXPERT IN NEURO-PSYCHIC RESEARCH... AND IT SEEMS TO ME THAT THIS DESIGN CAN BE USED NOT ONLY TO ***INTERFERE*** WITH MY POWERS...
...BUT ALSO TO ***AMPLIFY*** THEM.
EK
ERK
EEEK
ERK
ERK
EEEK

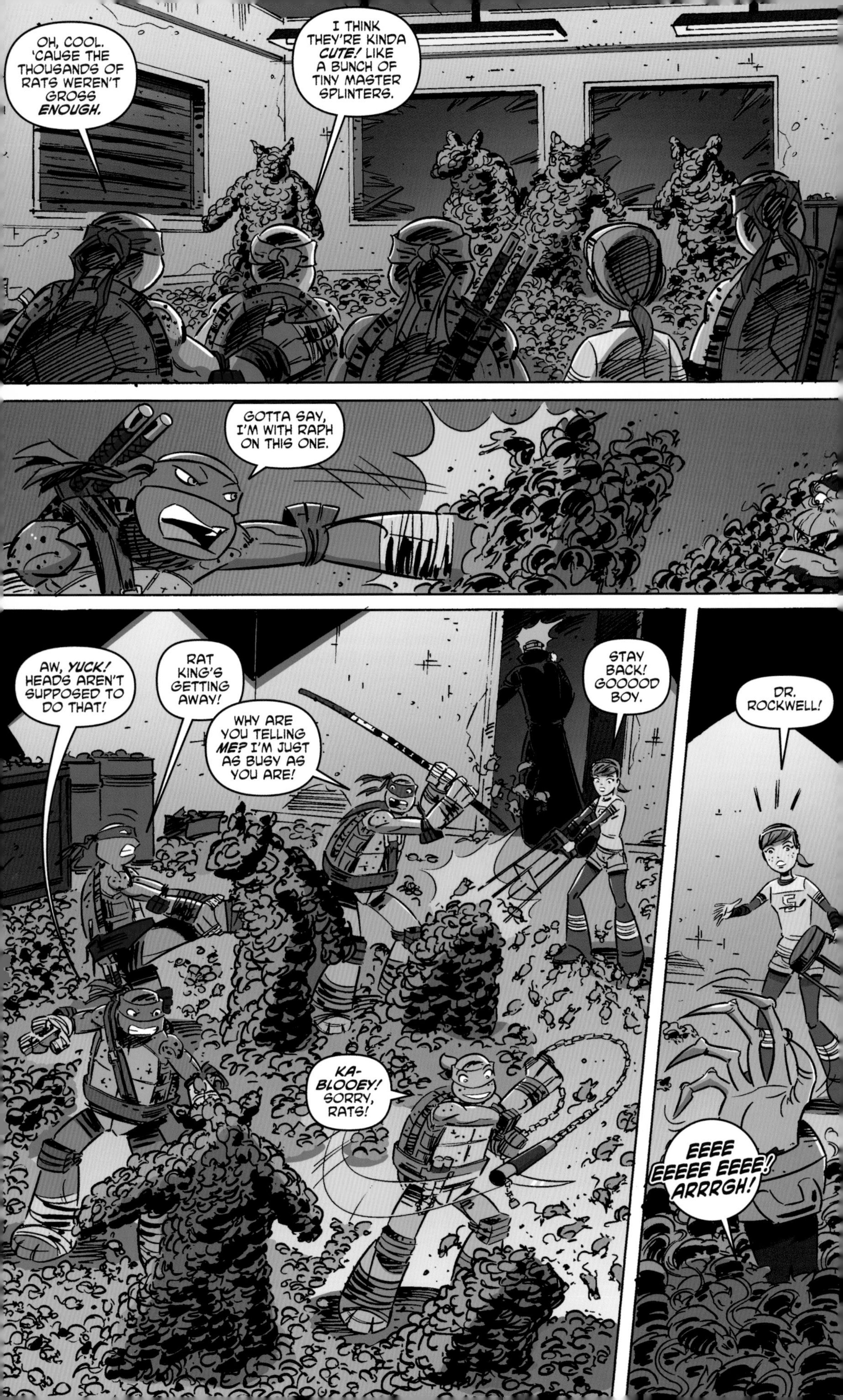
OH, COOL. 'CAUSE THE THOUSANDS OF RATS WEREN'T GROSS ENOUGH.
I THINK THEY'RE KINDA CUTE! LIKE A BUNCH OF TINY MASTER SPLINTERS.
GOTTA SAY, I'M WITH RAPH ON THIS ONE.
AW, YUCK! HEADS AREN'T SUPPOSED TO DO THAT!
RAT KING'S GETTING AWAY!
WHY ARE YOU TELLING ME? I'M JUST AS BUSY AS YOU ARE!
STAY BACK! GOOOOD BOY.
KA-BLOOEY! SORRY, RATS!
DR. ROCKWELL!
EEEE EEEEE EEEE! ARRRGH!

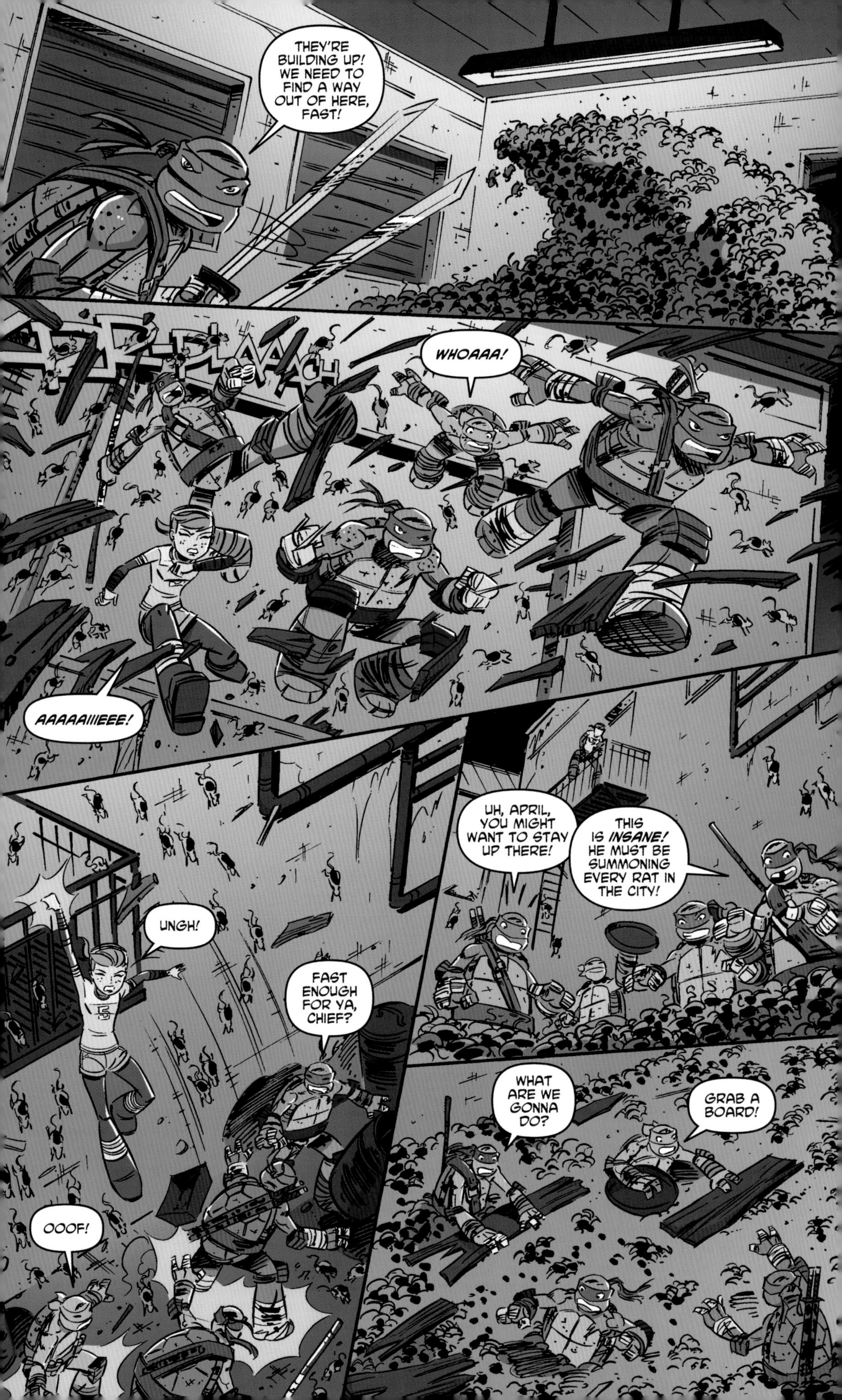
THEY'RE BUILDING UP! WE NEED TO FIND A WAY OUT OF HERE, FAST!
WHOAAA!
AAAAAIIIEEE!
UNGH!
FAST ENOUGH FOR YA, CHIEF?
OOOF!
UH, APRIL, YOU MIGHT WANT TO STAY UP THERE!
THIS IS INSANE! HE MUST BE SUMMONING EVERY RAT IN THE CITY!
WHAT ARE WE GONNA DO?
GRAB A BOARD!

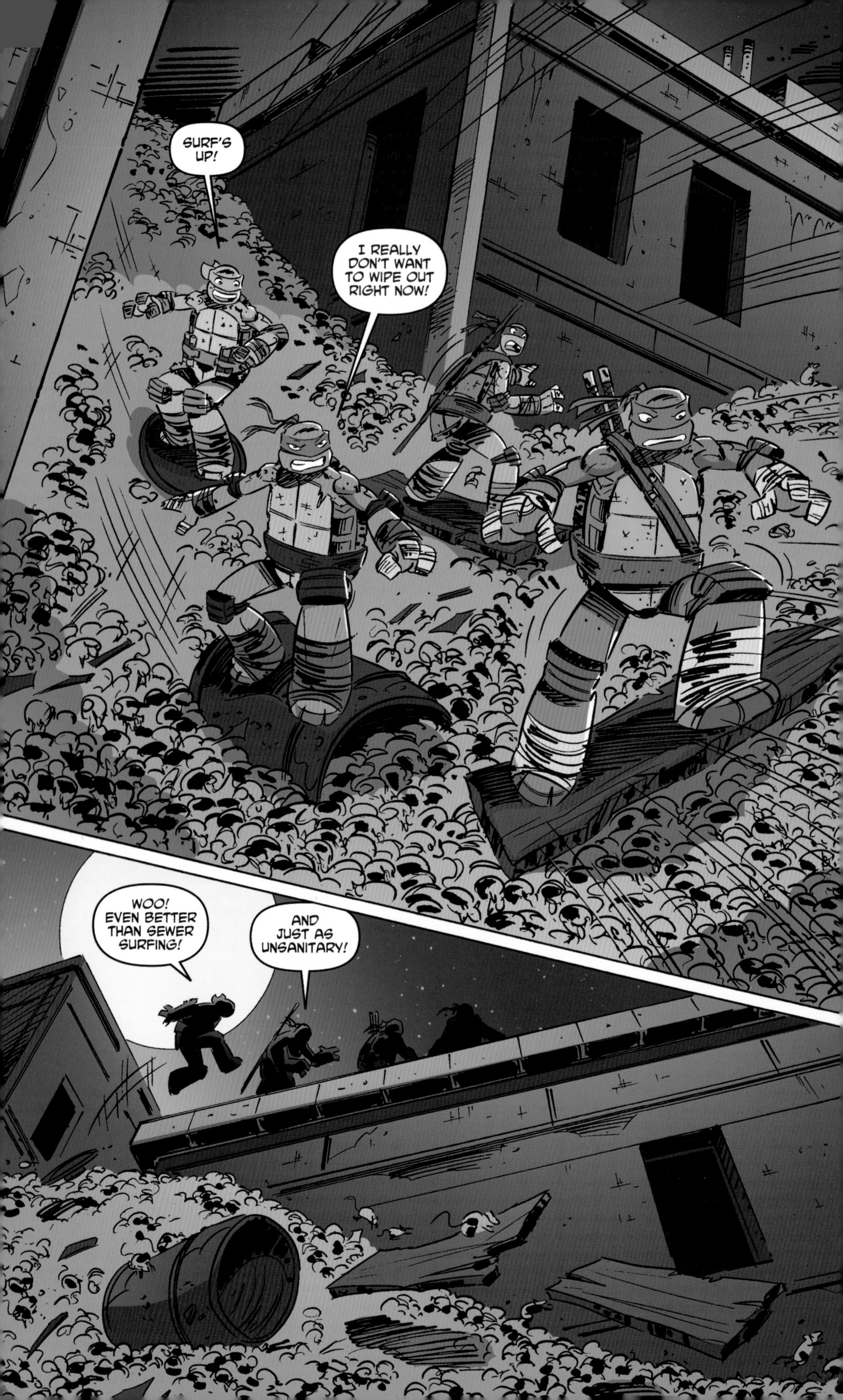
SURF'S UP!
I REALLY DON'T WANT TO WIPE OUT RIGHT NOW!
WOO! EVEN BETTER THAN SEWER SURFING!
AND JUST AS UNSANITARY!

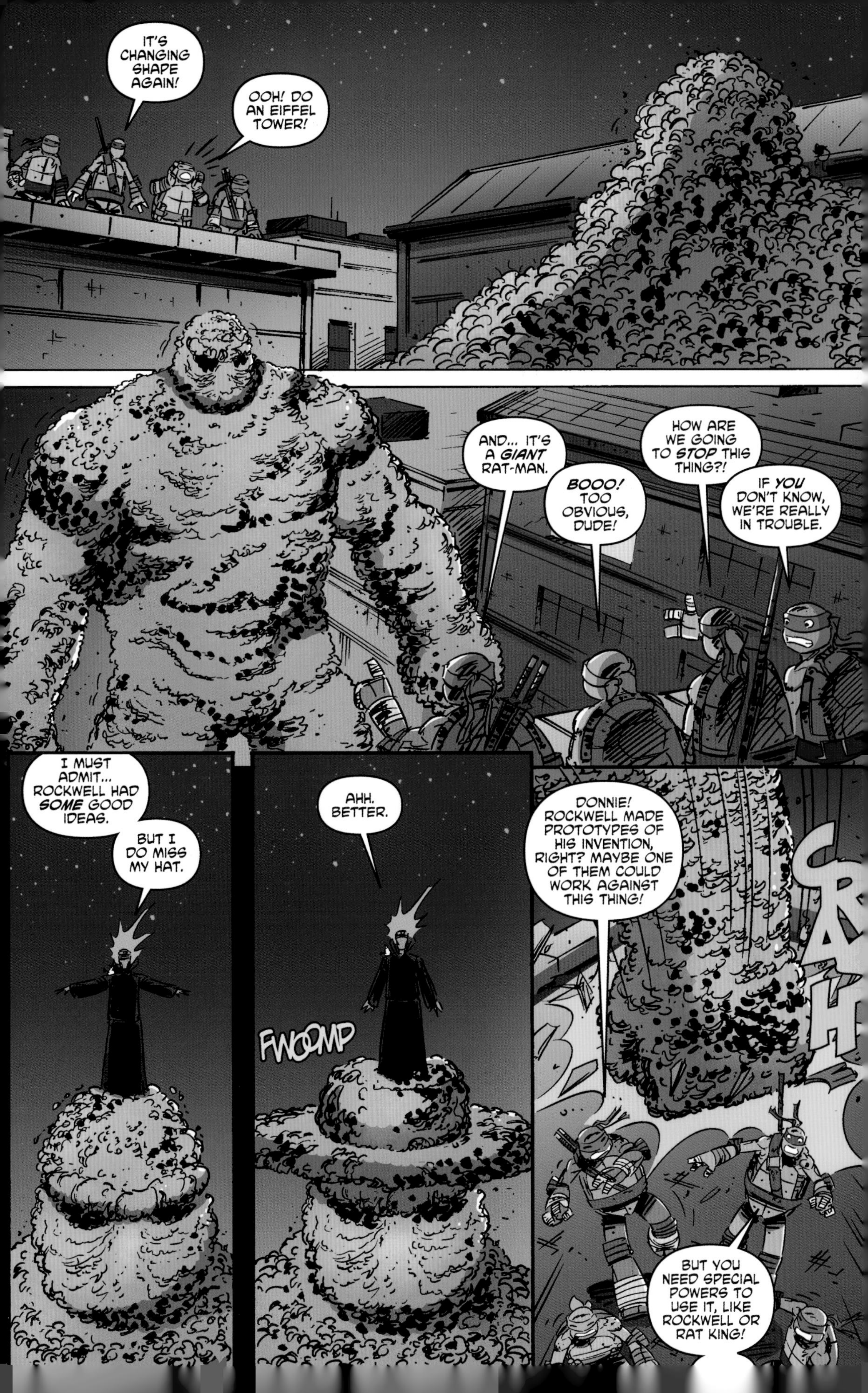
IT'S CHANGING SHAPE AGAIN!
OOH! DO AN EIFFEL TOWER!
AND... IT'S A GIANT RAT-MAN.
BOOO! TOO OBVIOUS, DUDE!
HOW ARE WE GOING TO STOP THIS THING?!
IF YOU DON'T KNOW, WE'RE REALLY IN TROUBLE.
I MUST ADMIT... ROCKWELL HAD SOME GOOD IDEAS.
BUT I DO MISS MY HAT.
AHH. BETTER.
FWOOMP
DONNIE! ROCKWELL MADE PROTOTYPES OF HIS INVENTION, RIGHT? MAYBE ONE OF THEM COULD WORK AGAINST THIS THING!
BUT YOU NEED SPECIAL POWERS TO USE IT, LIKE ROCKWELL OR RAT KING!

I'VE GOT AN *IDEA.* KEEP HIM BUSY!

YOU MEAN IF YOU HAVE AN IDEA YOU GET TO *LEAVE?!* IF I KNEW THAT, I WOULD'VE THOUGHT UP MORE IDEAS!

CRUNCH

APRIL! HOW YOU HOLDING UP?

ALONE ON A FIRE ESCAPE SURROUNDED BY RATS? WHAT'S NOT TO LIKE?

LOOK. YOU CAN COMMUNICATE WITH ROCKWELL. SO THERE MUST BE SOME *OVERLAP* BETWEEN YOUR ABILITIES.

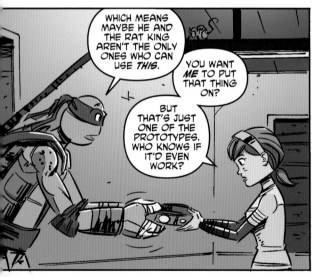

WHICH MEANS MAYBE HE AND THE RAT KING AREN'T THE ONLY ONES WHO CAN USE *THIS.*

YOU WANT *ME* TO PUT THAT THING ON?

BUT THAT'S JUST ONE OF THE PROTOTYPES. WHO KNOWS IF IT'D EVEN WORK?

I DON'T EVEN KNOW WHAT MY "POWERS" ARE! AND I *DEFINITELY* CAN'T DO THEM ON COMMAND.

COME ON, YOU DID GREAT COMMUNICATING WITH ROCKWELL. BESIDES, WE DON'T HAVE ANOTHER OPTION.

...YOU'VE GOT TO *TRY.*

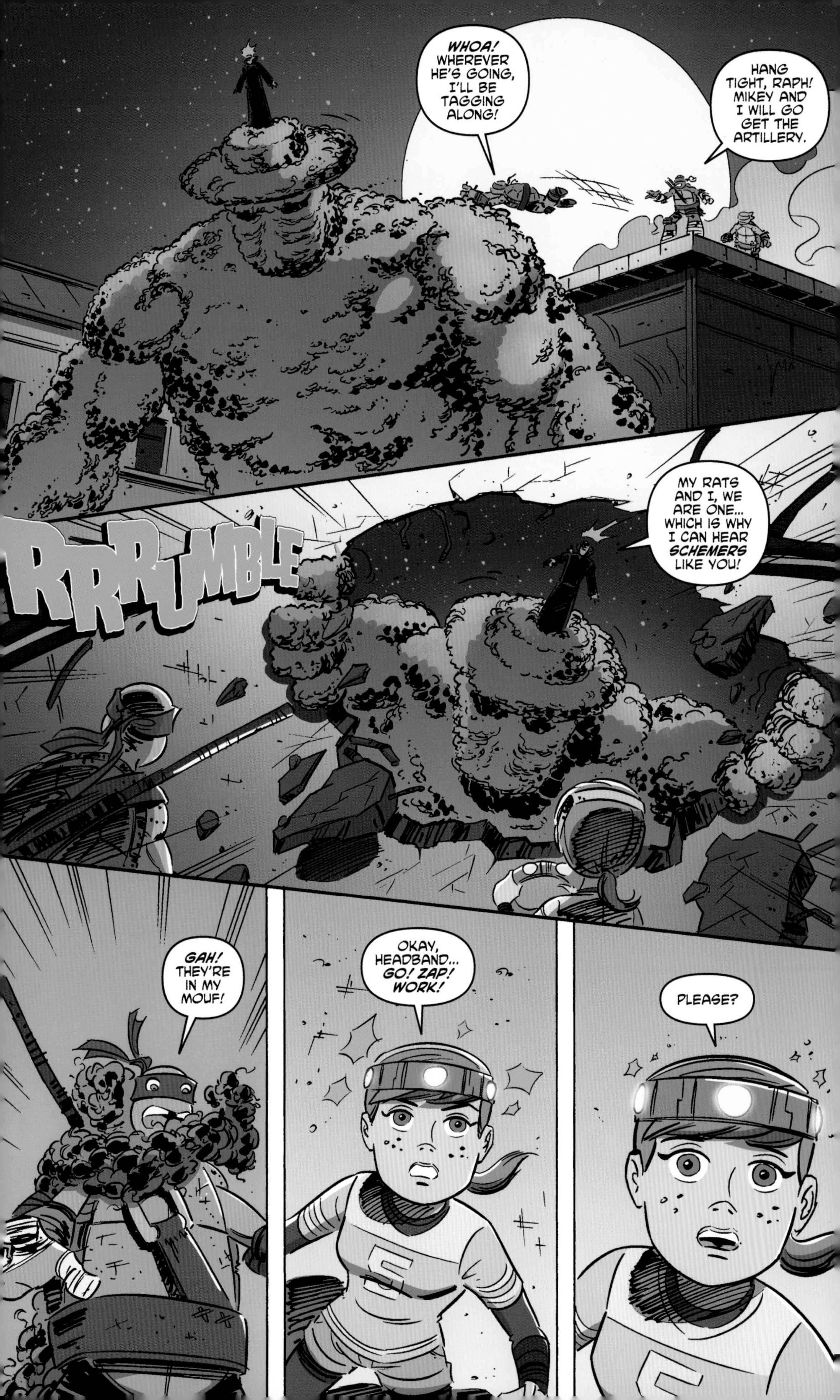
WHOA! WHEREVER HE'S GOING, I'LL BE TAGGING ALONG!
HANG TIGHT, RAPH! MIKEY AND I WILL GO GET THE ARTILLERY.
RRRRUMBLE
MY RATS AND I, WE ARE ONE... WHICH IS WHY I CAN HEAR SCHEMERS LIKE YOU!
GAH! THEY'RE IN MY MOUF!
OKAY, HEADBAND... GO! ZAP! WORK!
PLEASE?

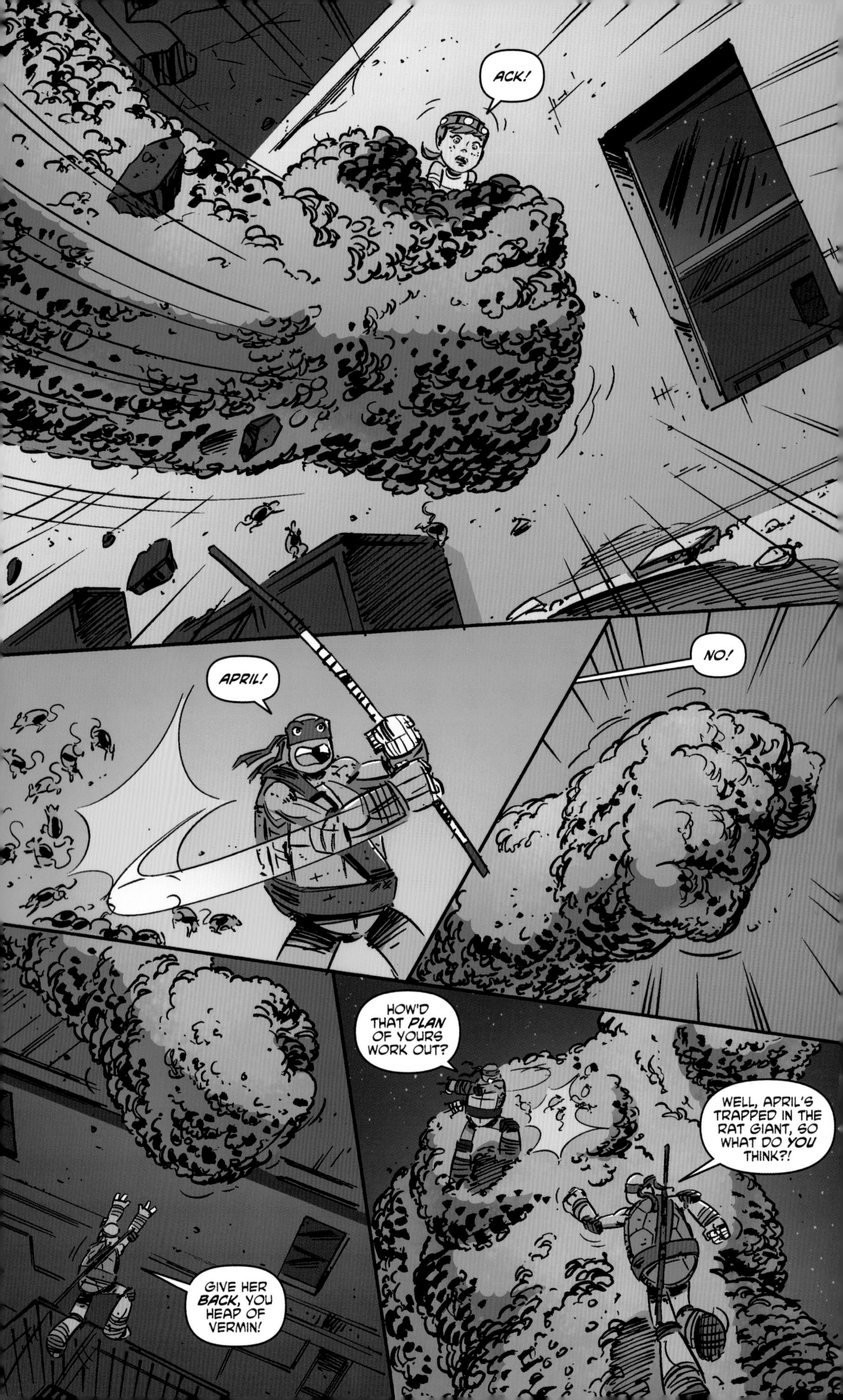
ACK!
APRIL!
NO!
GIVE HER BACK, YOU HEAP OF VERMIN!
HOW'D THAT PLAN OF YOURS WORK OUT?
WELL, APRIL'S TRAPPED IN THE RAT GIANT, SO WHAT DO YOU THINK?!

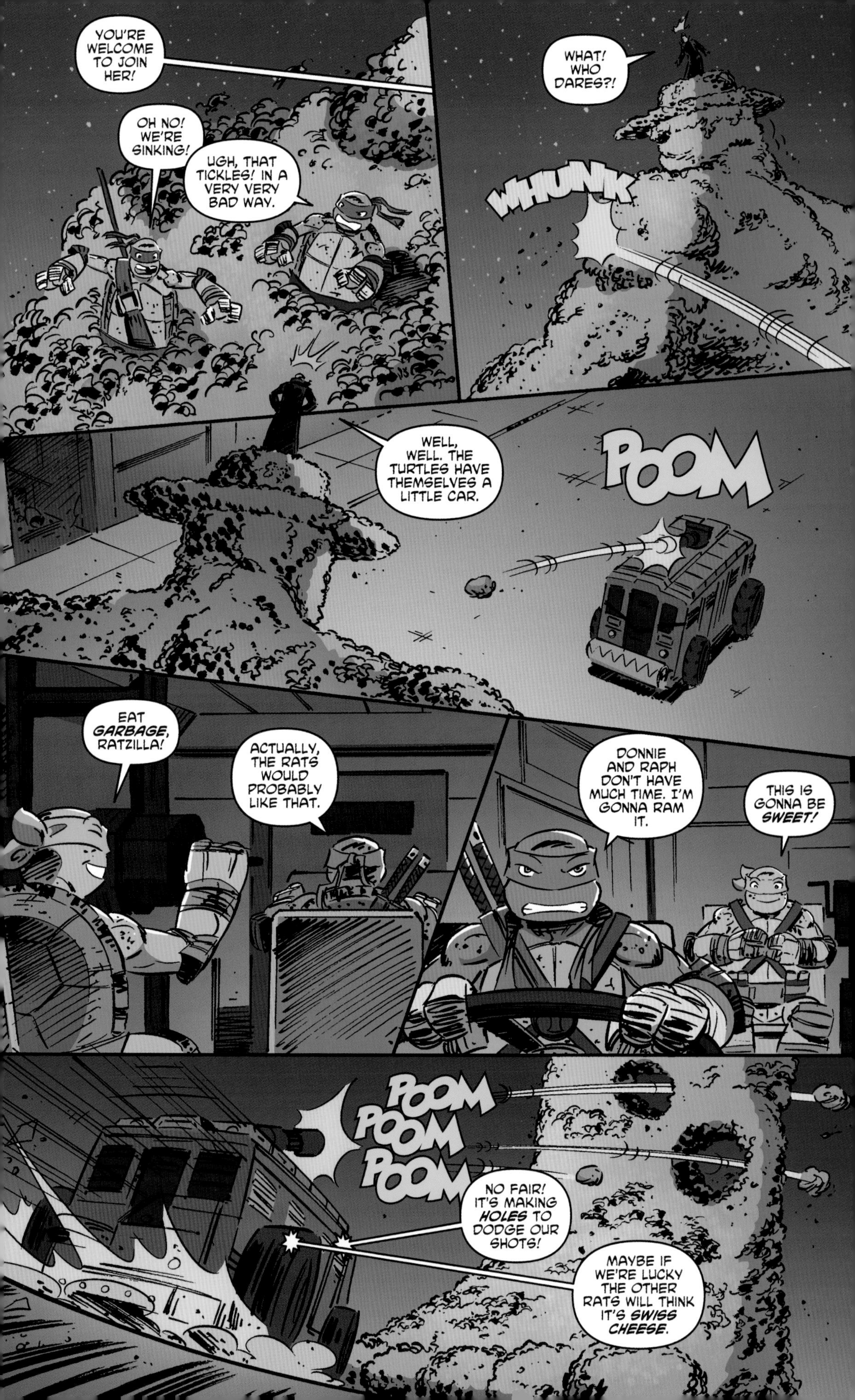

YOU'RE WELCOME TO JOIN HER!
OH NO! WE'RE SINKING!
UGH, THAT TICKLES! IN A VERY VERY BAD WAY.
WHAT! WHO DARES?!
WHUNK
WELL, WELL. THE TURTLES HAVE THEMSELVES A LITTLE CAR.
POOM
EAT GARBAGE, RATZILLA!
ACTUALLY, THE RATS WOULD PROBABLY LIKE THAT.
DONNIE AND RAPH DON'T HAVE MUCH TIME. I'M GONNA RAM IT.
THIS IS GONNA BE SWEET!
POOM POOM POOM
NO FAIR! IT'S MAKING HOLES TO DODGE OUR SHOTS!
MAYBE IF WE'RE LUCKY THE OTHER RATS WILL THINK IT'S SWISS CHEESE.

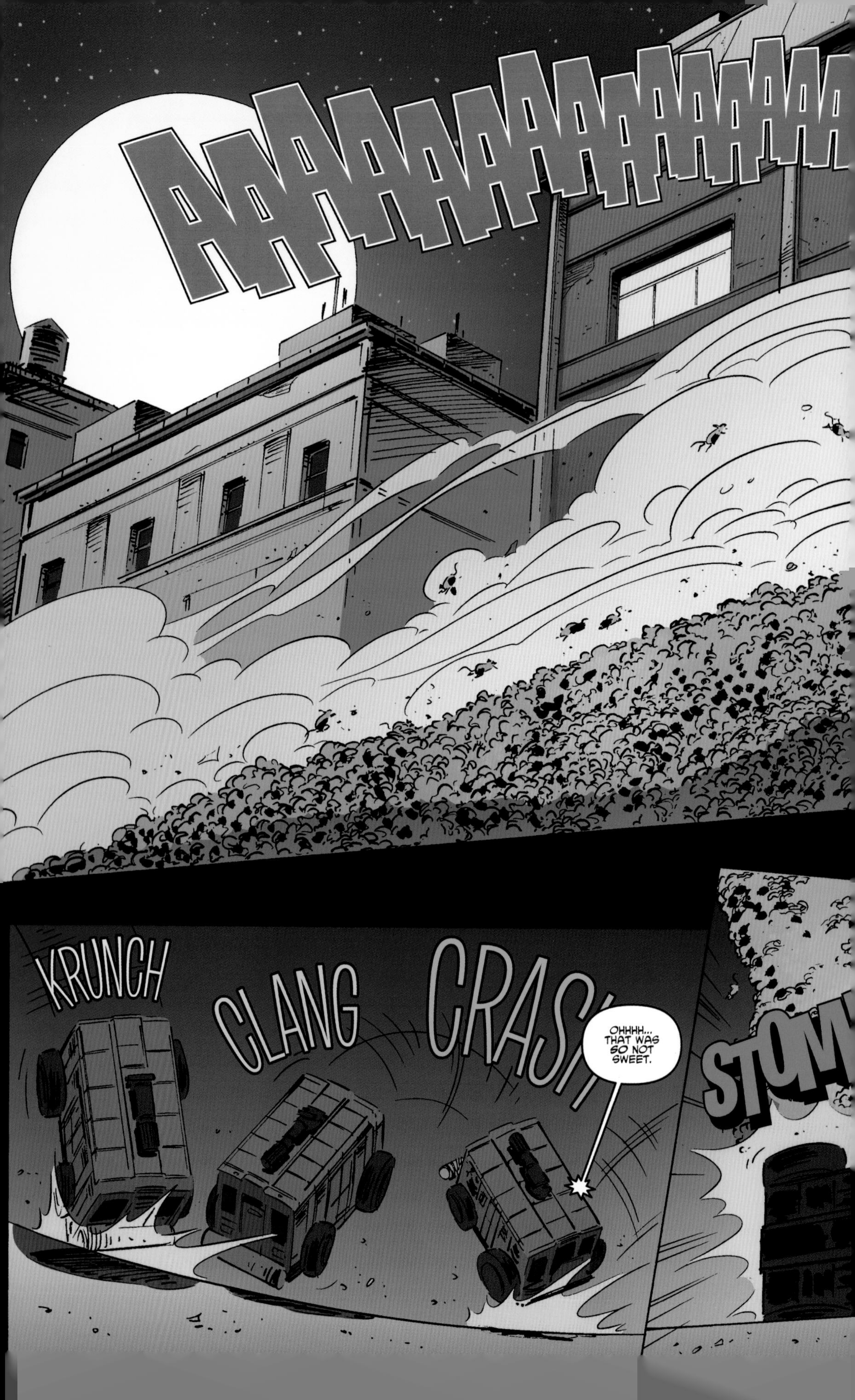
AAAAAAAAAAAAAA
KRUNCH
CLANG
CRASH
OHHHH... THAT WAS SO NOT SWEET.
STOM

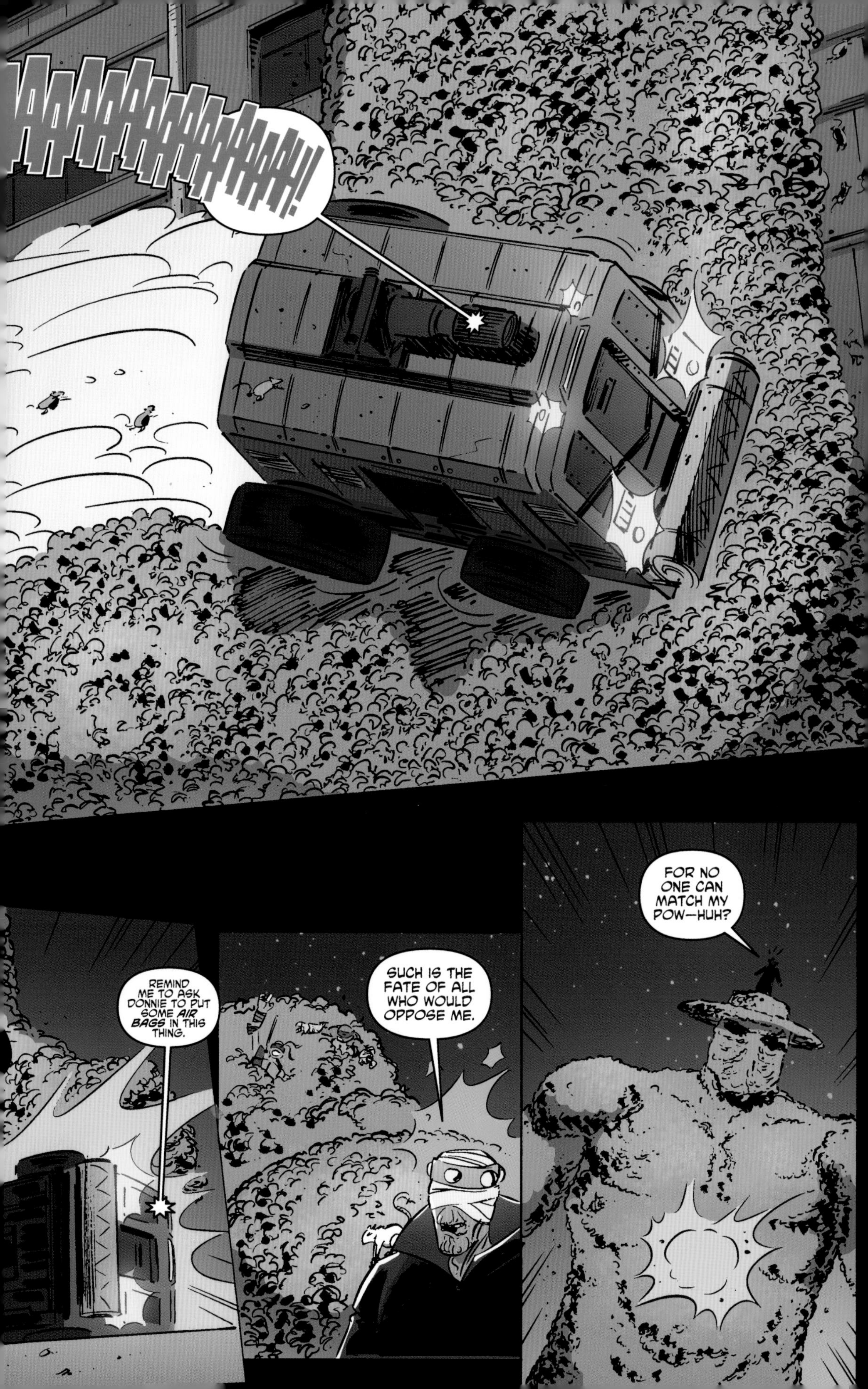
AAAAAAAAAAAAAAAAAH!!
REMIND ME TO ASK DONNIE TO PUT SOME AIR BAGS IN THIS THING.
SUCH IS THE FATE OF ALL WHO WOULD OPPOSE ME.
FOR NO ONE CAN MATCH MY POW—HUH?

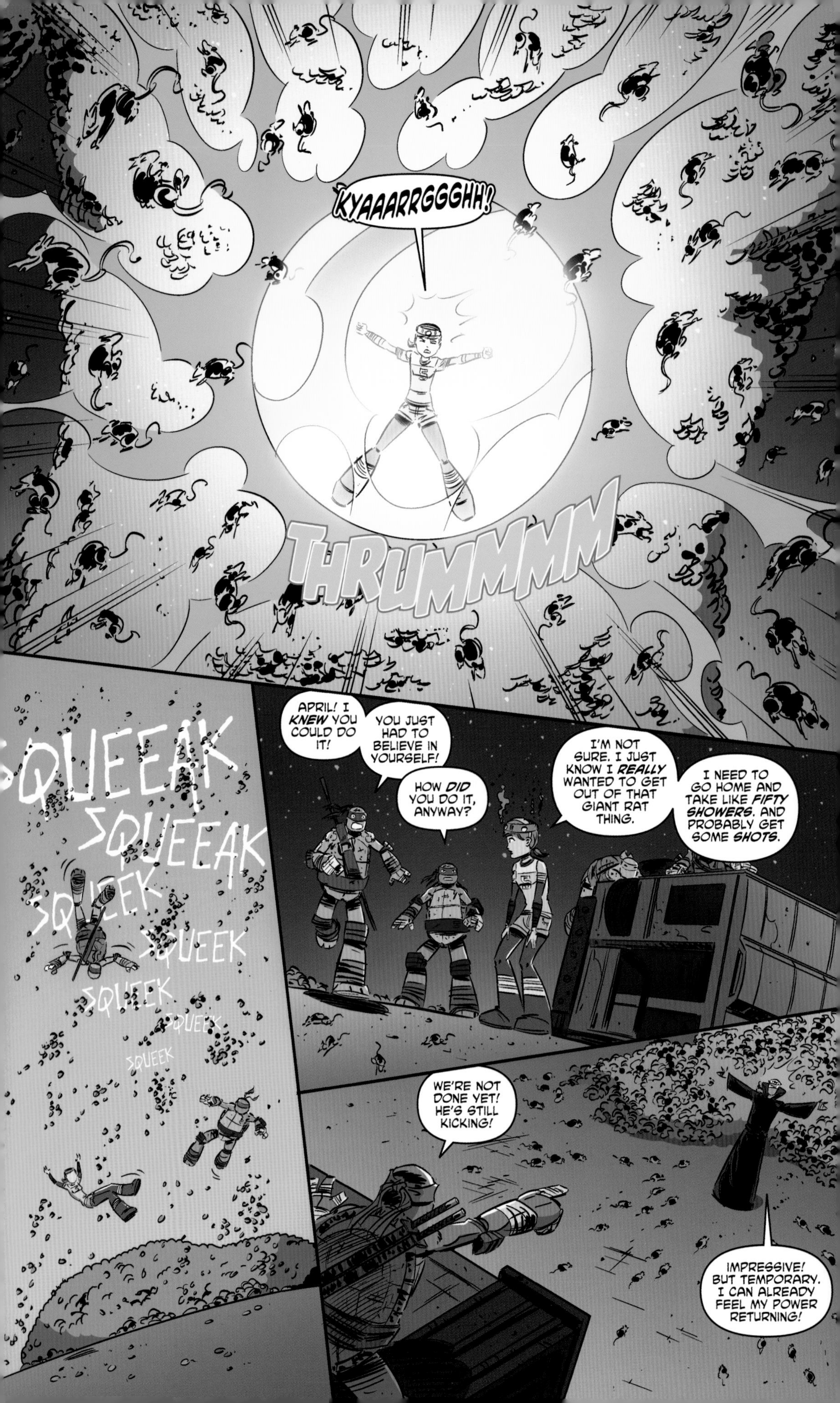
KYAAARRGGGHH!
THRUMMMM
SQUEEAK
SQUEEAK
SQUEEK
SQUEEK
SQUEEK
SQUEEK
SQUEEK
APRIL! I *KNEW* YOU COULD DO IT!
YOU JUST HAD TO BELIEVE IN YOURSELF!
HOW *DID* YOU DO IT, ANYWAY?
I'M NOT SURE. I JUST KNOW I *REALLY* WANTED TO GET OUT OF THAT GIANT RAT THING.
I NEED TO GO HOME AND TAKE LIKE *FIFTY SHOWERS*. AND PROBABLY GET SOME *SHOTS*.
WE'RE NOT DONE YET! HE'S STILL KICKING!
IMPRESSIVE! BUT TEMPORARY. I CAN ALREADY FEEL MY POWER RETURNING!

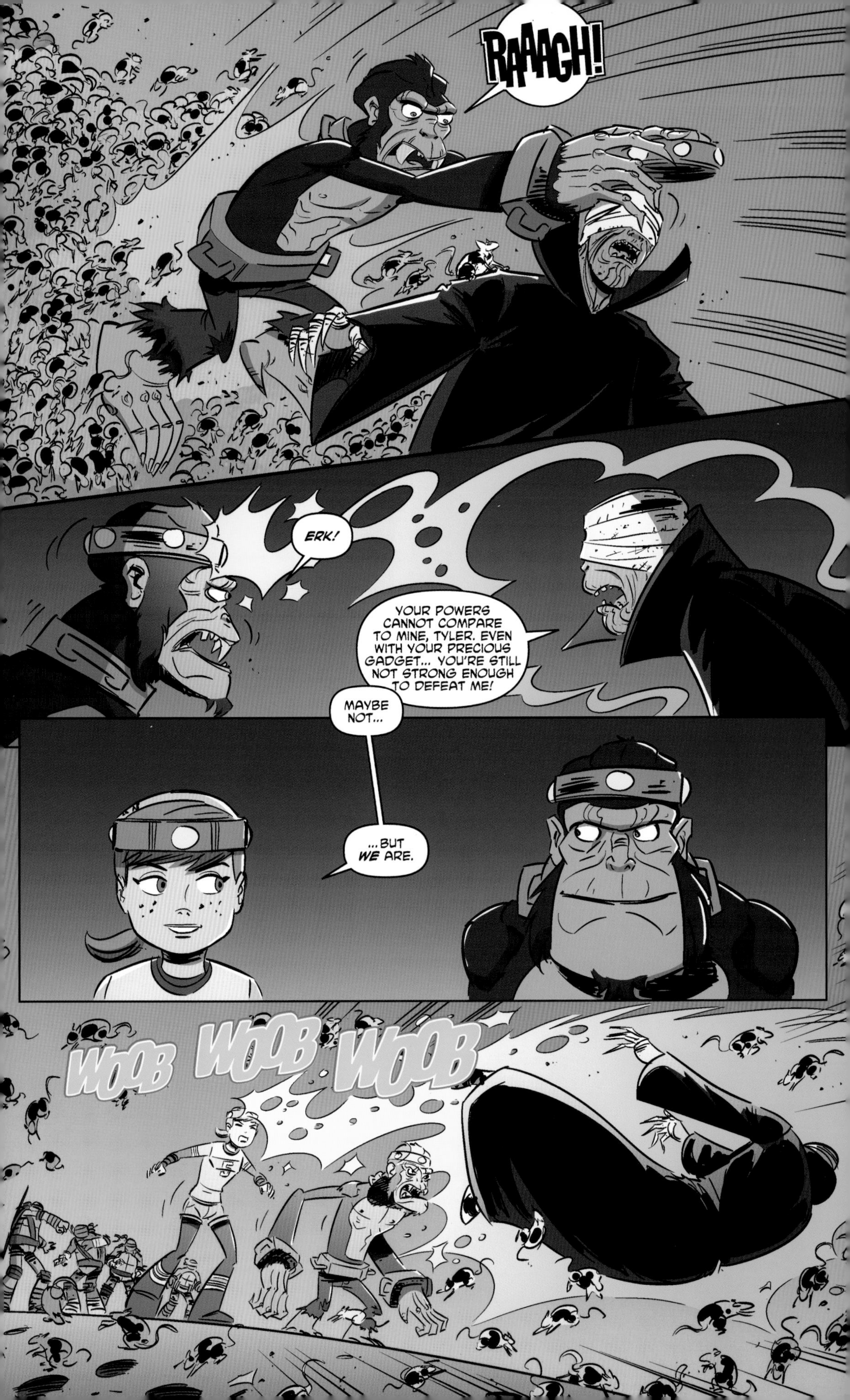
RAAAGH!
ERK!
YOUR POWERS CANNOT COMPARE TO MINE, TYLER. EVEN WITH YOUR PRECIOUS GADGET... YOU'RE STILL NOT STRONG ENOUGH TO DEFEAT ME!
MAYBE NOT...
...BUT WE ARE.
WOOB WOOB WOOB

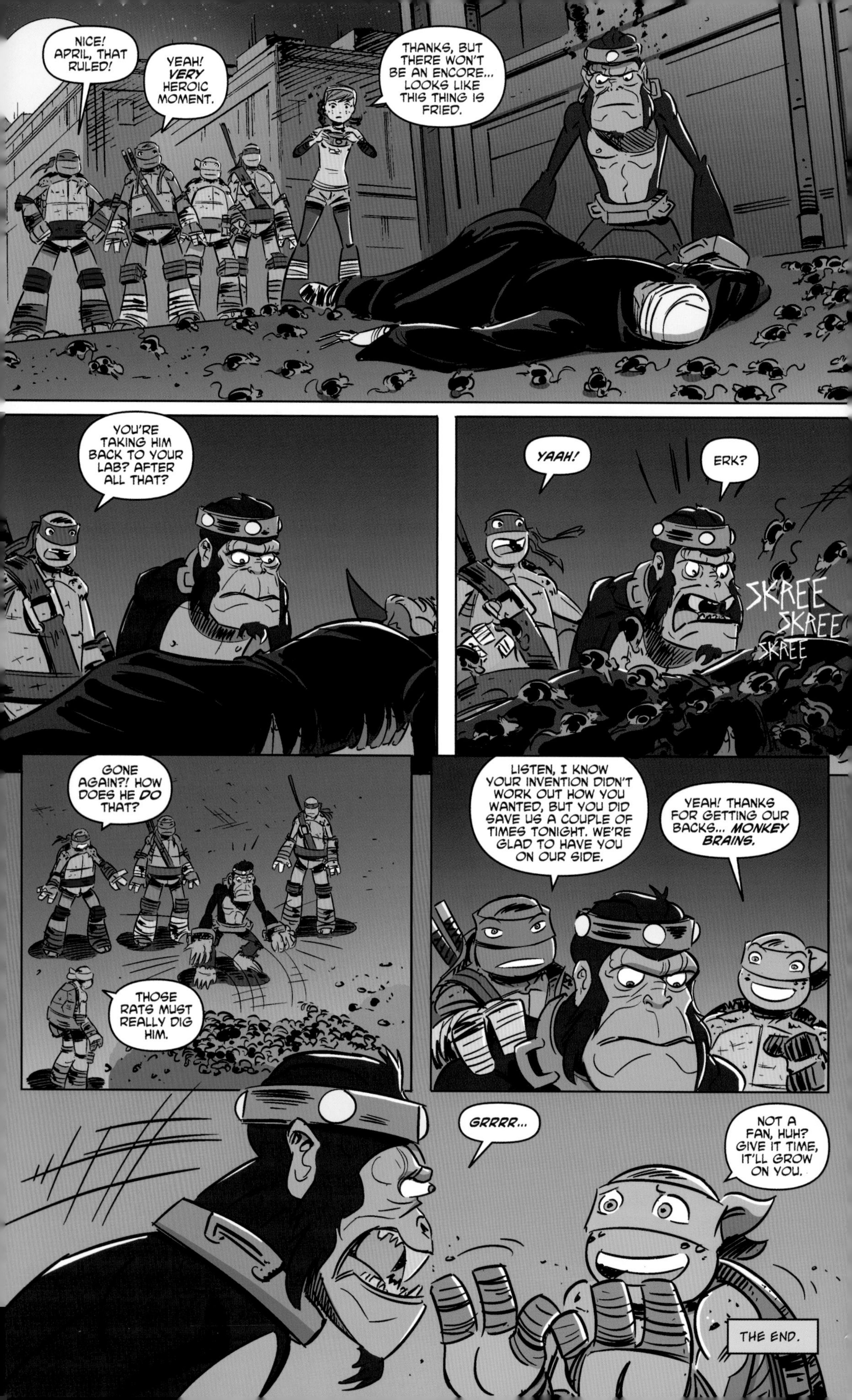
NICE! APRIL, THAT RULED!
YEAH! *VERY* HEROIC MOMENT.
THANKS, BUT THERE WON'T BE AN ENCORE... LOOKS LIKE THIS THING IS FRIED.
YOU'RE TAKING HIM BACK TO YOUR LAB? AFTER ALL THAT?
YAAH!
ERK?
SKREE
SKREE
SKREE
GONE AGAIN?! HOW DOES HE *DO* THAT?
THOSE RATS MUST REALLY DIG HIM.
LISTEN, I KNOW YOUR INVENTION DIDN'T WORK OUT HOW YOU WANTED, BUT YOU DID SAVE US A COUPLE OF TIMES TONIGHT. WE'RE GLAD TO HAVE YOU ON OUR SIDE.
YEAH! THANKS FOR GETTING OUR BACKS... *MONKEY BRAINS.*
GRRRR...
NOT A FAN, HUH? GIVE IT TIME, IT'LL GROW ON YOU.
THE END.

TEENAGE MUTANT NINJA TURTLES™

NEW ANIMATED ADVENTURES ART GALLERY

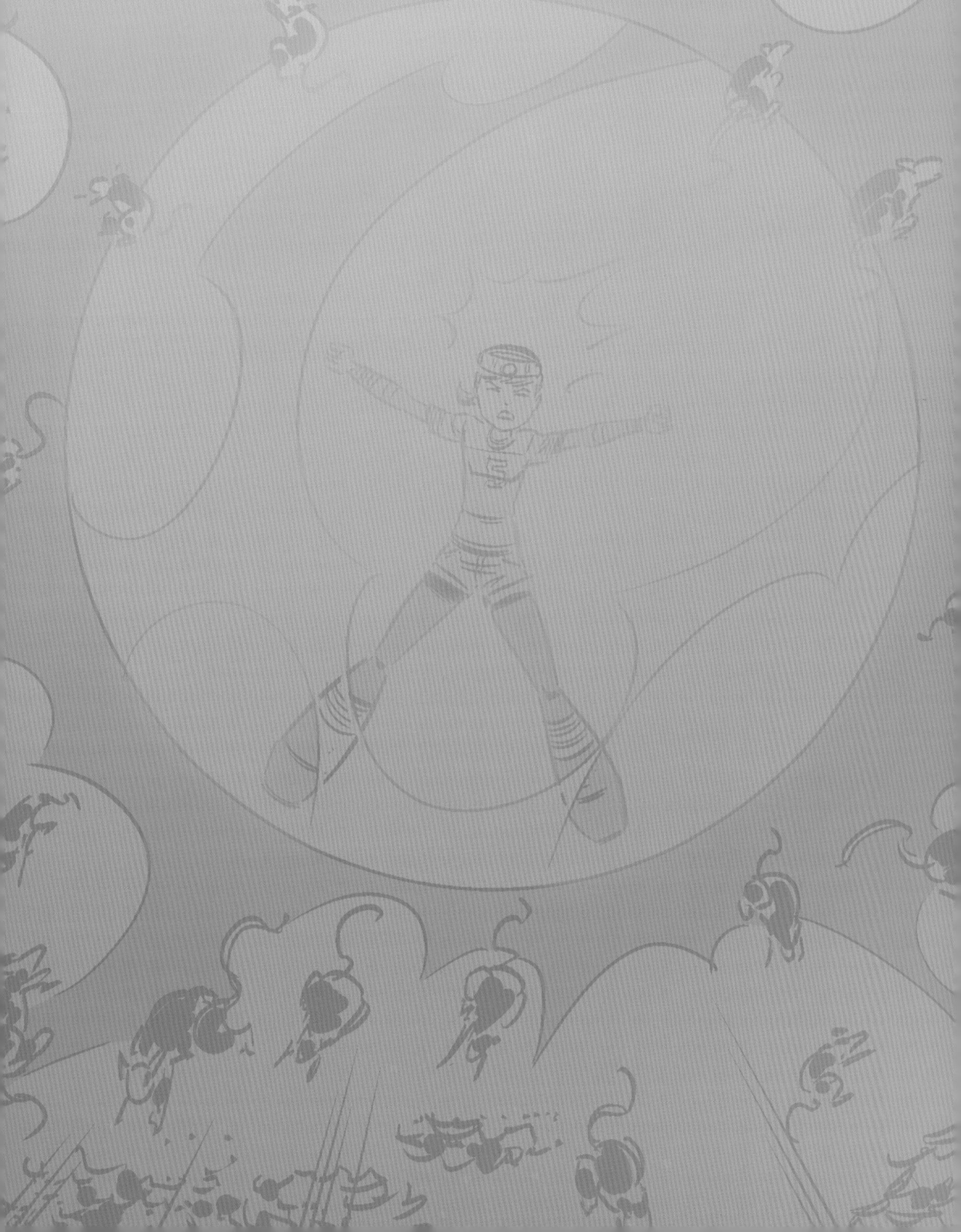

ART BY **MR. CHARLIE**

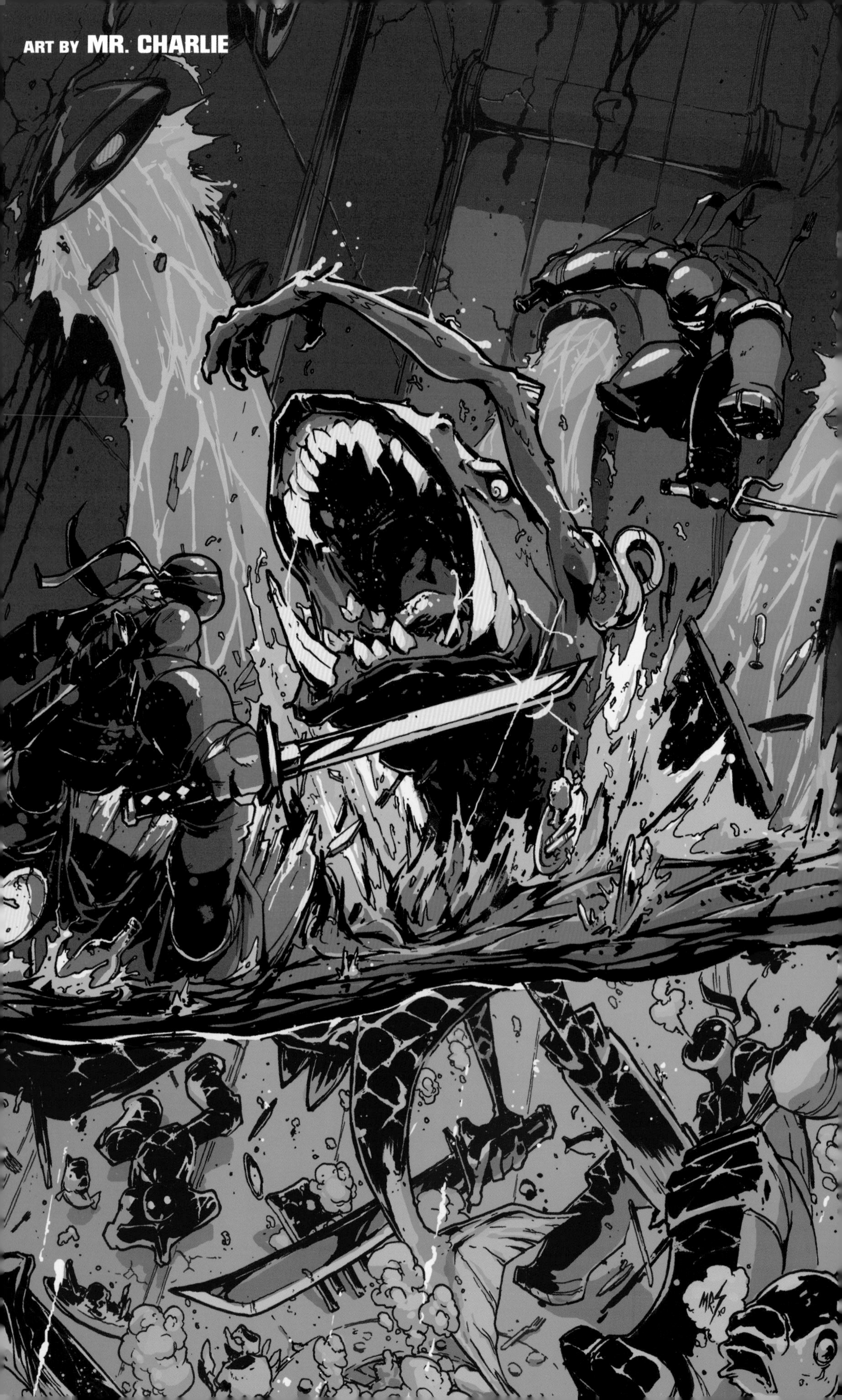

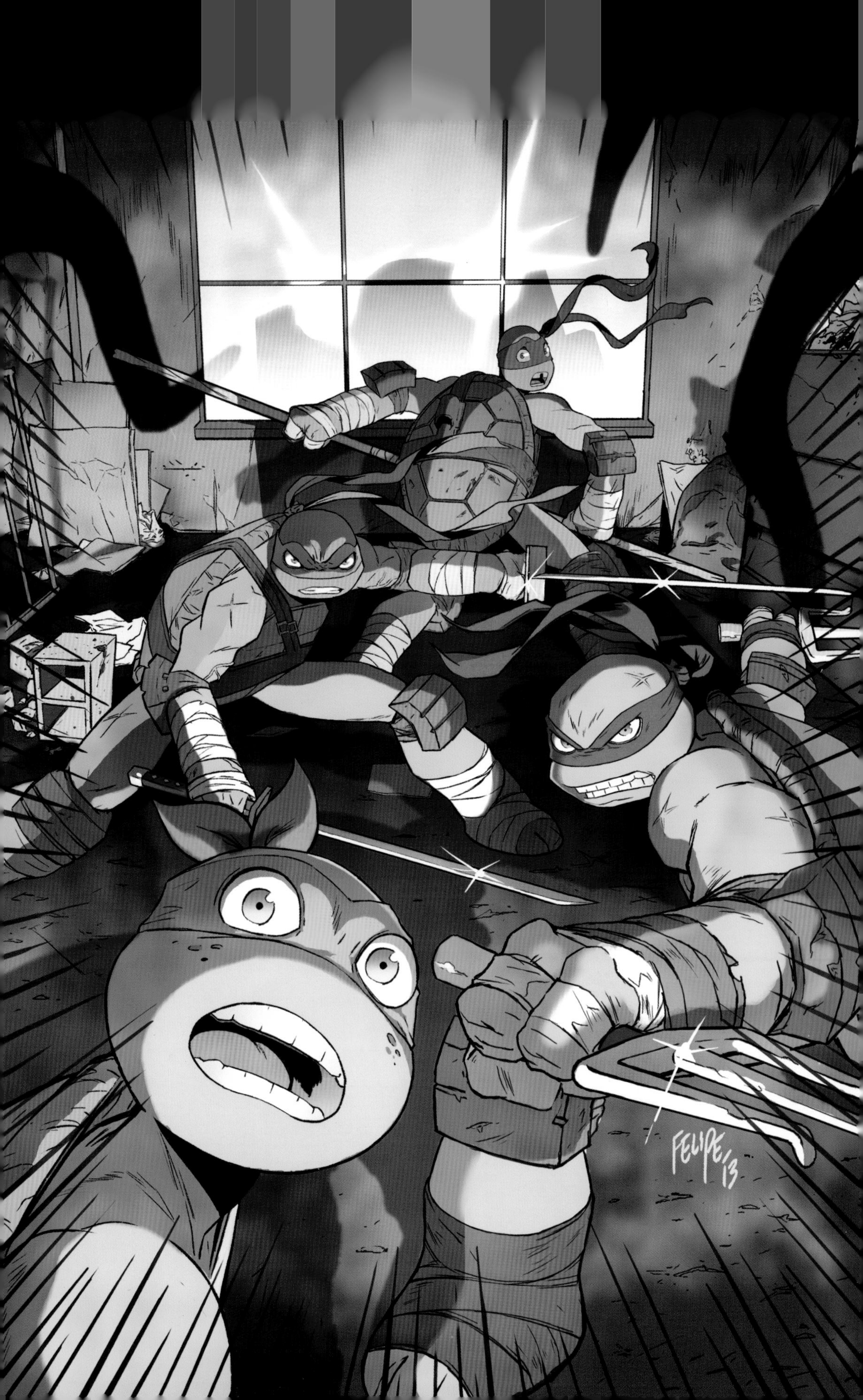
FELIPE '13

ART BY CHAD THOMAS

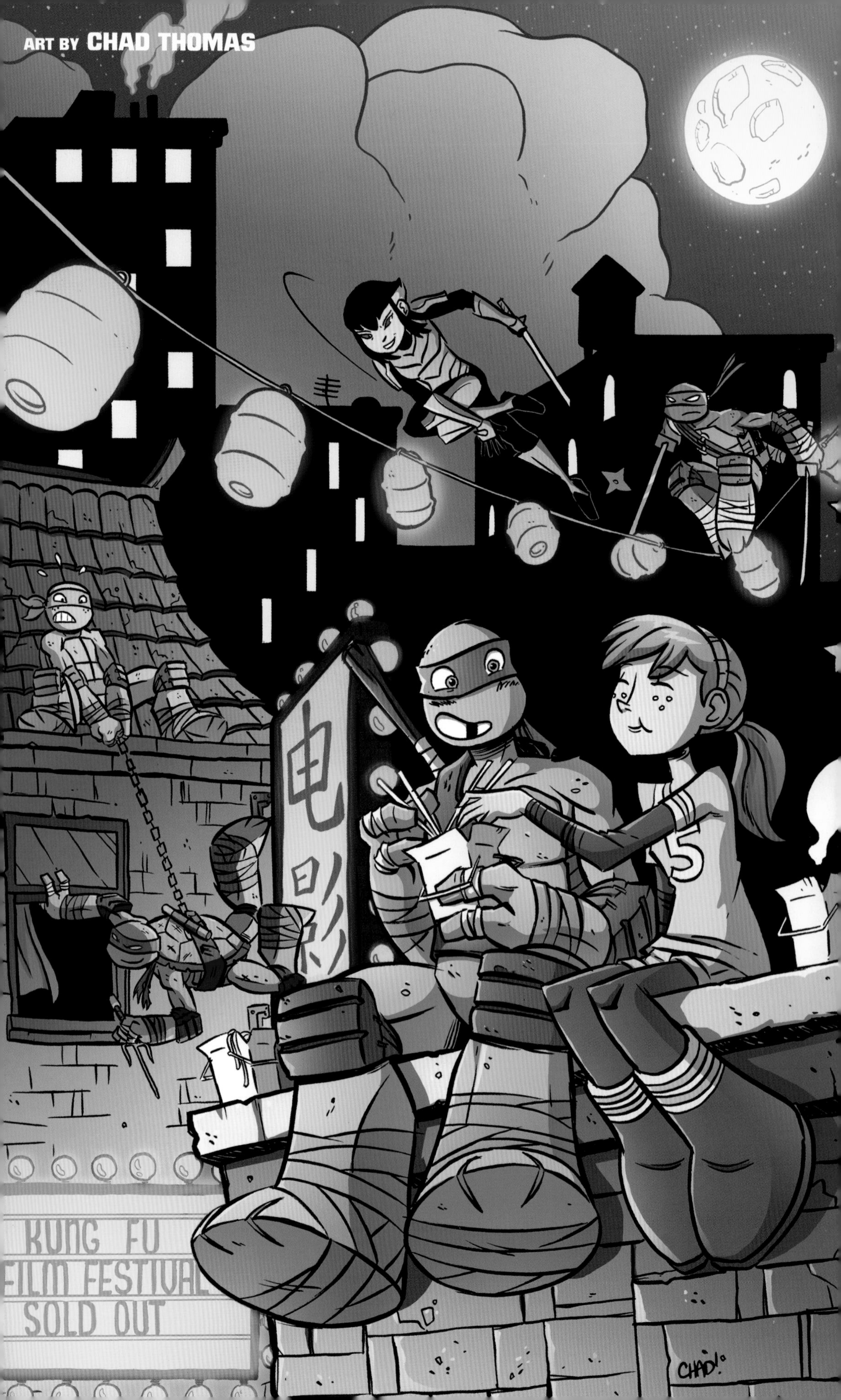

电
影
KUNG FU
FILM FESTIVAL
SOLD OUT
CHAD!

ART BY **CIRO NIELI**

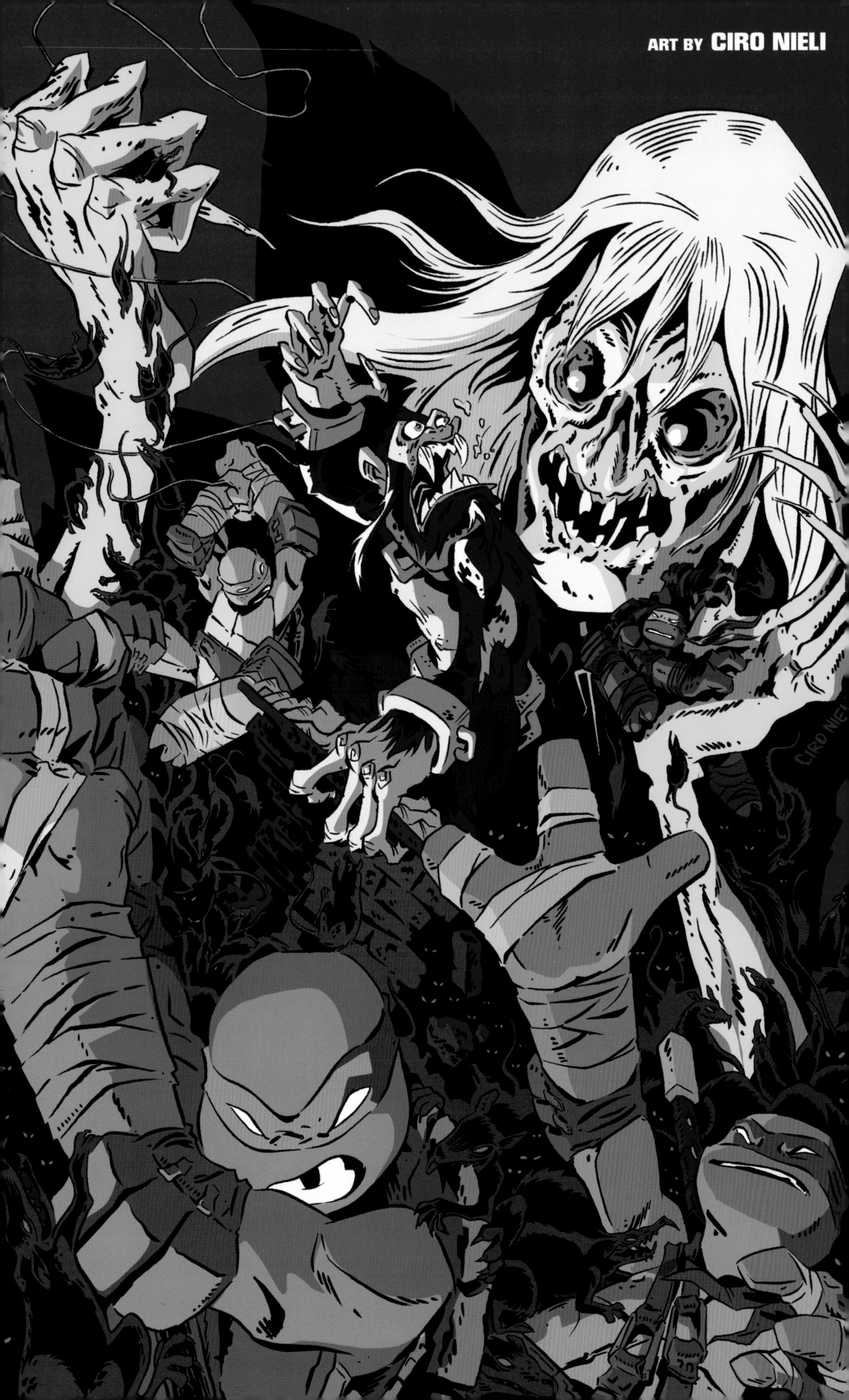
CIRO NIELI

TEENAGE MUTANT NINJA TURTLES
MORE TURTLE ACTION!

Teenage Mutant Ninja Turtles Adventures, Vol. 1
ISBN: 978-1-61377-289-8

Teenage Mutant Ninja Turtles Animated, Vol. 1
ISBN: 978-1-61377-613-1

ON SALE NOW

www.idwpublishing.com

IDW